To my friends everywhere,
wherever they are

》》》》》》》》》》 《《《《《《《《《《

Heinrich Böll

WOMEN *in*

a RIVER LANDSCAPE

A NOVEL IN DIALOGUES
AND SOLILOQUIES

Translated from the German by David McLintock

NORTHWESTERN UNIVERSITY PRESS

EVANSTON, ILLINOIS

》》》》》》》》》》 《《《《《《《《《《

Northwestern University Press
Evanston, Illinois 60208-4210

Originally published as *Frauen vor Flusslandschaft*. Copyright © 1985, 1987 by
Verlag Kiepenheuer & Witsch, Köln. English translation copyright © 1988 by
Alfred A. Knopf, Inc. Northwestern University Press edition published 1995 by
arrangement with Verlag Kiepenheuer & Witsch and Alfred A. Knopf, Inc.

Printed in the United States of America

ISBN 0-8101-1227-2 cloth
ISBN 0-8101-1205-1 paper

The paper used in this publication meets the minimum requirements of the
American National Standard for Information Sciences—Permanence of Paper
for Printed Library Materials, ANSI Z39.48-1984.

Women in a River Landscape

Wanderers Gemütsruhe

Übers Niederträchtige
Niemand sich beklage;
Denn es ist das Mächtige,
Was man dir auch sage.

In dem Schlechten waltet es
Sich zu Hochgewinne;
Und mit Rechtem schaltet es
Ganz nach seinem Sinne.

GOETHE,
West-östlicher Divan

Wanderer's Peace of Mind

Against the infamous and mean
Let none too much inveigh;
For baseness ever crowds the scene,
No matter what men say.

In evil circumstance it gains
High prizes with low skill,
Subjecting justice, where it reigns,
Entirely to its will.

The *characters* of the figures in this novel, their thoughts, lives, and actions, emerge from the conversations they conduct with others and with themselves. However, a few details must be added about their outward appearance, lest the reader gain any misleading impressions. Paul Chundt and Count Heinrich von Kreyl, though so unalike in character, are of roughly the same age—about seventy—and of roughly the same height—about five feet eight inches. Both are white-haired, with no hint of baldness. Both employ exclusive tailors and always wear waistcoats, etc.; both might be described as "immaculately groomed." Seen together, from a distance or even from behind, the one might easily be mistaken for the other. On closer inspection, however, one would be surprised to see how little they resemble each other: Kreyl is gaunt and has an air of suffering, though he is not sick in any medical or even psychiatric sense. Chundt, by contrast, has a full face that bespeaks what is commonly called "vitality"; he exudes health, yet a closer view reveals a surprising degree of sensibility.

The character known as the Sponge, who operates mainly behind the scenes and makes only one brief appearance, does not owe his nickname to any sponginess of appearance. He is tall, almost six feet, dresses in the same manner as Chundt and Kreyl, and is not even "corpulent"; despite his sixty-eight years, he might almost be said to be of athletic build. His background is somewhat obscure, since no one has seen his "papers": he could be Swiss, German, or Austrian, or a German-speaking Hungarian or Bohemian. His nickname derives from his facility for attracting and absorbing money. He constantly spreads the rumor that he is of gentle, even aristocratic, birth. The age of Wubler and his wife emerges from their careers. The men surrounding them and Chundt—Halberkamm, Blaukrämer, and Bingerle—are aged between fifty-four and fifty-nine. Tucheler, the literary scholar, who appears only indirectly, is fifty-seven. They are all respectably dressed, in waistcoat and necktie, etc., but not *quite* so gentlemanly in appearance as Chundt, Kreyl, and the Sponge. There are certain hints of "incorrectness" about Wubler's and Bingerle's dress—the way they tie their ties, their choice of shoes, etc. Krengel, a banker, aged sixty-six, has a more unobtrusive, more authentic elegance than Chundt and the Sponge, even than Kreyl, all of whom are a shade too obviously well dressed, whereas in Krengel's case everything appears to be "a perfect fit"—one might even say "perfectly fitting." He alone gives the impression of being an aristocrat, though in fact he is not. Exceptional among this group of men in their mid fifties and their sixties is Ernst Grobsch, who is forty-four, wears ready-made suits of indifferent quality, and, though not exactly ill groomed, clearly cares little about his dress. Karl von Kreyl is thirty-eight and quite unlike Grobsch; the six years separating their ages seem to amount almost to a generation gap. Karl von Kreyl, too, is indifferent to clothes, but in a sloppier and more nonchalant way. At parties, when not wearing a pullover and corduroys, he dresses conventionally, but in a casual manner that seems somehow like a disguise. The youngest of the male characters, Eberhard Kolde, the professional host or *animateur,* is thirty; he endeavors, without success, to affect the air of a medical practitioner. He is a personable and likable young man who tries in vain to appear serious.

The clothes worn by two of the ladies, Erika Wubler and Eva Kreyl-Plint, are sufficiently described in the text. Erika is sixty-two and Eva thirty-six. Elisabeth Blaukrämer (known as "Blaukrämer's ex") is fifty-five; she is quite tall, blond, tolerably well turned out, but somehow not "fully dressed": she tends to dress carelessly, having always forgotten to fasten one of her buttons or close one of her zippers. She is more corpulent than her bearing suggests. At times she even wears unmatching shoes. Dr. Dumpler is a rather nondescript woman in her late thirties. Adelheid Kapspeter, who is the same age as Eva Kreyl-Plint, dresses in notably "sensible" clothes. Katharina Richter is thirty, never wears an apron for housework, and has a certain indefinable chic, which makes her resemble Eva Kreyl-Plint. Either might be taken for a television announcer. Trude, "Blaukrämer's latest," is one of those women who delude themselves about their age (or let themselves be deluded by their advisers). She is forty-two but dresses as though she were a mere thirty-year-old who succumbs to absolutely all the latest trends; hence, in a rather contrived way, she appears somewhat vulgar. Not having learned the difference between décolleté and topless, and being rather generously endowed, she presents herself in a manner that might most appositely be called out of place. The youngest of the ladies, Lore Schmitz, is twenty, not in the least punk, but smart and modish, even in her hairstyle. She could be a student, a bank employee, or a shop assistant. She would not appear out of place in any social or professional ambience, not even at a reception for church dignitaries.

AUTHOR'S NOTE

Since *everything* in this novel is fictitious, except the place where the fiction is set, there is no need for the usual disclaimers. The place itself is innocent and cannot feel offended.

H.B.

Women

in a

River

Landscape

Chapter 1

The spacious enclosed veranda of an upper-middle-class villa built around the turn of the century, between Bonn and Bad Godesberg, early in the morning in late summer. There is a view across to the opposite bank of the Rhine, where large villas can be seen behind clumps of trees and shrubs. A breakfast table set for two, at which Erika Wubler sits in her dressing gown, the newspaper beside her. In her hands she holds a manuscript, which she is reading as Katharina Richter enters with the coffee. Katharina places the coffeepot on the table.

ERIKA WUBLER, *looking up:* Thank you. No egg for me. What's my husband doing? Is he up yet?

KATHARINA RICHTER: He's in the bath, having his coffee. Mr. . . . your husband says I'm to get your gray two-piece out of the closet and press it. . . . He thinks you might wear coral with it.

ERIKA *laughs:* He's got taste, at least. If you ever need any advice—in matters of dress, I mean . . . (*Seeing Katharina about to leave*) Don't go just yet, please. Leave the two-piece in the closet; I won't need a suit today.

KATHARINA *hesitates:* The high mass at the minster—I mean the memorial service for the anniversary of Erftler-Blum's death . . .

ERIKA *closes the manuscript she is reading:* I won't be going to the high mass. Don't tell my husband. (*Puts the manuscript down.*) I've just read your life story, your dossier. I know

I'm not supposed to, but I took the trouble to get hold of it. . . . I like to know whom I have around me. You realize you have to be screened if you work for us?

KATHARINA: Of course, in a house like this, which . . . (*Hesitates.*)

ERIKA: Which is frequented by so many people and where so many things are discussed. You probably also know that the security people advised us against employing you?

KATHARINA: Yes, I imagine they did. I (*hesitates*)—I'd like to thank you for taking me all the same. Karl's grateful too. It's Karl I have to thank, isn't it?

ERIKA, *with a scrutinizing look:* Yes, among others—including my husband.

KATHARINA: And you?

ERIKA *nods:* Yes, I had a little to do with it. I can't imagine that Karl would have lived for years with somebody I couldn't trust. In any case (*picks up the dossier and puts it down again*), I can't see anything in your dossier that would make *me* suspicious. You've trained as a waitress and worked in hotels as a chambermaid. You graduated from night school. You have a child—by Karl, I take it?

KATHARINA: Yes, by Karl. He's four. He's called Heinrich, after Karl's father.

ERIKA *laughs:* Yes, I read about that. Rather an old-fashioned name, I thought—who calls a boy Heinrich these days? (*Flips through the manuscript.*) And you've taken part in a few demos.

KATHARINA: And I was involved in a theft.

ERIKA, *casually:* Yes, so I read. You stole money that you thought was due you. Perhaps it really was.

KATHARINA: It *was* due me. Overtime. They deducted the wrong amount.

ERIKA: I used to steal too—whenever possible—during the war. Having been trained to sell shoes, I was called up for service with the army. Shoes, boots, leather goods . . . I was never caught. It could have gone wrong, of course—sabotage, theft of army property. I was hungry, and so was my husband when he was on furlough. He stole things too. (*Quietly, smiling*) Don't pass it on. I went on stealing after the war too, from the American mess. I decided that that was due me too—cigarettes and chocolate—for my husband, who was a hungry student with a craving for cigarettes. No, but there's something else I have to know. Do you go in for eavesdropping?

KATHARINA: No, but I do have ears, and I can't help hearing things.

ERIKA: And do you talk?

KATHARINA *hesitates, very embarrassed:* Karl and I have no secrets. (*She shakes her head. Erika looks at her in alarm.*) No, I don't tell him anything—anything political. He just happens to be very fond of you and Herr Wubler and likes to know how you're getting on.

ERIKA *sighs:* And how are we getting on?

KATHARINA *smiles:* Not badly, I gather—and (*points to the newspaper*) naturally he reads what's in the papers, and we talk about the news stories.

ERIKA: It says in the paper that my husband is not implicated in this Bingerle affair. But there's something else that might affect Karl. (*Katharina remains silent.*) You don't know what I'm talking about, then?

KATHARINA: No.

ERIKA: Last night, for the third time, a valuable grand piano—one that Beethoven is supposed to have played on—was dismantled and the parts were stacked up in front of the fireplace to be burned. This time it happened at the Kapspeters' place. You know . . .

KATHARINA: Yes, I've read about it. I've often served at the Kapspeters'. I was there last night.

ERIKA, *putting her hand to her head:* Yes—that must be why

you seemed so familiar. And you've served at Kilian's too, haven't you?

KATHARINA: And at Heulbuck's—and I've seen you too.

ERIKA: And you know that Karl specializes in chopping up grand pianos?

KATHARINA: Yes, he's told me. Seven years ago he chopped up his own and burned it in the fireplace. His wife left him, and you stopped seeing him.

ERIKA: He lost not only a few friends but a lot of sympathizers. I became afraid of him—there was something so cold about the way he did it, utterly cold, precise and deliberate. And there was a smell of burnt lacquer. He only kept the casters, for some odd reason.

KATHARINA: Are you still afraid of him?

ERIKA: No, not *of* him, but *for* him. I love him like the son I never had. (*With some emotion*) I even trust him—but then five years ago Bransen's piano was dismantled, and then four years ago Florian's, and now Kapspeter's.

KATHARINA: I know, and each time he came under suspicion, and each time was proved innocent.

ERIKA: Has he told you about the affair in Rio?

KATHARINA: Yes, he's told me everything, and I also know that he owes it to you that he got such a light sentence, and that it was suspended. He had nothing to do with this (*pointing to the newspaper*) or the thing at Bransen's.

ERIKA: I hope so, for his sake. I still love him, even if (*shaking her head*) . . . even his wife didn't understand him. And do you know about the things he does—how he earns his measly bit of money?

KATHARINA: No. Sometimes he's away for quite a time, and afterwards he has money, but I never know how he's earned it. He always says it's top secret—and ridiculous. Ridiculously top secret. We live very frugally.

ERIKA, *pointing to the dossier:* And you want to get away from here?

KATHARINA: Yes, *I* do, but *he* doesn't. (*Staring into the void*) Yes, I'd like to get out, if only I knew where to go. Not without him, of course—but maybe I can talk him into it. (*Listens.*) Your husband's coming. I'll bring his egg. (*She goes out.*)

Wubler enters, dressed formally in a black suit, etc. He embraces his wife, kisses her on the cheek, hangs his jacket over his chair, and sits down.

WUBLER: I gather you didn't sleep well.

ERIKA: Like you—I didn't sleep a wink.

Katharina brings Wubler's egg, places it in front of him, and goes out.

WUBLER: You'd probably been eavesdropping again, and then you were all churned up with fear, annoyance, and anger. Don't eavesdrop anymore, Erika.

ERIKA: Of course I'd been eavesdropping, as I always do when you have a meeting here, and you know I've always eavesdropped—for the last thirty-six years. I used to eavesdrop in Dirwangen. The stovepipe went from the kitchen into the living room, so all I had to do was to open the little soot flap. And at Huhlsbolzenheim I used to stand on the balcony, just as I do here. (*Points upward.*) You know—and you want me to know—last night there was somebody sitting here (*indicating her own chair*).

WUBLER, *anxiously:* No names, Erika, no names.

ERIKA, *laughing:* So now there are three people whose names mustn't be mentioned. Wouldn't it be better to give them numbers? Number One—that's *him,* you know. Number Two—that's *him,* you know. And the one sitting here was Number Three.

WUBLER: You've learned by now that politics is a dirty business.

ERIKA: Which doesn't mean, of course, that all dirt is political.

WUBLER, *looking at her in surprise:* Up to now you've been wise enough not to talk, not to gossip, and certainly not in front of journalists—as Elisabeth Blaukrämer did—and you've never gone around to all the cafés and restaurants and made trouble, the way she did.

ERIKA: She didn't just eavesdrop—she read documents and memoranda and made notes. And the man who was here last night—*she* saw him too. Number Three. I didn't see him clearly, but I recognized his voice. It was the same voice that used to make us all tremble, the voice that would have sent all of you to your deaths—all you soldiers, and the rest of us too. That voice, on my veranda—and that laugh . . .

WUBLER, *having just broken his egg, gets up and goes over to Erika, embraces her, and says softly:* Don't go on, I beg of you. You were mistaken.

ERIKA, *extricating herself from his embrace:* It was a murderous voice, the voice of a murderer. His henchmen would have strung you up if I hadn't quickly thrown a sack over you in the broom closet when they came searching for you.

WUBLER, *becoming increasingly anxious:* Keep your voice down. (*In an uncertain tone*) You're mistaken. (*Menacingly*) It was the same man that Elisabeth Blaukrämer claims to have seen and heard. She couldn't prove anything and only made trouble.

ERIKA: Until he put her into the nuthouse. No, she couldn't prove anything—but she was right all the same. You know better than I do that not everything one can't prove is untrue. Plottger's wife couldn't prove anything either, until the truth she couldn't prove drove her mad, and she killed herself. Don't worry, I won't go mad, and I won't talk either, precisely because I can't prove anything. After all, one knows only too well what things hysterical women imagine: being sex-starved and frustrated, they take to drink and start hallucinating. No, I won't talk, but I know what I know and I heard what I heard. And you know perfectly well that Elisabeth Blaukrämer was *not* lying.

WUBLER: She doesn't have an ounce of imagination, otherwise she wouldn't have gone on about what she called the truth. And you—you couldn't sleep after what you'd heard, could you?

ERIKA: I know perfectly well that my ears can't give evidence. (*In a severe tone*) You should keep out of it, Hermann. (*Very severely*) You've done enough, Hermann, quite enough. What do you intend to do about Bingerle? I'm allowed to use *his* name, I take it. It's even in the paper. Or should I call him Number Four? No, I'll reserve Number Four for God, whom you're all so fond of invoking: Number Four is our dear Lord and Father—you'd no doubt forgotten that He had one or two other names as well.

WUBLER: I've never heard you talk like this, Erika, in all of forty years.

ERIKA: Yes, you have, Hermann, once—almost forty years ago, when you deserted from the great German army and hid in the broom closet, and I threw an empty potato sack over you. You heard then how I spoke to the watchdogs, three days after Hitler's suicide. The watchdogs were the emissaries of Number Three, who was known as the Bloodhound. And you heard how I spoke to Chundt and slapped Blaukrämer's face and threw Halberkamm out of the house. My voice can't be all that new to you. And when I slapped the Sponge's face—you heard this new voice of mine then, too.

WUBLER: That was a long time ago, and I hope you won't talk about it—about my deserting, I mean.

ERIKA, *laughing:* No, I won't tell the Defense Committee about it, or the generals who invite us to their parties every so often—but I can mention it to you. And there were other occasions when you must have heard this voice of mine: whenever I asked you not to mention Chundt in my father's presence—remember?

WUBLER: Your father was a fanatic. He—

ERIKA: Yes, he was fanatical: he hated Chundt, and when I invited him for coffee he made me swear that the coffee and cakes had been bought not with Chundt's money but out of your fees as an attorney. He'd rather have starved than accept a piece of bread from Chundt—and he'd probably gone hungry often enough. And now I'll say it again: you've done enough, Hermann.

WUBLER: Since when this sudden liking for Bingerle?

ERIKA: I don't like him, I never have, and I could have foreseen—any of you could have foreseen—that he'd try to double-cross you. No, and I didn't much care for the way Blaukrämer laughed when he talked about him; or the way the other one laughed—you know, Number Three. It gave me the shivers—I always get the shivers when Blaukrämer laughs—and then, when the other one joined in . . .

WUBLER, *agitated and imploring:* Don't eavesdrop anymore, Erika, I beg of you. Don't ever do it again—think of Elisabeth Blaukrämer.

ERIKA, *putting her arm around him:* I stood there shivering until they left—Halberkamm, Blaukrämer, Chundt, and . . . Number Three. They were drunk by the time they left, staggering about and laughing. And you went on sitting there by yourself, getting quietly drunk.

WUBLER: You should have come to me. I thought you were asleep and didn't want to wake you.

ERIKA: Wake me? I lay awake until I heard Katharina come in and the smell of coffee began to come up from the kitchen. At last we've got a girl who can make coffee. I don't care if she's a full-fledged Communist—she knows how to make coffee.

WUBLER: She probably isn't a Communist—but at the same time she's not quite kosher. She did try for a time to emigrate to Cuba. Karl managed to prevent that.

ERIKA: She's Karl's girlfriend, and that's enough for me. You mention Elisabeth Blaukrämer rather too often. I've visited her twice, and I'm not going a third time. That sort of nuthouse is a bit too classy for my liking—an elegant cross between a luxury hotel and a sanitarium. And there are only women there, very rich women with diamonds and knickknacks. They go there to have their— what's the expression?—to have their memories corrected. So that's what you're threatening me with: do you intend to send me there?

WUBLER, *very frightened:* I'll never send you there—never. *I won't—*

ERIKA: *You* won't? But perhaps somebody else will? Chundt, perhaps, or Blaukrämer, or the other one? I hardly saw him—I only caught a glimpse of him when he lit his pipe: white-haired, distinguished, lots of Old World charm, like most surviving murderers. It just so happens that I can use my ears, and my eyes, and I sit upstairs on my balcony one balmy summer evening, having a glass of wine and looking down at the Rhine, which sometimes really does gleam like silver. Why do you meet here? Why don't you go to one of your official houses or one of your academies? The Johanneshaus or the Edelweiss? I know something that you don't know, Hermann: Chundt, Blaukrämer, and Halberkamm *want* me to eavesdrop. It's a kind of attempted rape—they *want* me to eat the filth I'm not allowed to talk about. Anyway, I'm the only wife Chundt hasn't been able to get, the only one Blaukrämer hasn't been able to—how do they put it?—"steer in his direction." And I'm not even a banker's daughter, not even titled, only the daughter of a fanatical village shopkeeper who never took more

than his ration, even though he was a grocer—not an
ounce of butter more than he was entitled to. It would
make Halberkamm collapse with laughter—a man who
was fanatical about justice and also had the misfortune to
be a pious Catholic. Do you know why my brother vol-
unteered for the forces? Because he thought that in the
army he'd get enough to eat—when he was still a mere
child, a boy who was caught stealing a few times by his
father, cutting himself a slice of sausage or helping himself to some bread and butter. My father virtually drove
him out of the house, and then they shot him, over in
Normandy. I think about him every day. I thought about
him a lot last night while the Bloodhound was sitting
down here: silver-haired, distinguished, old, drawing his
big pension, and laughing in that murderous way as you
talked about Bingerle. (*Wubler gives her a pained look.*) You
knew, of course, that Chundt was after me, right from
the start, when we were still at Dirwangen? You did
know, didn't you?

WUBLER *nods and sighs:* Yes, but I always trusted you. Otherwise I'd have . . .

ERIKA: You'd have done what?

WUBLER: I'd have strangled him.

ERIKA: Perhaps you ought to have done that early on. Not
on my account. He was always trying. The last time was
fifteen years ago, down at the Johanneshaus, by the lake—
at that time I was still one of the women he was keen to
sleep with. (*Lowering her voice*) It was misty—late in Sep-
tember, chilly, very early in the morning. I woke when
you got up. I went to the kitchen, made myself some
coffee, and went back to bed. I lay there with the window open and thought about my father, my brother, the
nuns at my school, whom I loved—and still do—about
my mother, and of course about us. And then I *saw* the
two of you. I've got eyes, you know, Hermann, not just

ears. I *saw* you drive out to dump the Klossow documents in the lake. (*Wubler stares at her.*) So you didn't know I knew? I saw you drive out, as though you were going fishing, with lots of tackle, but you also had diving gear, lots of lead belts. I thought: are *they* going diving on a chilly morning like this? But then I saw you had two sea bags. They probably contained the Klossow documents, which have never been seen since. Even the police haven't found them. You came back without the sea bags, without the lead belts, and you hadn't caught anything—not a single fish. But the documents were nine hundred feet below the surface of the lake. It was a beautiful morning, with mist over the lake, birds in the reeds. The mist slowly cleared, and it was a fine day. The sun broke through, and in the casino I heard the two of you laughing—drinking and laughing. And the great Herr Chundt, for whose benefit the great dumping operation was being mounted—that was no job for him; it was too dirty—he stayed in bed, and before you got back he tried to get into mine. Calm down, Hermann, before you go and strangle your best friend. I didn't let him into the room—I've never let anybody in, Hermann. In any case, I've never spotted the charm he's supposed to have. I've never understood what people were going on about; I've always found him rather lacking in subtlety. Blaukrämer and Halberkamm have always been ready to put their wives at his disposal—Elisabeth told me, at the Johanneshaus or the Petrusheim. You knew perfectly well that he was after me right from the beginning, at Dirwangen, when you were all starting out on your careers, and you yourself were working yourself to death for him. Bingerle was also one of the gang from the start—young, and as keen as an altar boy. And my God, how hungry you all were—how hungry *we* all were. So hungry!

WUBLER, *distraught, shakes his head:* I suspected it at times, but I never knew—I never actually *knew*. Why didn't you tell me?—about Chundt, I mean.

ERIKA, *in consternation:* Yes, why didn't I? Why? It would probably all have turned out differently. I couldn't have *proved* anything—and you know what people think about women who tell stories like that without being able to prove anything. He'd have said I was hysterical, and you might have had your doubts too. It's funny how women hardly ever tell people about things like that. But there's another reason (*speaks more softly*), one that's difficult to talk about but true all the same. There's no need for you to laugh at what I'm going to say, but it's true. You're so innocent. There's nothing sweeter than a man who's innocent, and you're one. . . .

WUBLER: In spite of the affair with the Golpen girl?

ERIKA: The affair with the Golpen girl just shows how innocent you are. Five days of written exams at the Academy—and then a woman with breasts like that! They sent her up to your room to put you in a situation of conflict, and *she* wanted to use you to help her career along. Oh, Hermann, that proves your innocence. Halberkamm put her up to it and sent her to your room.

WUBLER: And what about Karl, the little count who's living with our new help?

ERIKA: He's like a son to me, the son I've never had, or a younger brother I once had, whom they shot. When we met Karl I was forty-eight and he was twenty-four. And in any case he's anything but a ladies' man. But he has charm, and he— Oh, Hermann, I'd never have done that.

WUBLER: As age goes, he's probably more like a brother than a son.

ERIKA: When he was born I was twenty-four. The curious thing is that you love his first wife, and not the way one loves a daughter or a sister.

WUBLER: I love her the way a man loves a woman.

ERIKA: You've got a date with her this evening. Has she recovered from the shock over the piano? Does she want to play duets with you again? The Chopin arrangements?

WUBLER: She's never touched a piano since— No, I've got to warn her: she's about to do something very foolish. . . .

ERIKA: Does she want to leave Grobsch? For you? With you?

WUBLER: Oh, Erika—you know, I've no idea whether I love her *because* I don't have a chance with her or whether I'm afraid I might have. She's thirty years younger than I am. No, she's fallen in love with this Cuban and wants to go off with him—to Cuba.

ERIKA: Eva Plint going to Cuba! That's funny; Katharina wanted to go to Cuba. What do they expect to find there?

WUBLER: They want to get away from here and don't know where to go. In Katharina's case I can understand it: she's worked as a waitress here for ten years, in all the houses, on all sorts of occasions. Leading that kind of life makes you want to throw up. Don't you want to get away from here too?

ERIKA *nods, wearily:* Yes, but I know there's nowhere to go, and so I'll probably have to stay. It's not my home, but it's where I live. There are a lot of people I like here and wouldn't want to part from. I couldn't live anywhere else, yet I want to get away—and I want to stay with you: in so many ways you're still the nice shy young man I took up to my room all those years ago. As for Karl, I'm not worried about him. That rather surprises me. It's not important whether I'm near him or not.

WUBLER, *picking up the newspaper:* You've read what happened at Kapspeter's last night?

ERIKA: Yes, I've read about it. (*After a brief silence*) It's strange: I no longer find what he did to his own grand piano so dreadful. Is Karl under suspicion in the Kapspeter case?

WUBLER: Suspicion will automatically fall on him. I hope he has an alibi.

ERIKA *laughs:* He's sure to have. I'm not in the least worried. Ten minutes ago I saw him through the telescope. He was sitting on the steps of his trailer with a mug of coffee in his hand, reading the paper. He looked quite cheerful. (*Softly*) You won't get that one. And you didn't get him that time when you had him and he was supposed to go to jail.

WUBLER: Chundt hates him, without even knowing him—and you know what Chundt is like. Incidentally, you're wrong if you imagine that Chundt was ever as hungry as we were. He never suffered from hunger, and that was the great advantage he had over all of us—our mouths used to water, but his never did. He's never known the difference between appetite and hunger. Nobody knows to this day where he got to during the war, and how. There are just a few pointers to Italy.

ERIKA: Yes, I know what he's like, and not only from the angle I've been describing to you. I'll never forget the moment he first set foot in our attic apartment at Dirwangen, after that discussion at the presbytery. He told you that the only thing that really mattered was politics, that politics was a better bet than the law or any career in business. The old Nazis were trembling with fear, he said, whereas you were all young and had unblemished records. Power was there for the taking. Politics was like a deserted factory that was still completely intact, though the bosses had run away. It was now vital to resume production. He also said that the fear of the old Nazis was worth its weight in gold. You said "Yes," and from that moment you were in business, especially when you were joined by that American, Bradley. We had eggs for breakfast, and real coffee; we moved into a bigger apartment, and then into a really big one. You took your state exam in record time, and your doctorate in even less. Then we got a house, and you became head of the rural district of Huhlsbolzenheim, and then we got another house. The politics factory moved into top gear, and production never flagged. And then Blaukrämer appeared on the scene, a former Nazi, and Halberkamm, who'd never been a Nazi—Chundt managed it all very skillfully. And Bingerle, who was neither a Nazi nor a non-Nazi—just a greedy young dog. But now, Hermann, it's *got to stop.* Did I hear correctly last night—is Blaukrämer going to be made a minister? Blaukrämer?

WUBLER: Plukanski's no longer acceptable: there are disclosures circulating about him that can no longer be covered up. From the war in Poland. We can't go on supporting him.

ERIKA: How many Jews and Poles did he kill?

WUBLER: He didn't kill anyone, but there was some shady dealing with the partisans. *We* don't want to topple him; it's the Poles—quite an incredible story.

ERIKA: And so you have to give Blaukrämer a ministry? Blaukrämer?

WUBLER: It's been decided that Plukanski can no longer be supported.

ERIKA: But Blaukrämer! You can't do it. There are some things you just can't do. You know what he did to his ex-wife, Elisabeth, and what he's doing to his latest, Trude. He's the type of man I'd regard as a sex offender.

WUBLER: Has he tried . . . with you?

ERIKA: No, he hasn't. He's looked at me once or twice as though he'd like to, but one look from me—literally one look—and his hands began to tremble. That was when we were still at Huhlsbolzenheim. Since then—no; he's the sort even *I* would strangle. My God, Hermann, why does a man like that have to get a ministry?

WUBLER: Chundt calls it "stretching the bounds of toleration," continually extending them. If Blaukrämer becomes a minister and the public tolerates it, then . . .

ERIKA: Then one day the public might be prepared to tolerate Chundt, you mean. And you?

WUBLER: Don't worry, I'm not the type—and I don't want a ministry. I'm the spider that spins the web, not the web itself. And we really can't go on supporting Plukanski. We've always called him Apple Cheeks—and this particular apple is rotten to the core.

ERIKA: I see, and the apple's about to fall—and so now you pick an apple like Blaukrämer, whom everyone knows to be rotten. That was a good phrase of Chundt's— "stretching the bounds of toleration."

WUBLER, *wearily:* There was nothing I could do about it, nothing. . . .

ERIKA: And Bingerle—what's going to happen to him? Their laughter sounded like the swish of the guillotine. All three of them were laughing. You stayed so silent. I suppose smart little Bingerle appropriated a few documents before the rest were burned or dumped in some lake.

WUBLER: He's gone too far. He's taken money from us, and he's taken money from the others, and when he tried to get money from third parties, they pounced on him and put him in the calaboose. They couldn't prove anything against him, so today he's being released. It's the documents we want, not him.

ERIKA: And what if he were to stay in prison? (*Wubler gives her a significant and questioning look.*) You're right: he wouldn't be safe there either. So many suicides take place in prison. All the same, you could warn him. The warden at Ploringen is Stützling, an old classmate of yours from your student days. He was always hungry too, and while he was studying he got quite a few bowls of soup at our place. And if you gave him a few cigarettes, it made him feel like a millionaire.

WUBLER: Bingerle's been warned often enough. He knows the score.

ERIKA: And does he know his life could be at stake?

WUBLER: He must know that too. He's a gambler, and he plays for high stakes.

ERIKA: One thing I didn't understand last night—something about a count.

WUBLER: But surely you know Chundt's old trick? Whenever a delicate matter crops up, he presses some count into service if it's at all possible—some young, seemingly high-minded, dynamic count, preferably one who owns a smart car or, better still, his own plane.

ERIKA: Why not a prince—a royal highness?

WUBLER *laughs:* Surprisingly enough, a count sounds better than a prince or a royal highness. The word has a better ring to it; it sounds more serious. Royal highnesses are too reminiscent of operetta. . . .

ERIKA: Yes, I remember: there was that Count Praunheim. . . .

WUBLER, *almost in a fury:* And Count Treutz zu Stumm.

ERIKA: They were nice, and so was Count Klohren.

WUBLER, *really furious:* Yes, they were frightfully nice.

ERIKA: And now you've found yourselves a new count.

WUBLER: Count Erle zu Berben. He's young and dynamic, and he owns a smart car.

ERIKA: But now it really is time you had your egg and a roll.

Wubler sips his coffee, lights a cigarette, and pushes the egg to one side.

ERIKA: This is the first time in thirty-seven years that you haven't wanted your egg—the first time since we started

having eggs for breakfast. We didn't always have eggs—
only after Chundt appeared on the scene.

WUBLER: You're right; it's the first time since '45 that I
haven't felt like breakfast. I'm thinking about Stützling.
He's a decent, honest lawyer, but no telephone call I can
make will help Bingerle anymore: he's in the same danger whether he stays in jail or gets out. (*Smokes and sips
his coffee.*) Young Count Erle zu Berben will be outside
the prison on the dot of two. He'll simply escort him to
a plane. But tell me, why have you never told me about
Chundt and you, or about Chundt's affairs with Elisabeth Blaukrämer and Gertrud Halberkamm?

ERIKA, *softly:* Are you really telling me you didn't know?
Don't you know what men are like when they fancy
they're irresistible? (*She gets up, goes over to him, and takes
his face in her hands.*) Men who believe that everything's
there for the taking, absolutely everything? (*Hesitates.*)
Elisabeth told me the details. She did it out of hatred,
hatred for Blaukrämer and Chundt. She probably hu-
miliated Chundt—I don't know how—made him look
ridiculous somehow. And then, my dear Hermann, I
didn't want to spoil that innocence of yours; there's
nothing more touching than men who retain their innocence. It's always amazed me to see how innocent a
man can remain in spite of working alongside Chundt,
Halberkamm, Blaukrämer, and Bingerle. A man's innocence is something precious. You're the irresistible one.
It was dark, forty-four years ago, when you came up and
spoke to me. It was in the blackout, there'd been an air-
raid warning, and your rookie's uniform didn't fit very
well, and when I took you back to my room it wasn't
because I felt sorry for you or because I loved you: I just
had to have you, I had to know what it was like being
with a man. It was curiosity. I was a girl of eighteen,
with a religious upbringing, a salesgirl in a shoe shop—

and when I saw you in the light I was alarmed to see how ugly you were. Yes, your uniform was somehow awry, and your boots were too big for you. And you . . . you were alarmed to see how pretty I was—you hadn't had a good look at me—and you were alarmed by my fear that you wouldn't make a pass at me. One of us had to make a move, and I was afraid it would have to be me. But in the end you made the first move, and then I saw your eyes, your hands, and later your feet—especially your eyes, like a toad's eyes, the color of asphalt, gentle, sad, and clever. You've no idea how ridiculous the beaux are who try to make it with a salesgirl—what clumsy hands they have and what stupid eyes—and also the guys I met at Hilde's, the girl who had the room next to mine. They were always trying to fix me up with someone. Oh, Hermann, it's never been difficult for me to keep my promise and remain faithful to you. And was I to tell *you* what Elisabeth got up to with the irresistible Chundt in order to humiliate him? Was I to tell *you*? You, with your soft, innocent skin?

WUBLER, *looking at her in astonishment, softly:* It's time you started changing. How about wearing the gray two-piece? With the pink coral brooch? Blaukrämer will be here in twenty minutes; you can just make it. You have to look especially good today. (*Laughs.*) Television—live—the whole ceremony.

ERIKA: I'm not going to change, Hermann. I'm going to sit on my balcony in my dressing gown, unkempt, drinking coffee and looking through the telescope at Karl's garden, to see if he's still there and how he's looking. I'll watch the boats on the Rhine, see the skipper's wife bring her husband's coffee to the wheelhouse and put her arm around him. At the least hint of intimacy I'll look away and switch off the telescope.

WUBLER, *alarmed:* You mean you're not coming with me?

Erika, don't play games. You can't do this—you can't desert me. It'll be the first time you've sat next to Heulbuck, the first time you've been allowed to. The solemn mass in memory of Erftler-Blum, celebrated by a cardinal, assisted by three bishops—the whole mass sung in Latin. It'll cause a scandal if you aren't there.

ERIKA: Oh, Hermann, you really are a child still. There'll be a minor contretemps, a bit of trouble with Chundt and Blaukrämer—but not the least scandal. Okay, so I'm to be allowed to sit next to Heulbuck! Is that supposed to knock me out? Next to Heulbuck—perhaps between Heulbuck and Kapspeter, whose grand piano was given a going-over last night. And Blaukrämer's second wife, the ineffable Trude, Heulbuck's first, Halberkamm's third—and Plukanski, still just in office. Oh, Hermann, don't you go either. Call up Stützling or Count Erle zu Berben. I don't want to sit next to Heulbuck, I don't want to go to any more high masses, not even on the twentieth anniversary of Erftler-Blum's death. No, Hermann, I don't want to associate with VIPs anymore, or with vestals who end up moments later in the arms of Chundt. And no doubt the Sponge will be there too, touting his Heaven Hint shares. What actually *is* Heaven Hint, by the way?

WUBLER, *morosely:* Something to do with space weapons. Erika, what's come over you all of a sudden?

ERIKA: It's not all that sudden. You know I've never felt happy on these occasions, not on the tenth or the fifteenth anniversary of Erftler-Blum's death—always carried on radio and television, with Grüff as reporter and Bleiler as commentator: "And now we see, as always, the immaculately dressed Frau Wubler, together with her husband, the gray eminence. . . ." Last night I thought of my brother, whom they shot in Normandy when he was nineteen—and of my father, who was born embittered and died embittered—and of my mother, who died of exhaustion, tired, constantly tired, worn out by her husband's fanaticism. Oh, Hermann, don't say anything. And the cardinal will give another address extolling Erftler's services and Christian values, and Heulbuck, with his usual mindless Rhineland jollity, will sit there savoring the Latin he learned as an altar boy.

WUBLER: Chundt will be livid. He'll connect your absence with last night.

ERIKA: He won't have to make the connection—it's there already: he'll be right.

WUBLER: So you're ill.

ERIKA: I'm *not* ill. I'm tired, but I could survive the high mass.

WUBLER: Kapspeter really admires you, and so does Heulbuck; they're fond of you, and Erftler positively loved you.

ERIKA: But I didn't love him. He was always nice to me, that's true, but I never liked him. I know—he saw me as the embodiment of democracy: a shopkeeper's daughter, a salesgirl who worked her way through night school and almost became a pianist. And I know that Kapspeter is the greatest, wisest, and most pious of bankers, a really fine-feeling man, cultured, sensitive, and with exquisite taste—and yet (*darkly*) I presume that *somehow* he profited from the bullet or the grenade that killed my brother. And, Hermann, the dreadful thing is that I can't feel sorry about his piano being dismantled. And what's even more dreadful—I'm beginning to have some *understanding* for Karl. I've got an uncanny feeling that there was something solemn and significant about his destroying his own grand. It was a serious act, and we never understood him. Eva didn't either, though *she* loved him. I also know

that with Bingerle it's not just a question of a few documents. There are probably any number of documents
about Chundt. It's a question of—

WUBLER, *utterly scared:* Don't say the name, please. . . .

ERIKA: Okay, no names. Let's stay with Number One,
whom you could have saved but didn't. You wanted to
do two things—to show how hard you were and to make
sure of getting a victim. I know, Hermann: I've sat next
to you when you were telephoning. But you liked
him. . . .

WUBLER: Yes, I liked him, and his wife and children. It
wasn't a question of Chundt's crooked dealings, or of
Klossow and Plottger, or of Bingerle. It was a question
of something you resolutely refuse to understand—the
state.

ERIKA: And at his funeral you'd have preferred to have the
pope officiating, but an archbishop would do in a pinch.
And Heulbuck made a really touching speech. Kapspeter
sat in front and cried his eyes out—genuine tears. Even
Chundt's eyes were moist: you could see the tears glint-
ing on the television screen. Did they use glycerin?

WUBLER: Don't become cynical, Erika. He's dead; he was
murdered.

ERIKA: And the practiced way Chundt moved his missal
from side to side and made his genuflections. Hermann,
I'll say it again: you've gone far enough. I'm being serious, Hermann—it's not just a whim, not just the mood
I'm in. Stay with me and let's look down at the Rhine
together: there's dazzling white washing hanging on the
lines; there are dogs running to and fro behind the deck
rails and children playing in their playpens.

WUBLER, *with a sigh:* I can't, Erika. I have to go—perhaps
for the last time. For ages it's been no fun for me either.

ERIKA: For a long time I thought it was fun, or rather for
some time—even the solemn mass for the man whose

name mustn't be mentioned. I liked him too—I liked all the razzmatazz. He was a charming villain. I even enjoyed my own feeling of horror when Heulbuck turned the taps on and his revolting Rhineland grief came gushing out. And for a long time I enjoyed all the rest of it—the parties with all the gossip and whispering, the ceremonial and the intrigues and the petty conspiracies, the small talk and the brazen self-serving. I felt good in my pretty clothes and the jewelry you bought me; I could rely on your impeccable taste. It was fun having the canapés and drinks; playing the piano with you and Karl; the theater, the receptions, the balls. But then they shunted Elisabeth off to Kuhlbollen, where I visited her twice. And yesterday I heard that that nice Frau Bebber has ended up there too. Did you know?

WUBLER: Only that he wanted to get rid of her.

ERIKA: And now he has. Such a pretty little blond creature, a genuine blonde, a bit dumb, but amusing—tennis, dancing, the odd flirtation, canasta. He's gotten rid of her, just as Bransen has gotten rid of his wife: she does the rounds of all the hotels on the Riviera and the Côte d'Azur, sitting in front of the one-arm bandits with her little basket of coins, waiting for the jackpot she doesn't need. And at Kuhlbollen they even send a nice young man up to your room if you get too lonesome—all so tasteful and aboveboard. Stay with me, Hermann. Or let's go away.

WUBLER: But where to? (*They look at each other in silence for a while.*)

ERIKA: Anywhere, but not back home—not back where we came from. I don't want to have to lead the dancing with the mayor, or the champion marksmen at the hunters' ball, or the head of the rural district, or the local druggist, or the landlord of the local inn. I don't want to be photographed again with the local member of parliament, wineglass held high. No more folk music, no more collections for deprived children making their first communion. You ask me where we could go. I don't know . . . so let's stay here.

WUBLER: You can't leave me *alone.*

ERIKA: I don't intend to, not even if your little Eva were prepared to answer your prayers.

WUBLER: Oh, she's not just in love with her Cuban; she also loves Grobsch. Don't forget about him: he's her husband, and she loves him. (*Sadly*) He's an able chap. But they've finished him off too. They've saddled him with Plukanski; he won't last much longer. No, she loves two men, and she's still attached to Karl. There's no room for me as a fourth party.

ERIKA: I can't forget the little rookie with the droopy uniform who had the courage to touch me and seduce me. I was afraid I'd have to touch you and seduce you—but I'd have done it. It's something you learn, something you know, even if you've had a religious upbringing. After all, there was another girl living in the same attic; she used to tell me everything and explain everything to me. Anyhow, you didn't crumple up with shyness. You knew that it was not just men who had desires, but women too—that what they call chastity was a luxury we couldn't afford. And you think I'd leave you alone? All I ask is that we don't go back to Dirwangen or Huhlsbolzenheim—I couldn't bear that anymore. I couldn't bear being back home. The sad thing is that I couldn't have children; and it's a pity you couldn't remain an attorney or become a judge. . . .

KATHARINA *appears on the veranda:* A Dr. Blaukrämer is waiting for you in his car. He'd like you . . .

WUBLER *straightens his tie, takes his jacket from the back of the chair, puts it on, kisses Erika:* So I'll be going. There'll be trouble. (*Wubler leaves. Katharina remains.*)

ERIKA *goes over to Wubler's place and, still standing, spoons out the egg:* One thing I've never gotten used to is waste, in spite of my bank account, our grand piano, and our smart apartment with its view of the Rhine. In the old days an egg cost ten pfennigs, and as a salesgirl I used to earn a bare eighty-five marks, twenty of which went for the rent, and then there was electricity, heating, and laundry. (*She replaces the empty eggshell in the eggcup. At this moment Wubler returns with Blaukrämer.*)

BLAUKRÄMER *remains in the doorway:* You still seem to like the taste. You don't look all that sick.

ERIKA: I'm not sick—not even the sight of you makes me sick. What I'd most like to do is go with you just as I am, unkempt and wearing my dressing gown, and walk around the minster singing the All Saints litany while you attend your high mass.

BLAUKRÄMER *laughs:* Not a bad idea: committing a public nuisance, disturbing the peace—it might even be blasphemy. (*Looks at Wubler.*) And as we know, all are equal before the law. (*Seriously to Erika*) I'll give you ten minutes to change—we're in a generous mood today.

ERIKA: Yes, and then you can send me to join Elisabeth and the little Bebber woman—and all the others, whoever they are. . . .

BLAUKRÄMER: If you stay here and aren't sick, there'll be a scandal. Hermann, what have you got to say?

WUBLER: There's no shortage of scandals, worse ones than this, and they're all forgotten after three days. (*Goes up to Erika and kisses her.*) Just you stay here. There won't even *be* a scandal—just a bit of trouble.

BLAUKRÄMER: Are you encouraging her?

WUBLER: No, I'm not en*couraging* her. She's got enough courage of her own—if you need courage in a case like this.

BLAUKRÄMER: There are bound to be repercussions.

ERIKA: The only repercussion is that as from now I'm withdrawing from my public duties, my duties as a picture-book democrat. (*Wearily*) You'd better both be going if you . . .

Wubler kisses her again and leaves with Blaukrämer, who is furious.

KATHARINA, *who has heard the conversation, comes closer and says in a friendly tone:* Shall I clear the table?

ERIKA: Will you tell Karl about this?

KATHARINA: I don't think so. (*Smiles.*) That was a political matter—and in any case it would hurt him to think of you being victimized by Herr Blaukrämer. . . .

ERIKA: He's got a telescope too, and sometimes looks across here. (*Takes the telescope from the balustrade and looks through it.*) Nothing to see. Would you bring the coffee, milk, and sugar up to the balcony? And, my dear Katharina, once and for all: don't let anything go to waste. Take whatever you want—bread, milk, sausage. I hope the offer doesn't offend you.

KATHARINA: Not in the least, but please inform the security official outside. I'm not only politically unreliable; I have a previous conviction for theft.

ERIKA: Are you still studying? Do you intend taking a doctorate?

KATHARINA: Yes, if my dossier allows me to. On a subject to do with banking. As an economist I'm unemployed, but not as a waitress. (*Laughs.*) I worked for three years in Kapspeter's bank, and then I was dismissed. Don't ask me why—I don't know myself. So I went back to waitressing. When Karl was kicked out of the service, he only had his trailer and not a penny to his name, and nobody wanted to have anything to do with him. I worked in the crummiest sandwich bars and the smartest hotels, especially at parties—that was where I met Karl. After a long party at the Kilians', where he was one of the guests,

I was standing in front of the door, not knowing whether to take a taxi or not. Then he drove up, stopped his car, and drove me home.

ERIKA: And stayed the night?

KATHARINA: Yes, and we've been together ever since. Soon we'll be living together. (*Softly*) He talks about you and Herr Wubler, and about his wife. He only says nice things about you. I can't think of anybody he speaks ill of.

ERIKA: And what about you—do you speak ill of people?

KATHARINA: Yes, of Kapspeter: I failed him as an economist but am allowed to work for him as a waitress. I don't like him. I can imagine them giggling when they read the thing in the paper about the grand piano. I don't eavesdrop, and in our profession you mustn't gossip. What might I hear? What they say about Herr Chundt in the papers every now and then is worse than anything I might hear in your home. And Herr Blaukrämer ... Tell me, Frau Wubler, what could I hear? About Herr Halberkamm, for instance. After all, it's common knowledge that his hobby is inventing sauces and that they don't taste very good.

ERIKA: So, if you haven't been eavesdropping, what *have* you heard?

KATHARINA: I've done the rooms upstairs, and the bathroom, vacuumed the carpets and dusted, then done the kitchen—what is there to hear there? A name now and then: Chundt, Halberkamm, Bingerle, Blaukrämer—names that are in all the papers. And the only interesting thing was something you told me—that you're not going to the high mass. And soon the whole town will know that, without my having to say a word. We need the money I earn here. Every roll and every piece of sausage I can take home will be welcome. Even if I were inquisitive—which I'm not—and always had my ear to the door, I wouldn't put a good position like this at risk by being indiscreet. I hear things, I read things, and I put two and two together, but I've no time for gossip. In the evenings I work at my dissertation, and Karl helps me with it. The subject is one that wouldn't please Kapspeter at all—profit maximization in the third world. And I happened to be standing by the door when Herr Blaukrämer was ... when Herr Blaukrämer was very unpleasant to you. The high mass will be on the radio, by the way, *and* on television. Shall I bring the radio up to the balcony for you?

ERIKA: No, thanks, but if you want to hear it, do take the radio into the kitchen with you.

KATHARINA: Thanks, but I'm not keen on church services and that sort of thing. (*Softly*) That's the only respect in which I differ from Karl. He waxes quite poetical about them, and there's nothing wrong with poetry. But you see, I'm illegitimate, and so was my mother. And in those days they hadn't started chasing after every unmarried girl who got herself pregnant and sprinkling her with holy water. In those days, when my mother was born— her mother was a waitress too—the unborn life you were expecting was a source of disgrace: my mother was a source of disgrace, and so was I. Don't ask me to tell you what you perhaps know already: unmarried mothers and their children were not exactly sold on the fine pronouncements made by bishops. I'm sorry if what I've said offends you. Please forgive me, and if you think I've spoken out of turn ...

ERIKA: No, don't worry. I'll take the paper up with me, and please take a look at my grand now and then. Who knows whether the guy operates in daylight too? He'd only have to climb over the balustrade.

KATHARINA: You needn't worry about your grand.

ERIKA, *suspiciously:* How can you be so sure?

KATHARINA, *affecting something of the tone of a sociology lec-*

turer: From an analysis of previous dismantlings of grand pianos, it clearly emerges that in every case the piano belonged to a banker—Florian, Bransen, Kapspeter. This argues a particular intention on the part of the criminal. Herr Wubler is not a banker, and you are not a banker's wife. I would regard it as desirable to reinforce the piano security troops in all bankers' households. In your case I can see no danger. Anyhow, Kapspeter has already ordered a new grand. I heard that this morning—I still know a few people there.

ERIKA: You seem to be enjoying the whole thing a little bit too much, Katharina. And your dissertation on profit maximization in the third world does strike me as having some connection with the pleasure you get out of listing the cases of dismantled grands. I love my piano. I admit I was never a waitress, but I did work in a shoe shop, which is in some ways an even lowlier job—always kneeling in front of the customers and tending patiently to all the silly women who come in and try on three dozen pairs of shoes, even though you know in advance that they won't buy any, and they know it too. You can tell they're not going to buy anything the moment they come into the shop, yet you still have to fetch three dozen shoe boxes from the storeroom and be patient and polite, taking the shoes out of the boxes and helping the customers try them on, then putting them back in the boxes. And the customers haven't always washed their feet. What could have been humiliating actually gave me a feeling of pride, and sometimes, when I see some woman at a party, I ask myself: how would she have treated you if she'd been one of your customers forty years ago? It wasn't until I was twenty-five that I learned to play the piano, and it wasn't until I was over forty that I owned a grand. There were days—weeks, even—when it was my only consolation. Since then I haven't had much

sympathy with people who chop up such valuable instruments, take them to pieces or dismantle them—or
even burn them, as Karl did with his. In all conscience,
your hatred of Kapspeter—

KATHARINA: You've got me wrong: I'm against it too.
When I think of the money a thing like that costs, and
what one could get for that money . . . I don't understand
Karl. And yet, as a student or a bank employee, I've heard
so much about where money goes and where it comes
back from, multiplied threefold, tenfold, a hundredfold—
oil, armaments, tapestries. And about girls who have to
resort to alcohol or drugs in order not to throw up all
the time, and who then throw up because they've gotten
drunk so as *not* to throw up . . . And wherever you go,
you come up against that man they call the Sponge.

ERIKA *goes up to her:* I beg you, Katharina, for your own
sake . . . (*Shaking her head*) That sounds very much like
the class struggle. I know the Sponge too—on one occasion I even slapped his face.

KATHARINA, *very quietly:* What else is it if not a class struggle? At these parties you see people getting drunk and
throwing up—the same people who force the girls to
throw up. It's a class struggle fought out with vomit.
Sorry, I've let myself get worked up—I'm not normally
like this. But I heard you: not what you said but your
tone of voice. Didn't your voice sound like the class
struggle? Wasn't it the voice of the salesgirl who'd had
to kneel down too often and grit her teeth? Now I'm
putting my job at risk by allowing myself to interpret
your reasons for not going to the high mass—or not
going again: because you don't wish to go on playing
the part you probably never wanted to play anyway,
the part of the poor girl who made it. Forgive me, but I'm
saying all this because I like you, and when the time

comes for me to leave, I have a request that you may be able to fulfill.

ERIKA, *shattered and weary:* And that is?

KATHARINA: To give the party-goers a bit of advice. Tell them that the boys and girls who serve them are happy to take tips—or, to put it more elegantly, that we neither disdain them nor refuse them. You see, sometimes when we're serving we look so smart that we could be the daughters of the house or guests who are chipping in and helping. The result is that nobody dares to tip us. Tell them they can put the money in the pockets of our aprons or jackets.

ERIKA: I'll pass it on. The sad thing is, my dear girl, that I'll probably not be going to any more parties. Do you need money?

KATHARINA: Yes; I want to get away from here. (*Very quietly*) Sometimes, in the evening, I lie on the bed with my little boy, telling him a story or singing him a song, and then we'll play with the globe Karl gave us, turning it around and trying to pick out a country we could go to. We haven't found one yet.

ERIKA: So you don't like it here anymore?

KATHARINA: No; do you?

ERIKA: So you *were* eavesdropping?

KATHARINA, *vehemently:* No, I never do, but I heard your voice. You spoke for a long time, and very loud. Do you know somewhere to go?

ERIKA: No, and what's more, I know there's no point in looking for somewhere. And just one more thing: be careful. You frighten me with your ideas. What you have in your head will come out sooner or later—I discovered that myself today. Be on your guard. And you know, I'd have been willing to take tips, but nobody offers them to girls who work in shoe shops.

Katharina takes the tray and goes to the door.

ERIKA *continues:* There's another thing you must explain to me, since you're such a clever girl, with a gift for analysis. Why has my husband never become a minister? Do *you* know?

KATHARINA *stops in the doorway, holding the tray:* Don't *you* know? You really don't know—honestly? (*Erika shakes her head.*) Then I'll tell you: he's too good to be a minister—he really is. He's just too good! He's a brilliant planner, a real acrobat when it comes to ideas; he's built up the whole of Chundt's organization. His place is at his desk, at the telephone, at conferences, at secret talks. In public he doesn't come across—he's too shy and not much good at expressing himself freely; he's a planner and a policymaker, but he can't sell his policies. He's a born secretary—that's his métier. And you can console yourself: "secretary" is a distinguished title. The German Democratic Republic and the Soviet Union are run by secretaries—in fact, they're the leaders. Even the Vatican has its secretaries. And being secretary to Chundt . . . wouldn't you like me to make some fresh coffee and bring it upstairs?

ERIKA: No, but you can fix me a roll and honey.

KATHARINA: Wouldn't you like an egg?

ERIKA: No; one's enough at my age. And I'd better tell you: you're beginning to give me the creeps. When I'm upstairs I'm going to think a bit about Number Four and have a word or two with him. (*Katharina gives her a questioning look.*) Number Four is the one they always call God. Can I sing you a little song? (*Katharina looks at her in amazement and bewilderment. Erika sings:*)

> Heaven, send the just one down;
> Send him, clouds, in dew and rain.

Does that say anything to you? Does that stir anything inside you?

KATHARINA, *still standing with the tray in her hands, confused:*
Sounds quite nice, like an old-fashioned poem—and it
reminds me a bit of Karl. (*Smiles*) But it doesn't stir anything in me. I'm sorry . . . I'm sorry. Nothing.

ERIKA *smiles:* I think you're capable of learning—and now
to work. (*Exeunt.*)

Chapter 2

ERIKA WUBLER, *on the balcony above the veranda, the coffeepot and a cup of coffee beside her. View of the Rhine.*

This morning, for the first time since the end of the war, I was frightened. I was suddenly overcome by a strange kind of fear, quite unlike the fear I felt at the end of the war. Forty years without fear? No, I've often been anxious when Hermann became too involved in politics, and Chundt always frightened me with his boundless ambition to control both heaven and earth. Yes, he wants heaven too. Perhaps I have too much time to brood. After all, I don't have much to do: I have to perform my social duties at parties and dinners. At official banquets I always sit next to the second most important person present, sometimes the most important, and then I discover that even queens are real people, that they can even be stupid. I'm never bored on such occasions; I have no compunction about asking them about their husbands or wives, about their children or their favorite dishes, and obviously that's what's expected of the wife of the third most important person present—to be a nice, private individual. I'm not only allowed to tell people that I was once a salesgirl in a shoe shop; it's expected of me—after all, that's what democracy's all about. Some of them even pull their feet from under the table, and I have to give an opinion on their shoes.

The morning sun is pleasantly warm, the Rhine is calm

this weekend, and there are no pleasure boats to be seen yet. Over on the opposite bank there are already signs of fall, with red and yellow tints in the leaves of the cherry trees. The flags of the ships anchored on the other bank hang limply from the masts. I've come to like it here. At first I felt a stranger, but it was worse when Hermann was here all week and I was alone back home, always the first lady at balls, parties, and receptions given by the local dignitaries, at huntsmen's fairs and parish festivities. I don't yearn for the tootling of the local bands, which I never liked, or for the sweaty hands of corpulent mayors who felt obliged to invite me to dance and whisper to me, "Old Hermann's really quite a dog, isn't he?"

Herman was frightened, too, this morning. He still is. His hands were trembling so much that he didn't try to take a second spoonful of his egg. And as he was reaching for the coffeepot he suddenly stopped, and he lit his cigarette from the candle under the coffee warmer, for he probably wouldn't have been able to hold his lighter or matches steady. I know that it's Blaukrämer's wife who scares him, and the other wives up there. When I was about to mention Plietsch's name he gave me a look that was so imploring, so anxious and scared, that I stopped short. *(Puts the telescope to her eye, her hands trembling.)* No sign of the boy I'd have so much liked to have as a son. A Dutch and a Swiss ship are lying next to each other; a little farther down the Rhine, three Belgians are having breakfast on their terrace; a young boy is pouring milk on his cornflakes. *(Lays down the telescope, her hands still trembling.)* The last time I trembled was when the bombs were falling and the fighters were whizzing overhead, firing their cannon into the houses. I saw a young soldier hit as he was riding his bicycle; he was little more than a child. He was carrying his cooking utensils on the handlebar. He fell off and bled to death in the road, his blood mingling with the pea soup. And I trembled when the watchdogs who carried out Plietsch's orders came searching for Hermann. At that time I knew what I was scared of, why I was trembling. But what am I scared of now? What is it that frightens Hermann, whom I've never seen trembling before? He's not afraid for Bingerle. Is he afraid for me? Blaukrämer's ex really did have no imagination, but she told some fantastic stories. I've never told any, never, and I'd have needed no imagination to tell fantastic stories. *(Looks through the telescope again.)* Sometimes I envy the skippers' wives: their quarters look so cozy, with the pretty flowers at the windows and on the balconies. They always have their husbands with them, and they have their cars on deck in front of their doors. A Dutch diplomat once told me that they all do a bit of smuggling—quite a lot, in fact. *(Puts the telescope down.)* That was a good headline today: "Wubler's waistcoat obviously white." What's he scared of? My fear subsides for a time, then revives, and I get no pleasure from the view of the lovely Rhine valley down there. It reminds me of a poem I learned at school: "Where'er the world was fairest, it was but bleak and bare." The way they were laughing last night, the sound of Plietsch's voice, all the shouting—and Hermann so silent all the time! Then suddenly everyone became so glum—so heavy, grave, and apprehensive. At one time I took everything so lightly. Life had always been easy; for years we lived the life of Riley, and what a surprise it was when I suddenly—quite suddenly—turned sixty. I even joined in the laughter when Halberkamm said at the time, "The Americans are so naive, letting a thing like Watergate get so out of hand." But when he said, "My God, Vietnam— but they've got atom bombs!" not even Chundt laughed. That girl downstairs, Katharina—she's bright: she's right about Hermann being too shy to be minister material. He's no good at public speaking, whereas Chundt *is*, booming away and shaking his blond mane. How we laughed when

he got an actor in to show him how to shake his mane—
he needed no lessons on how to boom! Blaukrämer's a good
speaker too, when he's addressing a small audience. And
how they got control of all the various groups and the
media! Again that was Hermann's phrase: "First take control, then take action." "Omit nothing, neglect nothing,"
as Blaukrämer put it. It was Chundt who changed "take
control" into "strike."

That young woman downstairs I find reassuring and re-
freshing. She's got a heart, and a cool way of expressing
herself, and I admire her nonchalant attitude to what they
call sexuality. I always made heavy weather of it. Naturally
we'd been told by Sister Huberta that "men had desires,"
and then she added quite softly—but very clearly, so that
we could all hear—"And women have desires too." I knew
about the first from the antics of the boys in the village
when they tried to make a grab for us. I didn't get to know
the second until I was living in the town, in my shabby
attic, next to Hilde, who was a salesgirl like myself, in a
textile firm. She was nice, amusing, and frivolous, and
sometimes she took nice boys up to her room, boys she'd
met at dances. And on weekends she went away with men
for water sports, canoeing and what she called "terrific
necking sessions" in their tents on the riverbank. I always
blushed when she told me the details, and then she would
stop, because she was a really nice girl. Sometimes she
brought home reduced goods for me—underwear and
bras—and when I tried them on in her room she would tell
me, with a breathless admiration that was quite free of envy,
"Gee, with breasts like that you could go far." That made
me feel proud, but also apprehensive. I was scared by
Hilde's frivolous doings, and yet I liked her. We used to
tease each other, and sometimes I'd say to her, "Careful
you don't end up on the streets," and she'd say, "Why
don't you go into a convent and neck with your friend

Jesus." The village boys left us in no doubt about their sexuality. Some of them went in for obscene gestures, even while serving at mass. I was scared by their crude behavior, yet I knew that one day someone would have to behave crudely with me, even if he was the nicest, quietest boy in the world.

When we were sixteen, Sister Huberta said to us, "I've told you a lot about chastity, but if you're going out into the world to work, to learn a profession, to marry and have children, then you have to know that there's no chaste way of having children: a man has to desire you and you have to desire him." There were two things I found marvelous about the nuns—their singing and their lingerie. The way they sang their prayers was so soothing and entrancing; they sang a lot about love, which reminded me of folk songs. And their lingerie smelled so wholesome—it was so clean. Later on Hermann once told me that I was a secret lingerie fetishist.

Then Hilde stopped talking in her frivolous way. She said, "I don't want to lead you astray or corrupt you in any way; all I want is that you should enjoy yourself and have fun, and I can tell you, it's fun having boys. I hope you'll find one who really loves you." And that very evening I found him. I'd gone out into the street to find one— the best one available—and he turned out to be the best I could have found. I deliberately dressed up to look a bit nunnish—in a gray coat, a gray woolen cap, and the most sensible shoes I had. And when this little soldier took me shyly by the arm and said, "Say, miss, maybe we should get together"—which is just about the silliest way to address a girl—I answered in the same silly way and said, "Yes, maybe we should," and took him up to my room.

Yes, I was alarmed by his ugliness. It wasn't only that he was rather small; there was something wizened about him, and his uniform fitted so badly that I was scared he might be a hunchback. He wasn't, though, and later I was amazed at the difference between the skin on his body and the skin on his face: it was soft and white, like a child's, both on his body and on his hands, and his eyes didn't beg for sympathy. He was to be my husband: I'd already decided that I wanted to marry whoever came up and spoke to me and went home with me. As we were going up the stairs in the dark, he started running his hand up my legs, cautiously, almost tenderly, and that didn't strike me as at all improper. It was as though he wanted to feel for what his eyes couldn't see; it was a blind date, almost literally. Now I looked him full in the face, and he looked at me. His ugliness made me feel better about the shabbiness of my room—the old walnut bed, the tripod with the washbasin, the little table that was scarcely bigger than the chair.

I wasn't ashamed of the crucifix on the wall and the cheap print of the Madonna; in front of it, in a rickety brass candlestick, was a candle that I sometimes lit when I said my prayers. The few clothes I had were hung on nails on the wall; I even had a red-and-white-striped dressing gown, which I was quite proud of. On the table was the immersion heater, and under the bed was my suitcase. The heater had a rather brittle element, which sometimes came apart and had to be allowed to cool before it could be forced together again, loosely, so that it would come on long enough to warm up a cup of soup or chamomile tea. The element had been forced so often that it had become too narrow and sometimes jumped out of its housing. The only pretty thing in my room was the little cherrywood chest that my father had given me when I left school; it had a white varnish, with roses and daisies. I used it to store soup cubes, salt, bread, chamomile tea, and my few bits of jewelry—an amber necklace I'd been given at my first communion, and a bracelet made of glass beads.

He stood there looking at it all, and then we looked at

each other. We looked at each other for a long time, a very long time—not sizing each other up but absorbed in each other. He knew I was not a tart, and I knew that I was going to spend my whole life with him. It was very quiet, and now and then we heard the stairs creak, the cracking sound of the dry wooden floor in the hallway, the opening and closing of doors—Hilde taking somebody up to her room. The person who lived in the big room looking onto the yard was a war veteran who set the whole floor in the hallway vibrating with his crutch and the weight of his body.

As I looked at Hermann his ugliness vanished, and his wrinkled, rather old-looking face became smooth with happiness. I saw that he couldn't be much more than twenty. His hair was thick, fair, and smooth. I wasn't afraid as he looked at me. Hilde had repeatedly said to me, "You're good to look at, quite a feast for the eyes." I was only afraid that he'd behave clumsily when the inevitable happened. His shoes were of a superior kind, more expensive than any we had in the shop. They looked almost elegant against the pants of his uniform. I was so aroused that I almost began to feel ashamed. I wished he would make a move before I lost patience. I had thought too often about the inevitable physical contact, when the last trace of modesty has to be abandoned—and now I had abandoned it. His face was now completely smooth and full of happiness. He nodded, came up to me, and put his hand out to touch me—not down below, as I'd feared. He put his hand on my shoulder, drew my head toward him, and kissed me. I sighed for joy, and all the poisonous fear left me. The joy remained, and *he*'s still the best. Much later I ran into Hilde again. By then we were both over forty; Hermann had been in politics for a long time and was campaigning for reelection. Hilde came up to me out of the crowd, and it took me a while to recognize her. She'd become a plump, cheerful brunette. She whispered to me, "Your fear that I might end up on the street was unfounded, as you see. My husband has a building firm, and we have four children. He was also one of the ones I took up to my room."

When people talk about the twenties it always makes me think of Hilde, though it was the late thirties when we were living in our attic. We were so unalike, yet linked by the same situation: Hilde going on her canoeing trips and making love in the bushes on quiet riverbanks, while I was afraid of "human sexuality," yet so much looking forward to it, dreaming about nuns with their soothing singing and sweet-smelling lingerie, yet aroused by Hilde's stories and going where she never went—on the street.

Yes, Hermann and I couldn't help laughing when it came to unfastening our buttons. You can't do it without unfastening buttons. After all, we were both shy, and that can lead to disaster, as it did with the Küblers, who live next door. They had both, independently, read up on what one should do on one's wedding night, that decisive moment when even the tenderest and most romantic love has to become crude and physical. It went wrong for the Küblers: he was so clumsy and crude that she's never forgiven him.

In the morning I went to Klogmeyer's shop and asked for the day off. It was a miserable little shop, with everything in short supply. At the front of the shop I used to take in the shoes for repair; the shoe boxes were stacked up in the living room. At the back, Klogmeyer would sit at his workbench, and Frau Klogmeyer, who was always ailing, would be in the kitchen. Everything about the shop was sad and wretched. I had learned the trade at a smart shop where the women would come out of boredom and have dozens of shoe boxes brought to them.

(Speaking more quietly) This is a story I can only tell myself—about my desire driving me onto the street and Hermann being the best I could find. Was it love? It was more than that. And so is what I feel for the man over there, sitting in his trailer: he's the son I'd have liked to have, a son who was deserted by his mother, a son who has terrified me as only a son can. *He* cast a spell on my beloved piano, at which I would normally be sitting on a day like this. It's as though there were a curse on it. I'm sure he was at Kapspeter's last night, even if it can never be proved. It was him; and if by some chance it wasn't him, it must be his spirit haunting the place. I'm glad he's got that girl downstairs, and that he's got a child by her. His first wife, whom Hermann is so in love with, was too much like him—too pious, too poetic and spoiled. She'd have joined in lustily when I sang "Heaven, send him down." What can it be that frightens me? I'm afraid and I don't know what of. Something's going to happen. And it won't be to Bingerle. Before I forget, I must call Stützling up and tell him to release him a few hours early. *(Puts down the telescope and goes downstairs.)*

Chapter 3

The interior of a very large and slightly run-down trailer. From the front window there is a view across to the left bank of the Rhine. Karl von Kreyl is seated at the table, constructing a buggy out of slats and small wooden boards, using the appropriate tools. At present he is trying to fix some small wheels, like those used as piano casters, to a wooden board. He is dressed in a shirt, trousers, and pullover, and smoking a pipe; beside him is a mug of coffee. He hums a tune until his father, Heinrich von Kreyl, enters after a brief knock on the door. His father is dressed formally, with a tie, waistcoat, etc. Karl rises, embraces his father, and pulls up a chair for him. The older man sits down and lights a cigarette.

HEINRICH VON KREYL, *after watching his son working for a while:* Don't you find it just a bit macabre, messing about with the kind of wheels that are used as piano casters? (*His son looks at him in surprise.*) So you haven't read the paper yet?

KARL VON KREYL: Yes, I have; quite thoroughly, in fact. Being unemployed, I've plenty of time to read the papers. Am I supposed to stop making this buggy for my son after reading the paper?

HEINRICH VON KREYL: Have you also read what happened at Kapspeter's?

KARL VON KREYL: Yes, I have, and I've also read that the culprit apparently took the casters away with him. These are the ones from my—from our grand piano, which I chopped up and burned seven years ago. I kept them because at the time they seemed to be the only part of it that might be useful someday. I had no use for the rest of the instrument. . . .

HEINRICH VON KREYL: My mother loved that piano. And Beethoven is known to have played on it. But we don't need to discuss that piece of barbarity again—that was the start of the whole wretched business.

KARL VON KREYL: The business wasn't all that wretched— it freed my wife, Eva, from me. And in any case I'm not afraid of being judged by Mother, or by Beethoven. And the grand was my property. *Propriété oblige.* Seven years ago I was obliged to destroy it. I kept the casters, and now I'm making a buggy for my son. Children love toys that their parents make for them. I see nothing contemptible or macabre—and certainly nothing illegal—in the way I'm spending my morning.

HEINRICH VON KREYL: Kapspeter's grand was *his* property. You must realize that playing around with those casters might be seen as provocative, to say the least. Seven years ago you destroyed your own grand; five years ago Bransen's was destroyed, four years ago Florian's, and last night Kapspeter's—and you sit there playing around with those casters.

KARL VON KREYL: I was at Kapspeter's musicale myself last night. Oddly enough, I'm still on a lot of people's guest lists. Kapspeter's daughter played some Beethoven—not very well, by the way, but she's a sweet girl and tries very hard. Katharina was waitressing there. It was funny—almost hilarious, in fact—when she came up to me with the drink tray and said, "Would you like another sherry, Count?" (*Laughs.*) I made a great show of giving her a tip. Do you know the girls are hardly ever given tips? Something has to be done about that. I hereby challenge you to make a point of ostentatiously tipping the staff at parties. (*Stops short and peers at his father.*) Why are you looking at me like that? You look worried, almost angry. Am I under suspicion, by any chance? If so, they'd hardly have let Katharina go to work at the Wublers' this morning. (*Pointing to the telescope lying on the window seat*) I watched her setting the breakfast table at the Wublers'. By the way, you're not going to the memorial service for Erftler-Blum, are you? (*Goes to the window, picks up the telescope, and looks through it across the river.*) Erika's still sitting there in her dressing gown. Wubler hasn't surfaced yet.

HEINRICH VON KREYL *stands up, goes over to Karl, and puts his hands on his shoulders:* Have I ever abused your confidence?

KARL VON KREYL: No, never, and I don't think I've ever abused yours.

HEINRICH VON KREYL: No, you haven't, so tell me: is it you or not—was it you or wasn't it?

KARL VON KREYL *smiles:* It isn't me, and it wasn't me. (*They both sit down again.*) It must be someone who has— how shall I put it?—a spiritual affinity to me. It might even be that my spirit is abroad. You all made far too much fuss about that grand piano of mine. It was almost blown up into a scandal, yet all I did was to treat my own property in—let us say—a rather eccentric fashion. What a fuss it led to: meetings of the staff committee, and then the press! And all the time it was just a kind of private act of worship—a solemn sacrifice, a ritual. And then all the excitement: it's contagious, Father, it has an inflammatory effect that can't be checked. I'm a lawyer, Father, I'm passionately devoted to the law. Konkes, my teacher, tried to persuade me to stay on at the university and become a professor. I respect the laws of the land.

HEINRICH VON KREYL: You didn't have much respect for them that time in Rio.

KARL VON KREYL: Okay, I was negligent, but I didn't do it deliberately. Yes. I was temporarily in charge of the expense fund, and I gave that girl money to fly to Cuba. Yes. It was a moot point whether it was actually a punishable offense, but I *was* punished. Let's not talk about all the other things that were paid for out of the expense fund. I got caught and was thrown out—I was even given a few months' probation. And all because they were furious about my burning the grand. And in any case, the girl returned the money because she thought it would help me. With interest. Revolutionaries are often punctilious and loyal. None of the spies who got money from the fund ever returned a single mark.

HEINRICH VON KREYL: You were also having an affair with her, weren't you?

KARL VON KREYL: Yes, that's what it's called. We were in love for two or three days. And I think that was why she returned the money. That was something the papers didn't mention. (*Sighs.*) And now I'm not even allowed to make a toy for my little boy because—

HEINRICH VON KREYL: Mozart is known to have played Kapspeter's grand.

KARL VON KREYL: And Wagner's supposed to have tinkled on Bransen's, and Brahms on Florian's. And Krengel's got a piano that Bach's supposed to have played. (*Picks up the casters, immediately puts them down again, stands up, and starts pacing restlessly to and fro.*)

HEINRICH VON KREYL: All the same, you were sad when Eva left you and you lost all your friends.

KARL VON KREYL: Yes, it made me sad—especially Eva's leaving me. But then I had Assunta for a few days in Rio. I got over Eva—and now I have Katharina. What made me sad at the time was that it didn't strike any of you— Eva, you, the Wublers, or any of my friends—what day it was when I did the deed. (*Heinrich looks at his son ques-*

tioningly.) Okay, I'll tell you now: it was the day Konrad Fluh was accidentally shot when he put his hand in his trouser pocket during a police check. And I'll tell *you* what they've never found out so far and are just about to learn (*points to possible bugging devices*): that Konrad actually was in contact with them. He was on his way to rescue the man whose name mustn't be mentioned—and whose dossier has vanished. . . .

HEINRICH VON KREYL *looks around anxiously:* In contact with them—in his capacity as a priest?

KARL VON KREYL, *shrugging his shoulders:* They were so shocked by his death that they never thought to search his apartment. They assumed that it was all a regrettable accident, and the policeman himself was quite shattered. I visited his wife and tried to comfort her. And then, being an old friend of Konrad's and the executor of his will, I went and searched his apartment, and it became clear to me that Konrad had been on his way to rescue the man who wasn't supposed to be rescued but wanted to be. And so, if you look at it one way, the poor policeman, though he didn't know it, had a function in the whole dreadful logic, since Konrad *might* have succeeded in rescuing the man. I destroyed all the written evidence—all the addresses, telephone numbers, and coded notes. It was a premonition, Father—chance, fate, providence. (*Speaking very quietly and gravely*) When I came back from Konrad's place, Eva was sitting at the piano, playing a duet with Wubler, an arrangement of Chopin for four hands. Erika was sitting listening with rapt attention. I didn't say a word. I wasn't even worked up. I just asked them both to get up, went and got the ax, and chopped up the piano—quite calmly, almost decorously; coldly, they said. There was an open fire on the veranda. Of course, it came as a shock to them, because it was all done so quietly, as though it were the most natural thing in the world. They all fled, as if I were a madman. Nobody gave a thought to Konrad Fluh. Nobody had so much as an inkling of the connection it had with him—not even Eva—or wondered what it could all be about, what it *was* about. It was a sacrifice—a burnt offering, if you like. And when they'd all left, I sat down in front of the fire and smoked my pipe, thinking about Konrad Fluh, who'd been my best friend, and about that poor policeman, who had no way of knowing that there's no such thing as chance. I was alone. I've never played any musical instrument since—and these casters (*points toward the table*) are *my* property.

HEINRICH VON KREYL: So didn't Eva know Konrad?

KARL VON KREYL: Of course she did. She loved him. And she cried when he was shot. She was deeply grieved—what they call genuine grief. She really missed him. They'd argued so often about theological problems! And the Wublers liked him: they wouldn't have been surprised if I'd smashed something—some old piano perhaps, but not a valuable grand that was in perfect condition. They didn't see the connection.

HEINRICH VON KREYL: And that was the end of your career. They shunted you off to Rio, and you were overtaken by Plukanski.

KARL VON KREYL: It dragged on and on. Klunsch, my superior, wanted an explanation, but I couldn't give one—and yet it *was* my own property. It was as though I'd set fire to my car with my own hands. They even called in the staff committee, and they were all against me, even those who'd been so sympathetic to me before, the drivers and the office personnel. I refused to be examined by psychiatrists—you try explaining to a psychiatrist why you make a burnt offering for a friend who's just died: such an expensive one, a sacrificial fire. They couldn't dismiss me, and I continued to do my duty correctly and conscientiously.

HEINRICH VON KREYL: Except for what happened in Rio.

KARL VON KREYL: Yes, there they had me, because money was involved. Money is something real that even psychiatrists can understand, something rational. I'd given this girl money, and she'd taken herself off to Cuba, and I'd also had an affair with her. The whole thing was clear. Money that belonged to the German Federal Republic had been paid over to a Communist! There they had me, of course. Money from the hallowed coffers of the foreign service, from which so many other things are financed—including, of course, the occasional girlfriend. She paid the money back. She writes to me every so often—Assunta de la Torre. She's become a teacher, and she tells me that if ever I need asylum I'll be welcome in Cuba. But I don't need asylum, and I don't want to go to Cuba. I want to *work*, as a lawyer.

HEINRICH VON KREYL: There are rumors about Eva wanting to go off with a Cuban.

KARL VON KREYL: Eva in Cuba? Why not? She could sort out the government's relations with the Church, maybe even improve them. She's so sweet, so clever and so sensitive, and she's tougher than you might think.

HEINRICH VON KREYL: Why don't you get a divorce and marry Katharina, who's had a son by you?

KARL VON KREYL: *You* talking about divorce, Father? In that respect Eva's even more conservative than you. She still regards herself as my wife, till death us do part. She's living with Grobsch, but the last thing she wants is a divorce, even though *she* left *me*—I didn't leave her. In any case, Katharina wouldn't want to marry me. . . .

HEINRICH VON KREYL: Why not, for heaven's sake, why not? What reason could she possibly have?

KARL VON KREYL *sits down and starts working at the toy again, while his father stands in front of him. Karl, very embarrassed:* I'd rather not say. It might hurt you; you might even understand, and then it would hurt you even more.

HEINRICH VON KREYL: Tell me all the same; perhaps it won't hurt all that much. If I tell you that I no longer understand the world anyway, you'll probably find it easier to tell me how *I* could be hurt if Katharina didn't want to marry *you*.

KARL VON KREYL, *in great embarrassment:* How shall I begin? I think, like Katharina, that . . . that there are too many counts. She's a semi-countess, so to speak: her natural father was a nice young count and her mother a waitress. He would have married her mother, but *she* didn't want to bring any more counts and countesses into the world, and Katharina wants to keep up the tradition. (*Looking up*) Look, you're a count. That can't be changed, and there's nothing wrong with it. I'm one too—and even I find that a bit of a joke. The title produces a degree of respect in people that is seldom justified. And if we make our little Heinrich into a count, he'll beget more counts and countesses. But Katharina wants him to be called Heinrich Richter. I'd like to marry her if Eva would agree to a divorce, but I happen to be a count and can't get rid of the title that goes with my name. And when you consider how many counts Chundt has swarming around him! Whenever things get ticklish, some count suddenly pops up. It was only through being a count that I was mixed up in that damned Mottabakhani affair. They got me involved in it—remember?

HEINRICH VON KREYL: Something to do with oil, wasn't it?

KARL VON KREYL: Yes, a lot of oil. Klunsch wanted to do a little private deal, something quite legal, incidentally— he wanted to act as an oil agent. Legal, but embarrassing.

So I had to go to the embassy and see this man Motta-bakhani, because the name Karl Count von Kreyl has a serious ring to it. That was during my time in Brussels. Brussels, Father, three years in Brussels—that'd be enough to make even you think about chopping up grand pianos that Offenbach might have played on. Brussels, oil—in that context my title was impressive and useful. If I'd been plain Karl Kreyl, nobody would have dreamed of involving me. Nothing came of the deal; I don't even know why anymore. I think Chundt was smarter and got in first with *his* count. He sent Count Erle zu Berben, who was smarter than I was. I even understood Klunsch's motives: he was brought up in a cottage in the north and wanted to get into the big money in a perfectly legal way. So are you angry or sad that we don't want to turn our little Heinrich into a count?

HEINRICH VON KREYL: I can understand, but it still hurts. After all, one has a name and everything that goes with the name, even if the name is Richter. It's not a good thing to deny one's own name. Yes, it does hurt. All the same, Eva is still Countess von Kreyl, and if she had a child by Grobsch . . .

KARL VON KREYL: It would take Eva's maiden name, Plint, if I didn't acknowledge paternity.

HEINRICH VON KREYL: And would you?

KARL VON KREYL: Yes, if Eva asked me to and it would give you pleasure. And then you might have a count as a grandson who didn't have a drop of noble blood in his veins—Grobsch is a prole.

HEINRICH VON KREYL: And your little Heinrich would be seventy-five percent noble and be called Richter. Of course, I could adopt him.

KARL VON KREYL: Not against his mother's wishes. She likes you, by the way. . . .

HEINRICH VON KREYL: I like her too. I'm against allowing

names to die out. I'm surprised by what you say about Brussels. Was it really as bad as all that?

KARL VON KREYL: Eva made it endurable—and she played the titled lady to perfection. Naturally we gave parties and invited people from NATO and the EC. We arranged balls and excursions, danced a lot, laughed a lot, and poked fun a lot—and obviously we went hunting and shot a lot of animals. But a void remains a void, and I came to see that people go in for the most outrageous follies in order to escape the void—or else they shoot themselves and put an end to it all. And you meet people who own grand pianos there as well, people like Florian, Bransen, Kapspeter, and Krengel—in the lobbies or out hunting. And there it doesn't sound like Chopin at all. I met Krengel there too. He's a very charming man . . . and they all cried when that guy died.

HEINRICH VON KREYL: You really believe he could have been saved?

KARL VON KREYL: Have you any idea of the kind of notes and documents that led to that horrible creature Bingerle's being imprisoned?

HEINRICH VON KREYL: He's due to be released today.

KARL VON KREYL: May God have mercy on him!

HEINRICH VON KREYL: You really believe . . . or are you sure?

KARL VON KREYL: I believe I can be sure. Once again the state is at stake—and Chundt's own interests. What makes that man so disgustingly brilliant is his unfailing ability to combine his own interests with those of the state in such a way that the state can be equated with Chundt and Chundt with the state.

HEINRICH VON KREYL: Nothing has been proved, despite all the speculation and rumor.

KARL VON KREYL: No, nothing has been proved; none of it carries complete conviction. I really am a lawyer,

Father. But one can also destroy evidence, make it vanish. That's something every lawyer knows.

HEINRICH VON KREYL: You forget that I'm a lawyer too. No judgment can be passed on the basis of documents that have been destroyed or made to vanish.

KARL VON KREYL: Right. And no judgment *will* be passed. But you underestimate the *seepage effect.* (*Heinrich looks at him questioningly.*) There remain patches of fog, obscurities, things that haven't been cleared up. No real light is thrown on anything. The poison remains: it percolates downward, seeps into the popular mind. It percolates deep down, and it really is poison.

HEINRICH VON KREYL: I can't believe it.

KARL VON KREYL, *holding up the coffeepot:* Have a coffee, Father?

HEINRICH VON KREYL: No. I can't believe it, not even of Blaukrämer—or of Halberkamm either. . . .

KARL VON KREYL: And what about Elisabeth in her luxurious nuthouse?

HEINRICH VON KREYL: She really is crazy.

KARL VON KREYL: He *drove* her crazy.

HEINRICH VON KREYL: She couldn't prove any of the stories she told.

KARL VON KREYL: Nor can I.

HEINRICH VON KREYL: I only hope you've got an alibi for last night!

KARL VON KREYL: The best alibi a man can have: I was lying in the arms of the woman I love. Her class consciousness is so great that she didn't even return my tip, though I only gave it to her as a symbolic gesture. No, Father, it must have been an angel of the Lord who flew down to Kapspeter's, and the angel of the Lord always has an alibi. He leaves clues behind, but nobody finds them. A little silver dust from his celestial wings.

HEINRICH VON KREYL: Now you're confusing me again

with your metaphysical puzzles. You talk like your mother, even though you hardly knew her.

KARL VON KREYL: You're wrong; I knew her quite well. I was five when she walked into the Rhine up there, near Cleves, where Lohengrin stepped onto the swan. Red Ribbon Swan was the name of a well-known margarine they made up there. . . . Perhaps the swan was waiting for my mother *under* the water—and now she goes up and down the Rhine on her swan. (*Points to the opposite bank.*) Perhaps that's the spot where she parks her swan. She told me a lot about her family and yours, which both produced so many generals. She showed me all those dreary portraits of our ancestors: there was hardly any war in which a Kreyl or a Skogerage wasn't a general. None of them was less than a colonel. Right down to the battle of Worringen, where a Skogerage was on the side of the archbishop and a Kreyl on the side of his opponents. Sometimes they fought for the Spanish, sometimes for the Prussians, or against the Prussians; sometimes against the Czar and sometimes for him, and when Napoleon came along they also changed sides. It was only in 1870–71 that they discovered their noble sense of patriotism. Then again at Weissenburg or Sedan one of them was involved—no, two of them: a Skogerage as a general and a Kreyl as a colonel. And your father fell at Langemark, having attained the rank of a mere major. Finally you broke the mold completely—you were only a captain in the reserve. Why on earth don't you take down the portraits of all those old bores with their orders hung around their necks or pinned to their chests? In any case, the old boys must have done quite well out of it all—after all, generals get pretty good tips, don't they? Why not lighten your pack, Father?

HEINRICH VON KREYL: I've tried to get rid of the portraits, but it's no good—they're obviously of miserably poor quality. Perhaps you know somebody who's into nostalgia and looking for a family portrait gallery?

KARL VON KREYL: It's the sort of thing Plukanski goes in for. But oil on canvas burns well. The frames are more valuable than the pictures. Why don't you sell the pictures to Plukanski and keep the frames? Don't be sad because our blood (*laughs*) flows only in little Heinrich Richter's veins.

HEINRICH VON KREYL: We could have had more children, but I couldn't hold on to your mother. For so long I tried to hold on to her, literally. (*Makes the appropriate movement with his arms.*) It was really bad when Erftler-Blum and his friends turned up. He made me rural district chairman, then county manager, and we gave a reception at the castle. And she saw the faces of Schirrmacher, Rickler and Hochlehner. They'd just been released from prison—for good.

KARL VON KREYL: Yes, I now understand why, when I was five, she made me swear I'd never wear a uniform. I often think of her. She wasn't a beautiful woman, to judge by photographs of her.

HEINRICH VON KREYL: No, she wasn't beautiful, or at least she wasn't photogenic. We were impoverished, and so were the Skogerages, in spite of all our well-paid generals. A lot of the money had disappeared in the brothels of Amsterdam and Paris. With great difficulty we managed to preserve a minimum of gracious living—you know, hunting parties, with the correct gear, and all the nonsense of hunting horns and stirrup cups. We watched the guests like hawks, to make sure they didn't eat too much, and we shared the leftovers with the servants. Time and again we noticed that the ones with the biggest appetites were the priests, who were much better off than we were. This whole aristocratic charade was so forced that it made us sick. Yes, you remind me of your mother and myself. But then, when the Nazi plague was over, we thought the time was ripe for Jesus to come at last. We still had Christ Jesus in our bones; we cursed him but couldn't get rid of him—he really was in our bones.

The wedding festivities were sheer torture: the high mass, followed by hunting horns and a reception in the great hall. Your mother and I hardly knew each other, and when we finally left for the Dutch coast—both of us scared stiff—and found ourselves alone for the first time in the hotel room, we both burst out laughing, and suddenly we found we were in love. We loved each other, and that was what saved us. Scheveningen, the beach, the hotel, the pier—it was heaven, and we were in love. A member of the Spanish branch of the Skogerages gave us pesetas, and one of the Dutch Kreyls gave us guilders. And so we were able to indulge our love and enjoy ourselves. Nobility, my boy, is the only truly international connection. The other one is money, and more often than not the two go together. The man in charge of them both is the Sponge. I shudder whenever I see him, just as I'd shudder if I came face to face with the Grand Inquisitor.

KARL VON KREYL: And we belong to both, do we—the nobility and the money aristocracy?

HEINRICH VON KREYL: No, of course not. As nobles we have a long lineage, but otherwise we're *nouveaux riches* and hence don't belong to the money aristocracy. Ancient nobility but financial upstarts. Suddenly we had real estate—but of course you know all that, Karl. With the building craze, the building panic, the building madness, our lands became real estate, and the money rained down from heaven.

KARL VON KREYL: Don't you want to go to the high mass, Father? Shall I order you a taxi?

HEINRICH VON KREYL, *looking at his watch:* It's too late

now, and there's something else I want to discuss with you.

KARL VON KREYL, *going to the window and looking out:* Erika hasn't gone either; she's sitting on the balcony in her dressing gown. I can't see Katharina. She's probably in the kitchen.

HEINRICH VON KREYL: If Erika Wubler stays away, there could be trouble; nobody will miss me. You know that Plukanski's out and that Blaukrämer is to succeed him?

KARL VON KREYL: Blaukrämer, Father? Blaukrämer?

HEINRICH VON KREYL: Yes; incredible, isn't it? I only hope Chundt goes too far this time. Plukanski couldn't be supported any longer: an old wartime story has just emerged. No, it's not what you might think—only a matter of money. He was a rail transport officer and set a few points—literally, not metaphorically—at night, with his own hands. Not to help the partisans, but out of greed. Supply trains with consignments of arms and food disappeared into the sidings during the dark Polish nights. Polish officers who were related to half of Europe—nobility, my dear boy, nobility—paid money into Spanish accounts by way of Scottish banks. Honorable people. The Polish nobility has branches in every country of Europe. That's the advantage of having ancestors who were generals or colonels in foreign armies, or even mere captains. They go to foreign countries and win foreign wives for themselves, or foreign brothers-in-law for their sisters. In this way you are related, through the Kreyls and the Skogerages, to the Spanish Heredias and the Scottish McCullens. So if you ever need asylum, don't go to Cuba—go to Scotland or Spain. Or Italy, where we're related to the Vanzettis.

KARL VON KREYL: You've never talked to me like this before, Father. How can you endure it? The faces that drove my mother into the Rhine!

HEINRICH VON KREYL: How did you endure Brussels, where you found yourself in a void and couldn't do anything about it? And I haven't even got a wife. I couldn't remarry after Martha walked into the Rhine. It's still in my bones. But I've got you. (*Sighs.*) I'm beginning to understand why somebody I don't wish to name or to know dismantles pianos and leaves nothing but a smattering of silver dust behind him. When I came home from the war, Erftler-Blum was completely sold on me. I could have become a minister under him right away. A member of the Catholic nobility from the Lower Rhine—it was ideal. Then he came along with his old Nazis, meanwhile denazified. I never liked him. And now it wasn't just Erftler-Blum, with the old Nazis.

KARL VON KREYL: So there's to be another revelation. This time it's Plukanski.

HEINRICH VON KREYL: This time it's an international revelation, unearthed by a Polish historian—contrary to the wishes of his government, incidentally. In ten or twenty years the Vietnamese partisans will come clean about the tanks and guns and planes they bought from the American army. I *will* have a coffee after all. And in fifty years they'll come up with revelations about Chundt.

Karl pours him a mug of coffee from the coffeepot and pushes the milk and sugar toward him. At this moment there is a dull thud as something lands on the roof of the trailer, followed by two more thuds.

HEINRICH VON KREYL, *agitated and apprehensive:* What was that?

KARL VON KREYL: Don't get excited, Father. Those were two of your pears or apples—or perhaps one of each. I still don't know how to distinguish them by the noise they make. It's autumn, Father—harvest time. Sometimes they fall during the night. I like it when they do—it's such a homely, familiar sound.

HEINRICH VON KREYL: Don't you want to move into the house? Are you being well provided for?

KARL VON KREYL: I'm excellently provided for. Schnidhubel brings me my breakfast in the morning—toast, eggs, coffee, all nice and warm, and marmalade. And around eleven I get a second pot of coffee. Then I have lunch at Katharina's place, and if she has to work in the evening I stay on and play with the boy, and then I tell him stories until he falls asleep. Now I even have a telephone, and so there's nothing more I need. No, I don't want to move into the house. We're looking for an apartment, and when we've found one we'll finally move in together, for the boy's sake if for no other reason.

HEINRICH VON KREYL: And what do you live on? You don't have any income. Breakfast and the trailer—that can't be enough. And Katharina can't be earning all that much.

KARL VON KREYL: I still have friends in the service. There are more who like me than like Blaukrämer, for instance—though of course that's not saying much: no one likes *him.* I could tell you of more than a dozen who like me. They were shocked, but they were never really angry with me. Some of them thought it was a special kind of aristocratic snobbery that they hadn't previously suspected in me. Meanwhile they've come to realize that it was something *serious,* even if they don't understand my motives. Anyhow, the people on the staff committee know that it wasn't snobbery but at most a curious form of madness. Nobody's guessed about Konrad Fluh—although they knew he'd been my friend for ages—and that I've got the same thing in my bones as you have.

HEINRICH VON KREYL: And how do you earn your money? Do you get commissions from the service?

KARL VON KREYL: I get strange secret assignments from the people up there. (*Points to various corners where bugs might be concealed.*) Take this, for instance. (*Takes down a thick brown envelope from one of the shelves.*) Have a look at it and don't say anything before I've made a phone call. After all, I've always stayed within the law, even in Rio—for it's stated in the rules: "In exceptional cases help may be given to foreign nationals." (*Heinrich has meanwhile opened the envelope and taken out a Mercedes star. He looks in astonishment at his son, who prevents him from speaking by raising a finger to his lips.*) Wait before you say anything. (*Dials a number, then, after a short pause*) Karl here. Listen, I'm in an embarrassing position: my father wants to know how I earn my money. . . . No, I can guarantee his discretion—and I haven't even told Katharina. . . . You think no one will believe it anyway—and I don't have any proof. . . . Okay, thanks. (*Replaces the receiver and addresses Heinrich.*) I steal Mercedes stars. This will be the last for a while—I have to restrain myself for a time. This one was particularly hard to come by. It's from a car belonging to a certain Dr. Wehrli, a big fish in the Swiss banking world. I'm assuming that the family tradition of discretion will be maintained in this case too.

HEINRICH VON KREYL, *holding the Mercedes star and shaking his head:* You're not putting me on, are you? You do that for the service?

KARL VON KREYL, *in a matter-of-fact tone:* I've been doing it for some years. At home I get five hundred marks per star, plus expenses; abroad I get fifteen hundred plus expenses, because abroad I have to work at my own risk, so to speak, whereas here I can be given cover if necessary. It would be difficult for them to help me if I were caught abroad. I even have to sign a receipt for the fee and the expenses—all proper and aboveboard.

HEINRICH VON KREYL, *still astonished and incredulous:* Is it a test of courage or something? A kind of training that requires a test of courage?

KARL VON KREYL: No. It's like so many other things that are crazy on the face of it but quite logical when you know the background. They've obviously got a Russian on the hook who has a perverse craving for these things. He doesn't want money or women or little boys, but Mercedes stars. But they have to be stars belonging to highly placed personalities. Obviously he supplies information in return.

HEINRICH VON KREYL: But there surely must be an easier way to acquire the stars?

KARL VON KREYL: They've offered him whole boxes of brand-new stars, but he only wants ones that have been stolen and can be guaranteed to have been stolen. He—or they—call up anonymously, pretending to be police, and ask—in this case—Dr. Wehrli if he's noticed his star is missing and for how long. The person in question only has to look at his radiator to realize that the emblem is missing. In Wehrli's case it's already been confirmed, and tomorrow I get the money. (*Takes the star from Heinrich and returns it to the envelope.*) This one will cost them quite a lot: I had to fit myself up with completely new clothes and wait around for days at an expensive Zurich hotel, where the cars are very carefully guarded. I didn't dare take any risks, until this solid citizen finally went off with his mistress to a little village, booked himself into a small hotel, and parked his car in a barn. While he was enjoying the body of this nice lady—and perhaps her mind too; who knows?—I went and got the thing. It was very simple. In Zurich it was too risky: the Swiss police can be very nasty. Even the newspapers are no longer to be trusted. "Cars waylaid by shady German count": that wouldn't have been good for the family honor. Meanwhile the Russian must have a collection of about two dozen stars. He's obviously a sick man with a severe trauma brought on by capitalism. I've noted it all down and written up the accounts scrupulously. (*Laughs.*) What seemed like the hardest job turned out the easiest—getting Heulbuck's star. That jolly Rhinelander, who's so quick to turn sour and throw up (unfortunately Katharina is very discreet, otherwise I'd know more about it), was invited to a party at his friend Walter Mesod's place, and so was I. Heulbuck's car was standing in front of the door, with the driver at the wheel. I pretended to be drunk and fell across the radiator. By the time the driver rushed to my aid I had the star in my pocket. Incidentally, it's not at all easy to pry these things out of their casing: you've got to bash them fairly hard with your fist and then twist. I always wear gloves for the job. I practiced doing it at a scrapyard owned by a secondhand-Mercedes dealer. I had his permission, of course, and paid the cost of the damage, plus a small *douceur.*

HEINRICH VON KREYL: You practiced doing it—you say you actually practiced?

KARL VON KREYL, *calmly:* Of course. One has to learn one's trade and make oneself proficient—and since it's decently paid, I want to do a decent job. It's my profession at present. Whatever I have to do I do properly, even if it's not always quite proper. Katharina doesn't know anything about it. Incidentally, the service always sends the injured party a new star anonymously. Everything's done according to the book.

HEINRICH VON KREYL: Heulbuck would undoubtedly have parted with his star voluntarily for the greater glory of the fatherland.

KARL VON KREYL: That wouldn't have been any good. The Russian insists that the stars must be stolen. In Heulbuck's case I got hardly any expenses, by the way. Just the taxi fare there and back, and it's not far to Mesod's place. I'm punctilious in such matters too. I really am a lawyer, with a legal cast of mind.

HEINRICH VON KREYL, *pointing to possible bugs:* And you do it on their orders?

KARL VON KREYL: I am observed by them and paid by them. It brings in quite a decent living. Incidentally, it's always a minister, at least. The Russian won't settle for anything less.

HEINRICH VON KREYL: So before long you'll have to steal Blaukrämer's star.

KARL VON KREYL: I'll be keeping a low profile for a time. They always demand a solemn assurance and the receipt. Double indemnity, you understand.

HEINRICH VON KREYL: And how are you indemnified?

KARL: By the receipt. I even pay tax on my earnings.

HEINRICH VON KREYL: But they have the receipts, not you. Have you got anything from them in writing? Obviously not. And you describe yourself as an outstanding lawyer! They've got two dozen pieces of evidence against you—two dozen admissions of theft! If it comes to the crunch, who's going to believe that you've been acting on their orders? That would be a way of getting you out. The whole story's too crazy for anyone to believe—a Soviet who collects Mercedes stars!

KARL VON KREYL: He clearly has a positive craving for this particular symbol of capitalism and German efficiency.

HEINRICH VON KREYL: That may be, but can you prove that he exists?

KARL VON KREYL: I can't prove anything.

HEINRICH VON KREYL: Are you sure of your client?

KARL VON KREYL: He's an old friend of mine.

HEINRICH VON KREYL: In a high position?

KARL VON KREYL: Fairly high; in a responsible position, at any rate. He won't welsh on me.

HEINRICH VON KREYL: But there may be others who want to welsh on him.

KARL VON KREYL: I really can't tell you his name; there's more than one of them anyway, and they're well disposed toward me. On one occasion I even informed on myself, using his cover name—and claiming lots of expenses. (*Heinrich looks at him in disbelief.*) Yes, I wrote down precisely who visited me, who called me up, where I went, whether by taxi or by bicycle. Everything correct.

HEINRICH VON KREYL: It couldn't be Hermann Wubler, could it?

KARL VON KREYL: No. I do the odd translation for him, and get well paid for it. And he's taken on Katharina, although *they* (*points to the ceiling*) were opposed to it. And he's still in love with Eva—more than ever—but he won't get her. I often see her at parties. I also go and visit her now and then.

HEINRICH VON KREYL: When Grobsch is there?

KARL VON KREYL: Of course. I like Grobsch; he doesn't quite trust me, but I like him. He's correct, sharp, cynical, but not corrupt. That's the new nobility, Father— proletarian, like Katharina. The new nobility have names like Richter, Schmitz, Schneider—or Grobsch—and quite a lot of them are in prison. (*Heinrich looks at him in surprise.*) Yes, why not? Members of the nobility are always being imprisoned—for political reasons. Grobsch is one of the people who prevent me from walking into the Rhine.

HEINRICH VON KREYL: I'm getting worried: I'm just beginning to understand why grand pianos are chopped up or dismantled. . . .

KARL VON KREYL: That's over for the time being. Krengel's piano is probably so secure that even the silver dust from an angel's wings will set off the alarm. There may soon be a grand piano protection policy, though to be precise, it should be called a banker's grand piano protection policy. (*Speaking more quietly*) There's something very sad about it all, Father, something almost tragic, which affects even me—it even moves me. These people love art; they really adore it. Kapspeter's daughter is someone I could be quite fond of, and she's already got a new grand, with a safety device and comprehensive insurance—perhaps even one that Wagner's supposed to have strummed on. But a curious spell hangs over these people, and I assume that the person who dismantles their pianos is trying to break the spell. Yet the only thing that upsets them is the financial loss, which isn't the important thing at all. . . . I don't begrudge Adelheid Kapspeter the new grand. And I'd like to know what to wish upon Chundt.

HEINRICH VON KREYL: I wish he were dead. He's ruining our republic.

KARL VON KREYL: There's a spell on him too—I don't know of what kind. He keeps on having to . . .

HEINRICH VON KREYL: That's the spell I'd like to break, Karl. I no longer understand Hermann Wubler.

KARL VON KREYL: Wubler has one terrible, awesome quality: he's loyal. So is Katharina, and so is Erika Wubler. Wubler is loyal to Chundt, and Chundt is even loyal to Wubler—oh yes, he is—and if a man like Wubler is also loyal to the state, you end up with something like what used to be called the doctrine of divine right. No harm must come to the state or to him; he stands above the law. You surely know that. I don't know what Bingerle knows or what evidence he has, but if he endangers the state he'll have everybody against him. The most decent people and the least decent, the pure and the corrupt. Heulbuck and Wubler—and all the sea-green incorruptibles you can think of—will be on the side of Chundt, because if he's in danger, so is the state. The believers and the unbelievers, the faithful sons of the state, the Mafia and the Church—they'll all be on his side. That's why scandals are never fully cleared up in this country. Somewhere deep down, there's this god they all worship, to whom sacrifices have to be offered—and have already been offered. And because of this god who sits deep down there, idolized by them all, many of the pure in heart end up in the nuthouse, write embittered letters, issue appeals, and compose defamatory pamphlets, which never come before the courts. They become petty-minded and start informing on people, scenting corruption where there isn't any. There are hundreds, if not thousands, of the pure in heart who only *scent* corruption, and become destructive, malignant, stupid, and intolerable. That's not the way I want to go, Father. Wubler won't go that way either. For him there's only one possible situation of conflict—one in which his loyalty to Erika comes up against his loyalty to Chundt. I know them both, Father; we've been friends for too long. You needn't worry about Chundt—or about murdering him. You're not going to kill him—you couldn't anyway. Not even Bingerle poses a danger to him. The only one who does pose a danger is Wubler. (*Picks up the telescope and looks through it.*) She really has stayed at home: that could turn out to be dangerous. Do you really not want to attend the high mass, Father?

HEINRICH VON KREYL: I'll slip in during the sermon. . . .
But tell me: do you really think he could have been saved?

KARL VON KREYL: They needed a victim—but it had to be one for whom the other side, not they, would be held responsible.

HEINRICH VON KREYL, *leaving:* If you ever get orders to

steal my Mercedes star, let me know. We can settle the matter peacefully, without violence.

KARL VON KREYL *embraces him:* Don't be angry or depressed if I say that you're never likely to be the kind of person whose star is in demand.

HEINRICH VON KREYL: Who knows, who knows? (*Exit smiling.*)

Chapter 4

The Rhine Promenade between Bonn and Bad Godesberg. Dense fog. In the background, a thick high wall with a small iron gate set into it. About three yards from the wall, a bench by the river. An old woman with an old dog appears from the left, quietly scolding the dog: You bad doggy, *then disappears into a gap in the wall, from which Eva emerges.*

Eva, wearing a white duffel coat with a hood and carrying a white handbag, goes over and leans against the back of the bench.

EVA PLINT: This fog is so welcome. It soothes my fears, dulls the glare of the lamps, and softens the cubic shapes of the neighboring bungalows; it deadens the noise and is sufficiently thick to bring most of the traffic to a standstill. Only an occasional car comes slowly and timidly round the corner from the avenue. When I left the house, Ernst called after me from the doorway, "Mind you don't tell him too much," and his voice sounded as though it came across a great expanse of water. (*She points to the Rhine, in front of her.*) Nothing to be heard from out there—no ship's engines, no rumblings of tugboats, not even a foghorn. Everything quiet, even quieter than the normal quiet at the quietest time of the day—the time when the evening news is on television, the time when I leave the house every evening because I'm sick and tired of the news, the time when Ernst switches on and catches the last minute of the droning commercial before the important issues of the day are trumpeted forth: freedom, falling stock prices, force reductions in NATO, festivities, failure of disarmament talks—due to Russian intransigence, of course—fiscal reform, footballers' calves, fashionable weddings. And to round it all off, the fine and the foolish—culture—or, as a lyrical finale, a deeply troubled banker, apparently anxious about where his next meal is coming from. The one thing they don't announce is that we're frail creatures of dust but destined for higher things.

The bankers are all worried about their precious grands, now that some person unknown—unknown so far—has been dismantling their instruments at night and leaving the parts neatly stacked in front of their fireplaces. Recently, I'm told, he's taken to leaving matches and kerosene beside them as an invitation to their owners to start their own little bonfires. I know, of course, what a burning grand smells like, and I know what it's like to hear one being chopped up—chopped up quite coldly and systematically, with a kind of grim determination. I was married to the man who did it—and I still am, because only death can part us. At the time, I got scared and ran away from him. Yet I still see him from time to time, when he comes across on the ferry and sits on this bench and tells me about the woman he's living with, who's borne him a child, and I tell him about the man I'm living with, who doesn't want children. He had a lousy childhood; I didn't. I love them both—and now I'm in love with a third man. And if the friend of publicans and sinners, who spoke to the woman taken in adultery, were to sit here and ask me how many men I'd had, I'd have to tell him I'd had two. I wish he were sitting here and could tell me what I should do. The one who doesn't want children is a politician. He's a serious person and takes his job seriously. That's all to the good, even if I myself don't take everything seriously. Perhaps the only people who do take politics seriously are those who've had a lousy childhood; for the others it's just a game, a profession, a business.

Ernst and I have no communication difficulties whatever, except at suppertime. He likes to eat while the news is on. He doesn't have much time to spare, with so many meetings and committees to attend, and so many speeches to make and to write—he writes Plukanski's speeches as well as his own. I understand all that, but at seven o'clock I get hungry, and that's too early for him, and in the evening I always get an appetite for soup—I'm famous for my soups. He can't eat soup in front of the television, though, as it makes his glasses cloud over, and soup has to be steaming hot if it's to be called soup at all. So I have my soup around half-past seven, and then I make him open sandwiches and a salad just before eight. That's the only complication in our lives. Even when we're invited to a party, I have to have my soup before we go out. I never get enough to eat at parties, although there's usually plenty available. So I have to have my soup between seven and eight, and he likes to have supper around eight, when he has to watch the news in any case. So he sits there alone and takes in the information. And this evening, because the news is followed by a political discussion, which I've no desire to watch, he'll be sitting there till half-past nine. This gives me an hour and a half to myself. He can't see that these discussions are pointless, just window dressing. This evening it's a discussion about modern youth, who according to Gröbentöckler and Kromlach have lost all sense of values, whereas Breithuber and Ansbucher maintain that they're only just discovering the true values. And then there's the presenter—usually Hussper—droning on in his self-satisfied way, and whenever one of them says anything to the point he gets interrupted, and if he persists in saying it he's accused of talking out of turn. So I presume there's a set routine, and whoever speaks out of turn is breaking the rules.

(*Lights a cigarette.*) On a normal evening, or in normal lighting, I couldn't risk smoking a cigarette, but it's all right in the fog. In this country, women who smoke in the street are still regarded as little better than whores, and I'm not a whore, even if I *am* an adulteress and have a rendezvous with a politician who is an admirer of mine—yes, I can call him that. But Ernst knows I'm meeting him. (*Sits down on the bench.*) Now there's nothing of the whore about me anymore: German women are allowed to smoke if they're sitting on a bench; it's only when they're walking or standing around that it's not done. No lights on the water, and none on the opposite bank—only the fog surging across from where my dear Karl lives with his father. No red or green lights to be seen on the ships, which are not allowed to cast anchor. Somewhere around here, perhaps, lies the treasure of the Nibelungs, washed down from higher up the river—mutilated crowns, whose little bit of gold was long since washed away by the waters of the Rhine or rubbed off by the stones on the riverbed, buckled by the swirling pebbles and turned into something like carnival decorations, so that they can't even be polished up to serve as a champion marksman's insignia. Oh, Kriemhild and Brunhild, to think of your gold bracelets being hammered by the Rolling Stones, whiskered with algae, and perhaps lying next to a Nazi emblem that some anxious citizen discarded in haste as the American tanks rolled in. To think of all the different objects that jostle one another down there in the green slime: SS skull and crossbones, and swords with black, white, and red tassels—Germany's erstwhile honor—jettisoned in those historic moments of terror as grinning Negroes searched for "fuckin' German Nazis." Oh, you black brothers of NATO!—there are still plenty of them around—

my Ernst could tell you a lot about the Nazis, but you don't want to hear it; now you're only after Communists. Ernst is a good, hard-working man, and he specializes in Nazis. At present he's after a man named Plietsch, who now calls himself Plonius—and used to be known as the Blood-hound. But nobody listens to him. Dragon's blood was shed over there. Oh, you seven dwarfs beyond the seven mountains, what stories you could tell! But nobody would listen to you. Perhaps you even know where my cousin Alois is buried, who is said to have defended the autobahn. I know him only from photos: a handsome boy with blond curls and dark, deep-set eyes. Who's interested in him any longer, apart from my father and my uncle—and Karl over there? The water is far too cold, far too deep, and perhaps we no longer care for each other all that much.

(*Looks at her watch.*) Oh well, he's probably watching the news, too, and won't be here until a quarter past. It's now only ten past. The man I'm meeting is a politician. He's small and wrinkled, but he has beautiful eyes and beautiful hands, and he's said to have beautiful feet, but I haven't seen *them* yet. I only played piano duets with him, and he always had his shoes on and worked the pedals. Duets played on a grand piano that was later hacked to pieces and burned! It was hacked to pieces like some gigantic black insect, and there was a smell of lacquer. Karl kept nothing but the casters—I wonder what for. The hands of a child, the eyes of a toad. Whenever I leave a party he's standing by the cloakroom, this Alberich figure, and tries to help me on with my coat, but someone else always gets in first— the little Cuban I'm in love with. I've asked this man, the one who's in love with me, to get me some information on the one I'm in love with. Is that a cruel thing to do? I've never been cruel, and I rather think he's glad to meet me and be alone with me. But that could be cruel: there's no room for him in my life. Karl and Ernst agree in their judgment of him—that he's shrewd, but not a villain. The river is enticing. Karl's mother walked into it—yes, actually *walked*. She was never found. I've always imagined she was wearing lead shoes on her feet and wandered farther and farther downstream toward the North Sea. She wasn't a beautiful woman, my mother-in-law, but she had an imposing appearance, with blond hair and a voluptuous figure—a real Valkyrie or Rhine maiden—and she never emerged again. She found the Rhine more enticing than Erftler-Blum's postwar Germany. There wasn't one of her ancestors who hadn't been a general or a colonel—a real ancestral gallery, all with orders on their chests, almost like the Nibelung treasure. Some of them were stupid, a few were shrewd, perhaps even villains. "To walk into the Rhine"—it's a beautiful phrase. Perhaps I'll do it myself one day. Not that I'm tired of life—I'm not—but it must be good down there, wandering through history in the green mud, then across the seabed and around the British Isles, to emerge again in Brittany . . . and always hearing that shrill, distorted Chopin, that savage, dislocated music that Karl produced when he took an ax to the keyboard before tearing it out—and the strings melted into a black tangled mess in the fire.

(*Looks at her watch.*) Now the discussion's starting, and he'll be sitting there with pencil and notepad, writing down what he calls key statements, so that in the next debate, or at the next meeting, he can say, "At 8:19 p.m. on such and such a date, Herr Gröbentöckler, you said our young people must learn how to make sacrifices again—but at 9:03 p.m. *you* said, Herr Kromlach, that the readiness of our workers to make sacrifices had not yet reached the stage it has to reach if it is to produce stability." Yes, he's precise, and that's a good thing; he's serious and incorruptible, and his cynicism is born of sadness. He would never walk into the Rhine. Karl would be more likely to do that.

Wubler enters quietly through the iron gate and sits down silently beside her. She gives a start.

EVA PLINT, *turning to him:* Oh, it's you. You're punctual, but you might at least have announced yourself by clearing your throat.

HERMANN WUBLER: I'm sorry; it's because I'm shy. In daylight or in normal lighting I'd never have had the courage to sit down next to you. Thank God for the fog. Though of course we know each other and no one would suspect any impropriety. (*Points to the gate.*) I've never had such a short journey to meet somebody. It was forty years ago that I first went up and spoke to a woman. It was during the blackout, and the darkness gave me the necessary courage. I was twenty at the time.

EVA PLINT: Was she a whore, the woman you spoke to?

HERMANN WUBLER: No, she was a salesgirl in a shoe shop.

EVA PLINT: Erika, your wife! Her story's well known from election leaflets, poor thing. The career of a model democrat—it must be painful. I've always liked her. How is she?

HERMANN WUBLER: She wants to get away from here, and at the same time she wants to stay. It's strange how many people want to get away from here. You probably do too, don't you?

EVA PLINT: I'm beginning to have second thoughts when I think of Ernst. It depends on what you have to tell me. So what's his name?

HERMANN WUBLER: His name is Jesús Pérez Delegas, aged thirty-five, a Cuban, and of course a Communist. He speaks excellent German, as you know—learned it in the GDR. He knows his Brecht and his Anna Seghers, and he's with the trade mission here.

EVA PLINT: Married?

HERMANN WUBLER: That's something we can't discover. In most cases they don't bring their wives with them, and we never see their personal documents. I'm warning you, my dear Eva.

EVA PLINT: Is he a spy?

HERMANN WUBLER: Well, in a sense all diplomats are spies. They have to try to get information, as discreetly and legally as possible. If they go about it in an indiscreet or even a stupid manner that's not quite legal, they're called spies and expelled. He certainly won't question you directly.

EVA PLINT: I've only danced with him twice, and God, can he dance! And he always helps me on with my coat before you try to: he puts his hands on my shoulders and looks at me. What information would I have to give him? Ernst tells me nothing about politics. I know no more than what I read in the papers and hear on the radio.

HERMANN WUBLER: Any information would be welcome: about Karl, your father-in-law, Grobsch, and above all Plukanski, whom Grobsch works for. Plukanski is a very promising figure—it's known that he used to take bribes and might be vulnerable to blackmail. . . .

EVA PLINT: Oh yes, I know. Oil, arms, tapestries . . . belly dancers—but he hasn't started doing deals with the belly dancers, has he? (*Hermann Wubler does not answer.*) Or has he? Perhaps he only provides them. They're artists after all, and if it comes to acting as an agent in a small way . . . You're not saying anything.

HERMANN WUBLER *sighs:* I'm not saying anything.

EVA PLINT: That's what's called neither confirming nor denying, which probably means confirming.

HERMANN WUBLER, *vehemently:* No, if it means anything it means I'm denying it. Do you mind if I smoke?

EVA PLINT: No. Do you still smoke a pipe?

HERMANN WUBLER *nods, takes his pipe from his pocket, fills it, lights it, and holds the dying match in front of Eva's face:* Yes, cigarettes in the morning, a pipe in the evening. Your soups were the best I ever had, Eva. Your grand piano, the conversations I had with you and Karl and Erika . . . What a pity we only see each other at parties these days: that way an old man's fancy could lightly turn to thoughts of lechery. I'd even forgo the news bulletins or let my spectacles steam up—if I needed to wear them. Discussions like the one this evening you can tape and study later in peace.

EVA PLINT: So you were eavesdropping, were you?

HERMANN WUBLER: Yes; I even missed the news.

EVA PLINT, *softly:* Don't say anything about Ernst Grobsch, please, and we don't need to talk about Karl. And Jesús, this Cuban . . . It's strange, but he's beginning to fade out of the picture. And I'm frightened, now that I'm beginning to understand Karl.

HERMANN WUBLER, *softly:* I've always understood him—but understanding someone doesn't signify much. When I came back from the war at twenty-five and took refuge at home, I'd have gladly destroyed all the towns and churches that hadn't been destroyed already—and certainly all the grand pianos. I even understand people who set cars on fire. Be careful: don't talk about Bingerle, Plukanski, and Blaukrämer at receptions—and don't whisper about Blaukrämer's ex. Did you know her?

EVA PLINT: Only slightly. I can't remember clearly. I only know his latest. Yes, her I know. And what I have to chat about is nothing more than what appears in the papers.

HERMANN WUBLER: When a politician's wife chats about something that's also in the papers, it becomes more than just what's in the papers. She becomes a source, and everyone assumes that she knows more than what the papers print.

EVA PLINT: There's something about documents—and Bingerle. The papers describe it as explosive.

HERMANN WUBLER: Mines are explosive, and so are duds, and if you step on a mine or strike it accidentally you can be blown sky-high. The press can write what it likes about explosive situations, but you're living with a politician who sits on important committees and is private secretary to Plukanski, and if you talk about Bingerle and Plukanski, someone may get the idea that you know where the mine's been laid.

EVA PLINT: But Bingerle and Plukanski are the number one topic of party gossip.

HERMANN WUBLER, *urgently:* It mustn't be the number one topic with you. You know what happened to Blaukrämer's ex?

EVA PLINT: There's some talk of her having been sent to a nuthouse and given the full treatment. Yes, I've heard. And recently a new name has surfaced: Plonius. . . .

HERMANN WUBLER, *with a start, very seriously:* Not a word about Plonius, Eva, not a word. Has Grobsch talked to you about him?

EVA PLINT: No. Didn't I say he tells me nothing? But he knows a great deal.

HERMANN WUBLER: "Nuthouse" is not the right expression. It's called the Kuhlbollen Spa Hotel.

EVA PLINT: There are only women there, I'm told.

HERMANN WUBLER: Yes, women who hear a lot, see a lot, read a lot, who leaf through their husbands' notebooks and eavesdrop on their telephone calls. You should observe Karl—and Grobsch too—when they go to parties: they talk about nothing but the weather, antiques, fashion. Yesterday at Hüstermann's you talked too much. You should keep quiet, smile sweetly, and chat about pop songs and films. Incidentally, the red outfit you were wearing at Hüstermann's doesn't really suit you—red's a rather ticklish color—but the bright green outfit does, with the rock crystal brooch shaped like a daisy.

EVA PLINT: I'm nearly forty, I know. You haven't aged at all in the last six years.

HERMANN WUBLER: The last seven years. At twenty-five I looked almost fifty, and now I'm sixty-two and I look every bit of fifty. I've often sat up there, waiting for you to turn up here at eight. I've wished I had Siegfried's helmet of invisibility—not to eavesdrop on you but just to look at you without being seen, as often as possible. And I know that Karl has sometimes come across on the ferry and sat on this bench with you. Bright green suits you, and so does pale blue. White always suits you, and whatever goes with beige. Can we spend a bit longer together, please? Is there somewhere we can go?

EVA PLINT: You could take me for a beer, at Krechen August's bar. I often wish I could go there, have a beer and a quiet cigarette at the bar, and think about somebody who wrote in the sand. But unfortunately there's no end of men who think themselves irresistible, and if you're a woman drinking beer at the bar, there's a six-to-four chance they'll put their hand on your arm, and I find that even more disgusting than all their talk about their wives not understanding them. Misunderstood wives are bad enough, but misunderstood husbands are even worse. If a woman is sitting by herself on a barstool, these lonely men—who are slightly tipsy—immediately have to make a grab for her. "Lonesome today, lady?" they say, or, "I'm lonely too—why don't two lonely people get together?" It's impossible just to sit and have a quiet beer. . . . So let's go to Krechen August's.

HERMANN WUBLER *stands up:* Sometimes I sit there at the bar, alone.

EVA PLINT *also stands up:* We could meet there; that's not a bad idea.

HERMANN WUBLER *takes her arm:* Come on, Eva, let's go.

EVA PLINT: Please don't get too familiar, and please don't hold my arm so tightly.

HERMANN WUBLER: Do you mean now or never?

EVA PLINT: Probably never. I've never deceived a man—not Ernst, not Karl, not Jesús.

HERMANN WUBLER *stops with her by the old wall:* And yet you have the reputation of being free and easy and something of a coquette. That's what happens with many beautiful and many pretty women: people think they're free and easy, and it's seldom true. The others are usually worse, more dangerous.

EVA PLINT: I take it you speak from experience?

HERMANN WUBLER: Not from personal experience, but from knowledge acquired in the course of my profession. Sometimes I have to deal with whole hordes of diplomats and diplomatic wives, and that can lead to enough embarrassments. No, I'm not a ladies' man—do I look like one?—but I'm open to temptation, and sometimes I'm tempted. However, like your Ernst, I take politics very seriously and behave accordingly.

EVA PLINT, *putting her hand on the damp wall:* You won't have any luck with this property. It's not going to be sold.

HERMANN WUBLER: Are you so sure? I'm conducting negotiations on behalf of a sheikhdom where they're mad about the romance of the Rhine and our curious climate—a gray sky sends them into raptures. Blue, even sky blue, can be monotonous—in fact, it *is* monotonous. There's an offer of three or four million, which could go up to five. And after all, the property has become something of a disgrace.

EVA PLINT: Disgrace is the right word, and that's what it will remain—a disgrace, a monument to shame. Every day I walk past this mossy wall, which is so dilapidated and in places subsiding and overgrown. The garden has grown wild, almost become a jungle; for decades every-thing's gone to seed and grown almost to tree height. There are pools, little ponds—genuine biotopes almost—and in the evening I can hear the croaking of the toads. It's been impossible for ages to make out that the garden gate was once green—dark green—fifty years ago. Wood pigeons fly up when I walk past, and the sign saying "Danger" has been superfluous for ages, as the house collapsed long ago. Sometimes tramps would venture through the undergrowth and find a dry spot in the cellar where the ceiling hadn't caved in. And of course it was one of the places where they searched for terrorists, churning up the weeds and trampling the rotting pears with their boots; everything floodlit. It looked as if they were filming something out of Poe. A lot of people have been after the property, wanting to build a house with a view of the Rhine—and of the opposite bank, where, once upon a time, dragon's blood was shed. What do you call it when somebody is killed in the name of a higher law? Did Blaukrämer's ex know too much . . . do I know too much . . . did Siegfried know too much, just as Bingerle does? Someone's plotting revenge, and one of these days he might chop up the television set on which Chundt and Blaukrämer appear with increasing frequency—always Gröbentöckler, Kromlach, and Ansbucher, with Breithuber droning away in that self-satisfied way of his.

HERMANN WUBLER *presses her arm:* Pull yourself together, Eva. We were talking about the sale of property.

EVA PLINT: Property that has to be paid for in dragon's blood. And I must ask you again: please don't get too familiar, and don't hold my arm so tightly. Yes, we were talking about this property. (*Knocks on the wall.*) You, Wubler, represent the prospective purchasers, with an offer of three, four, even five million. Why not ten? After all, there's no shortage of oil. But Ernst—Ernst Grobsch—represents the prospective vendor, whom he's managed to track down after a search that took years, after the most fanatical and painstaking investigation. He's Jeremias Arglos, fifteen years old, living in New York—the heir to those who were burned to ashes at Auschwitz and Treblinka or returned to dust in the cemeteries of Jerusalem, California, and New York. He's been to stay with us—a thin, pale, lanky boy. I took him for an evening boat trip on the Rhine—Chinese lanterns, singing, songs about the jolly Rhineland. He had an ice cream, drank lemonade, and ate sausages. He walked around this ruin and through the garden, wearing jeans and a purple shirt, and when we were having supper he said, "Don't sell it, don't ever sell it. I want it to remain a monument to my great-grandfather who built it, to my grandfather and father who were born here, who spoke the local language and drank beer at Krechen August's. I want it to remain a monument to them—a disgrace and a monument, a monument to shame. . . ."

HERMANN WUBLER: From what I've heard, he could do with the money.

EVA PLINT: He certainly could. He lives with relatives in New York who are called Henry and Clodagh. They don't actually live in dire penury, but in somewhat reduced circumstances all the same. But the boy knows what monuments are worth, and he's prepared to pay the price for the wood pigeons, the weeds, and the falling pears. "Disgrace" is the right word, and so is "monument." Maybe Henry and Clodagh would like to sell, but it can be proved that Jeremias is the rightful owner, and he's fifteen. You'll probably have to wait a while yet, though he might be killed when he's eighteen—in Nicaragua—and then the oil sheikhs could start building a bit sooner. And now let's go and have that beer. . . .

Both are sitting on beer crates at the bar, each with a glass of beer, looking at each other.

HERMANN WUBLER: I didn't know Ernst Grobsch was a Jew.

EVA PLINT *looks at him in astonishment:* He isn't a Jew. Where did you get that idea?

HERMANN WUBLER: Because he's blocking the sale of the property, wanting to preserve the monument, as you call it—the monument to shame.

EVA PLINT: Grobsch's grandfather was murdered at Auschwitz, but he wasn't a Jew—he was a worker and a Communist. He was in the resistance, together with Polish Catholics.

HERMANN WUBLER, *pensively:* Hats off to him! He could earn a lot of money as a broker and an attorney if he chose to; he could be a rich man. . . .

EVA PLINT: Don't put it down to any possible idealism. He's very realistic and has a healthy respect for money, because his family never had any—and a monument is just as real as money. He simply prefers the one reality to the other.

HERMANN WUBLER: So, cheers! (*They drink to each other.*) I'm not pushing it; I can wait. And let's hope the boy doesn't die at eighteen, in Lebanon or Honduras. Let's drink to his staying alive!

EVA PLINT: Yes, good idea!

HERMANN WUBLER: I'm an attorney. I simply represent my clients' interests. (*Takes an old-fashioned gold watch from his pocket.*) At this moment Kromlach is saying how spoiled today's youth is.

EVA PLINT: How do you know that?

HERMANN WUBLER: It's 8:45, his turn to speak. Were you spoiled in your youth?

EVA PLINT: And how! My father was an engineer. For a long time he was unemployed, but after the war, when I was growing up, he earned a lot of money. I can't remember the bad times. I always had enough to eat, and warm blankets to sleep in. At night my father and mother always came and tucked me in. That was when I was three or four. My father was working in a factory where they made sewing machines and accessories. Everything was in short supply, especially the needles, and of course all the women wanted to sew and alter their clothes. He started up a big black-market operation in sewing machine accessories, and by the time the currency reform came, he had a small factory of his own. It was the familiar story of the *nouveaux riches:* a smart school, piano lessons, tennis, dances, canasta. After I graduated I worked for a time with my cousin Albert Plint in the Catholic Bureau. Then I met Karl and became a countess—Eva Maria Countess of Kreyl—and that's what I still am. Yes, I'm spoiled—except for the shock over Karl and over my mother-in-law's walking into the Rhine. Yes, I'm spoiled—and Grobsch spoils me: he's very kind to me.

HERMANN WUBLER: A spoiled countess in Cuba ... My dear, that really worries me.

EVA PLINT, *quietly:* Being a countess and being spoiled— that wouldn't matter, but just dancing, with our hands on each other's shoulders ... and Grobsch sitting here alone, the lapsed Catholic with the proletarian face. No, I'm also a lapsed Catholic. They're not as bad as they're sometimes made out to be, the Catholics.

HERMANN WUBLER: I'm one too. Lapsed and Catholic.

EVA PLINT: I know, and so are Erika and Chundt and Blaukrämer—and so is Karl. It was a lot for Grobsch to take, considering how much he's opposed to the aristocracy—a countess, and a Catholic into the bargain.

HERMANN WUBLER: And now you're going to leave him?

EVA PLINT: No, probably not. I'd just like to have Cuban

children, to wipe their noses and their bottoms and ladle out soup to them, to dance with Jesús and feel his hands on my shoulders.

HERMANN WUBLER: I'm prepared to show you a few hundred children here that you could feed, whose noses and bottoms you could wipe. Maybe we could do it together—you, Erika, myself, and Karl. I've never had children of my own, whose noses and bottoms needed wiping. Another beer?

EVA PLINT: Beer? No, thanks. Sometimes I think I could drink five beers one after the other, only to find that one is almost too much. Ernst has nephews and nieces: I sometimes feed them and wipe their noses and bottoms. They don't have a spoiled youth. Did you?

HERMANN WUBLER: No. My father was a minor official in the post office. We weren't exactly poor, but everything was shabby. I suffered from having to wear other children's clothes—hand-me-downs from my elder brothers that had been altered to fit me. And I never got new shoes, and being the youngest of the family and having such small feet, all my shoes were too big for me. Nobody knows what a lot clothes can mean to people, especially to children. And then my uniform: I never had the right size; nothing fitted me properly. Yet I've always been interested in fashion, maybe for that very reason; I don't know. Please wear your bright green outfit at Blaukrämer's tomorrow, the one with the daisy brooch in rock crystal.

EVA PLINT: Perhaps you should have gone in for *haute couture* rather than serving with Chundt and having to keep company with Blaukrämer and Halberkamm.

HERMANN WUBLER: Maybe I had a talent for *haute couture,* but I'd have been put off by the sadness of it. (*Eva Plint gives him a questioning look.*) What's so sad about it is that so few women have model figures, and the discrepancy would have made me unhappy. Now I have to contend with other discrepancies, which are probably more serious. And please, I beg you in all seriousness: forget about the man you called Plonius. And maybe you should also forget about your friend Jesús.

EVA PLINT: He's such a good dancer—and even if he *is* a Communist, he's not one of the ponderous German variety. And I shouldn't gossip about anything anymore? Including Plukanski? They say he won't be in office much longer. Too much oil, too many arms and belly dancers.

HERMANN WUBLER: Even that won't cause his downfall. Now remember my advice.

EVA PLINT, *finishing her beer:* I have to go now. We've got an invitation to a musicale at Kapspeter's. His daughter Adelheid is an old school friend of mine, and this evening she's playing Beethoven on a brand-new grand piano. She's coming over specially from New York to try it out.

HERMANN WUBLER: May I pay for your beer, then?

EVA PLINT: Yes, you may. It was nice being with you; let's do it again. (*She leaves. Hermann Wubler stays and sits pensively over a second glass of beer.*)

Chapter 5

---

*The bedroom of Ernst Grobsch and Eva Plint. A large double bed
placed at an angle to the spectator, two chairs, two bedside tables,
and a dressing table. On the wall are two posters, one of Che
Guevara and one of a Baroque angel. Grobsch is lying in bed, his
face turned to the left. Eva sits at the end of the bed, on the right-
hand side. On one of the bedside tables are bowls, towels, and
bottles. It is about 3:00 a.m. The room is dimly lit by a standard
lamp.*

ERNST GROBSCH, *who has just woken up:* What a nice smell!
  What is it—sage or rosemary or something?
EVA PLINT: No, lavender—and a little camphor. (*Leans over
  and lays her hand on Grobsch's forehead.*) It seems to have
  passed.
ERNST GROBSCH *tries to sit up, but Eva prevents him:* Have I
  been asleep long?
EVA PLINT: Three hours. It wasn't easy getting you into
  bed. Warm compresses and massage with oil of lavender.
  I massaged you and fed you some hot soup, and then
  you went to sleep. And naturally I prayed—I said the All
  Saints litany over you. That helped too. Stay calm; it's
  only three o'clock, and tomorrow you're going to spend
  the day in bed.
ERNST GROBSCH: Have you been sitting here all the time?
EVA PLINT: Yes, and I'll go on sitting here. You talked a

lot in your sleep: you said some horrible things, lots of obscene things, things about your life that I didn't know—and I was amazed at how pure all the dirty things seemed. (*More quietly*) Words I'd never heard or read, yet I knew what they meant. It's strange to think that we have all that inside us.

ERNST GROBSCH: And so Wubler told you everything about the Cuban, put on his languishing lover act, and also talked about the property: that's a real 3-D performance. So what about this Cuban of yours?

EVA PLINT, *embarrassed:* He's gone—flown away. (*With some emotion*) Oh God, you Germans are all so ponderous, so leaden—including Karl. Yes (*seeing Grobsch looking at her*), I know he doesn't give that impression, but he really is like that—the brooding type, nice though, and he can be frivolous when he chooses. But all you Germans . . . you always seem to be carrying the whole weight of the world on your shoulders, whereas he—Jesús—is so free and easy, so smiling—he can dance—and he's always cheerful, though he has a hard time of it here, harder than any of you.

ERNST GROBSCH: Jesús? Is he also called Pérez Delegas? (*Eva nods.*) He's one of the toughest boys they've got here: I know him from discussions I've had with him. Oh, Jesús, Jesús—if only I'd known. My dear Eva, I'm sorry. No, he certainly isn't a German. And what about you—aren't you a German, then?

EVA PLINT: Oh yes, without any doubt. My great-grandfather had a job in a brick factory up north—a worker, in other words. His ancestors were cottagers, poor tenant farmers who went in for a kind of superstitious mysticism—all genuinely German, gloomy and ponderous. My grandfather was a locksmith, my father an engineer—also German, but not quite so ponderous. And my mother was a town girl, as they say where I come from—pious, but freethinking and anticlerical, the daughter of a salesman from the Rhineland. And now . . .

ERNST GROBSCH: Now you dream about Caribbean dancing partners. . . . Yes, I understand. Oh, Eva.

EVA PLINT *sighs:* I'll probably have to stick to German men. I've sat here for maybe three hours, Ernst. You had the shivers, but you didn't have a fever, and you didn't develop one either. It wasn't a virus, and it wasn't brought on by the cold or anything. There was another cause. You were sweating—look at these towels: they're wringing wet. Fortunately it was a hot sweat. We shouldn't have gone to Kapspeter's—it was too much for one day. The normal day's work, then pumping Plukanski up, the annoyance over the TV discussion—and then having to go to that musicale . . . We won't go again, Ernst, never again. When you were dreaming, you said things to do with your childhood and youth, obscene things, and there was one thing you kept on repeating aloud—almost shouting it out. "Beethoven doesn't belong to them. Do they have to own everything—everything, including Beethoven?" It was uncanny, dear—it almost reminded me of an exorcism: it was as though you were possessed, really possessed. The soup, the warmth, my hands, the oil of lavender, and my prayers—perhaps they drove out the demon.

ERNST GROBSCH: What demon can you have driven out of me?

EVA PLINT: Your rage, your fear, your hatred . . . the feeling of being lost. And now all the trouble you took over Plukanski was in vain.

ERNST GROBSCH: I'd like to retain a bit of each of the things you've just listed—just a bit. And what I did for Plukanski wasn't wasted. I learned a lot.

EVA PLINT *stands up:* I'll warm up some more soup for you, and then you can go back to sleep.

ERNST GROBSCH: No, stay here. Pray if you want to pray, but not aloud; I don't want to hear you pray. Did I cause a scandal?

EVA PLINT: No, you were quite quiet, too quiet. . . . We won't go there again, Ernst. I'll stay with you. One thing's clear to me now: Cuba isn't kitsch, but it would be if I went there. (*Smiles.*) Let's forget about little Jesús.

ERNST GROBSCH: A sensitive, spoiled, educated woman—a pious countess—in Cuba. Why not? Educated, sensitive, pious noblewomen have been revolutionaries often enough—they've sometimes made it possible for revolutions to happen. I could understand it. Don't be sad, don't cry, Eva, but believe me: they're not fastidious about the way they treat their womenfolk, their wives included. You'd have cried even more there than you could possibly cry here over a lost dream. It's better not to come out of the dream. So I said, "Beethoven doesn't belong to them"—but I didn't say it there, did I?

EVA PLINT: No, here—and I thought to myself: now he'd probably like nothing better than to chop up grand pianos too.

ERNST GROBSCH: When I was sitting there I thought I'd go crazy, that in another moment I'd flip. Those people! So sensitive, so refined and unpretentious, so tasteful and cultured, so fine-feeling—all of them so *genuine*—and that young woman Adelheid sitting at the grand, playing Beethoven! And then I really began to think about Karl—your husband, Count von Kreyl. The way he hacked his own grand to pieces—I'd always taken that to be a peculiar brand of upper-class snobbery; it had struck me as merely funny. And then when he gave that girl money from the diplomatic fund so that she could flee to Cuba to avoid torture and death, I thought: well, well! And he was even thrown out of the service and sentenced to probation. And then, as I was sitting at Kapspeter's, I suddenly felt like doing the same—me of all people! What was it your father called me?

EVA PLINT: The prole with the face of a sociologist.

ERNST GROBSCH: Good. Not at all a bad description. Old man Plint has wit and understands human nature. Yes, at Kapspeter's I had to take hold of myself or I might have gotten up and smashed something, even if it was a piece of Meissen china, which in any case I find impossible to distinguish from the trash one buys in department stores. No, Eva, it had nothing to do with all the work I'd done, or with pumping up Plukanski, or with my annoyance over the TV discussion. I suddenly had an idea that scared me: even Plukanski, whom I detest—even he was closer to me than these fine, noble people surrounded by all that fine, noble furniture. Worse still: even that swine Chundt, whom I could happily murder, and that dirty little punk Blaukrämer—they were all closer to me, because we politicians collaborate in producing all the shit and then clearing it all away, so that they can do the dusting without getting any dirt on themselves. Fine! And they go off to auctions to rescue valuable crucifixes for the nation and don't give a moment's thought to the blood, sweat, and shit their money is made from. And there was another thing, Eva: your seemingly dreamy school friend Adelheid almost confirmed what I was thinking when she whispered to you, "Daddy didn't find it easy inviting that Grobsch of yours." And had she really flown over specially from New York to try out the new grand with a bit of Beethoven and to see you again? Tell me, Eva, am I "that Grobsch of yours"? Was she trying to persuade you to drop "that Grobsch of yours"?

EVA PLINT, *shattered, blushing:* Yes, you are that Grobsch of mine. I should have gotten up and left when she called you that. I just hoped you hadn't heard. I betrayed you, Ernst, but now you really are *my* Grobsch, don't you see? She made you that Grobsch of mine—she married us, so to speak. And all my life I'll be ashamed that I didn't get up and leave. I'm ashamed at having to tell you how stupid I've been. Forgive me; I'm sorry. I just couldn't. I hate scenes, I hate scandals. It was—oh hell!— it was an aesthetic problem. Now you're closer to me than Karl ever was.

ERNST GROBSCH: All the same, I'd have understood it if I'd been just the prole with the face of a sociologist. You see it from a social angle; I see it from a political angle. After all, I'm a member of the federal parliament and adviser to a minister—that's the problem. They don't like me—I can see that plainly enough, even though to this day I can't tell the difference between batik and a piece of printed cotton. She didn't say "Herr Grobsch" or "your friend and lover"; she said "that Grobsch of yours." At that point I should have got up and at least thumped the piano with my fist. It made me shudder, Eva, and I felt the age-old proletarian fear in the face of their impeccable taste. We're both equally spineless. . . .

EVA PLINT: You were shaking, and your teeth were chattering. . . . It must have been more than that stupid remark.

ERNST GROBSCH: It *was* more than that. (*Sinks back on the pillow and speaks more quietly and thoughtfully.*) In a way that I can't quite explain to you, it was . . . you mustn't be alarmed. It was a metaphysical shudder: it was as though I'd been touched by an angel—one of those angels I've been cursing and mocking ever since I was nine years old. We used to pee on the pictures of angels we were given for diligence at school. In the midst of all that

tasteful cleanliness I longed for the dirt of politics. It was
my job to pump up Plukanski; it's my job to do everything to ensure that Chundt disappears from public view.
Just tell me one thing: how many more banker's daughters were there at your convent school? Adelheid Kapspeter, Hilde Krengel, and who else?

EVA PLINT: Now *you* are joking again. There's a grand-
daughter of Erftler who'd like to meet you. She's called
Marion, she's unmarried, and she doesn't play the piano.
She has nothing to do with banking—she runs a rubber
factory. She's hard-working and severe. But she has a
sense of humor; she always wags her finger at me when
I meet her.

ERNST GROBSCH: She doesn't sound a bad sort. Presum-
ably she wags her finger because of me.

EVA PLINT: Yes, probably, but mainly because we're not
married, I suspect. Cheer up—you're rid of Plukanski.

ERNST GROBSCH: And of my job as his adviser. Blaukrämer's hardly likely to take me on. And I got a certain
perverse pleasure out of ghostwriting Plukanski's
speeches. But you haven't told me anything about Wubler.

EVA PLINT: The thing with Jesús is over. Wubler warned
me, in general terms, not to gossip too much. He also
advised me on how to dress, and he told me about the
Arglos property and about that woman Elisabeth Blaukrämer. Do we know her?

ERNST GROBSCH: He's not likely to get much joy out of
Arglos. The boy's adamant. And Blaukrämer's ex? You
should know her actually, through Karl. You *must* have
met her when Blaukrämer was still president of the co-
ordinated personnel committees. Think back—they used
to live right next to the ferry.

EVA PLINT: Oh, her! Grand receptions: lavish buffet, but

tastefully done. She had style. She used to stand in the middle of the reception hall, smiling in that unconcerned way, almost contemptuously—tall, ash-blond, pale complexion, the eyes almost turned inward. Not the type one would have called hysterical at that time; confused, I'd have said, disturbed, defiant, almost like a big schoolgirl who'd been raped. She used to wear a silvery gown with a big ruby brooch, and she had a way of smoking that seemed a bit too artificial, a bit too brash. Some people might have found her forbidding, but I liked her.

ERNST GROBSCH: She was a countess or something—but a genuine one.

EVA PLINT: I'm a genuine one too, though not by birth. When Wubler mentioned her it sounded like a warning.

ERNST GROBSCH: It's a warning to be taken seriously. Where she is now is where all the discarded wives live—in a high-class prison. I'm told there are even nice young men there who are sent up to your room if the authorities get the impression that that's what you'd like. Don't worry, you'll never end up there—I won't let you.

EVA PLINT: I'm afraid for you . . . I'm not even afraid for Karl.

ERNST GROBSCH: Last night I realized I'd done him a grave injustice, and I've stopped being envious of him. I used to envy him his audacity, his elegant way of doing things—the age-old self-assurance that I could never acquire. Your father was right: I'm a prole with the face of a sociologist.

EVA PLINT: I don't want to go to any more parties or musicales. I couldn't bear it if somebody hurt you again—and I was a coward again.

ERNST GROBSCH: There's one reception we're definitely going to—when Blaukrämer invites people to celebrate his appointment.

EVA PLINT: If you say so, but I won't let you out of my sight. Blaukrämer! Doesn't anyone realize that he's just impossible?

ERNST GROBSCH: He's not impossible, as you see. Plukanski could also have been called impossible, and Blaukrämer will fall—he'll come a cropper too. The only people who'll never fall, who'll never come a cropper, are the gentlemen who don't rule us but control us. Even Heulbuck will fall one day, but Florian, Kapspeter, Bransen, Krengel, and Blömscher never will. They don't rule, you see, they only control, and none of them will ever see the inside of a prison. They go on forever—by the divine right of money. And they're well assorted: Florian's a Protestant, a churchgoer, a bit loud, while Kapspeter's quiet and a Catholic; and Krengel's a Protestant too. And there's even an atheist among them—Blömscher. And they're all collectors of notoriously valuable objects, and Kapspeter even has a rather idle daughter who zips over from New York to have a good look at that man Grobsch, the political monkey they're obliged to tolerate in their zoo, but who's also an attorney, not just a sociologist, (*sits up suddenly*) and has a certain amount of influence over a dreamy Jewish boy who owns a property by the Rhine. Dear Eva, your friend Wubler's not just in love with you; he's also Kapspeter's attorney and a member of his board of directors—his partner, even—and you can be sure the oil sheikhs would pay any price, any price at all, for a view of the Drachenfels. But what they're offering the boy is merely a *good* price—all by the grace of God. Which is why I felt the angel touch my shoulder—Kapspeter, Wubler, love, politics, business. Hence my metaphysical shivers. No, they never rule and can never be toppled; they always remain pure, like those who reign by the grace of God. They'd even topple Heulbuck and throw Wubler out if they no longer did their bidding. I'm a hard-boiled atheist who has to take a firm hold on himself when he catches sight of a priest. Did Wubler also talk about a man called Bingerle?

EVA PLINT: Yes; he says I mustn't mention him.

ERNST GROBSCH: He must have gotten hold of something that makes them all tremble, good and bad alike, the nice guys and the villains.

EVA PLINT: And maybe even the bankers?

ERNST GROBSCH: No; he can't make them tremble, not even this time—at least not for their reputation or for their existence. That's been taken care of for them by the politicians—*they* are the people who do the trembling. I may be a prole, but I'm discovering more and more things that link me with Karl.

EVA PLINT: He'd be glad to hear it. He likes you more than you like him.

ERNST GROBSCH: Okay, I'll tell him sometime. Are you actually jealous of the woman he's with now?

EVA PLINT: I'm jealous of the child she has.

ERNST GROBSCH: The kid isn't a count.

EVA PLINT: Perhaps you and I will produce a count.

ERNST GROBSCH: No; he'd be a Plint. If we did have a child, I'd like him to be a little Grobsch—but on second thought I'd rather not, even if Grobsch does sound a bit better than Plint—no, rather not.

EVA PLINT, *removing the spectacles from his nose*: Funny how your gray eyes become darker and bigger. And suddenly the prole isn't there anymore—the analyst, the sociologist. All I see in his place is someone who's anxious, disturbed, hungry, and freezing. Don't forget: we're married to each other, even if it's not official. Adelheid Kapspeter married us—you're that Grobsch of mine. I'm not leaving here, or you, unless you leave me.

ERNST GROBSCH: I'm not leaving here. This is the state that made me, and I want to go on being involved with it until it's no longer controlled by those who don't rule it. I'm not leaving here—I've got things to do here; I want to go on working. Of course, I'm afraid. I didn't have a happy, settled childhood in which to build up the necessary reserves; it's only later that you realize they're missing. And I want to retain my anger, maybe even the hatred that has so far been reined in—had a framework imposed on it, so to speak—by my analytical faculty. Sometimes I can't keep within the framework. Did Karl have a settled childhood? Was he happy as a child?

EVA PLINT: He was five when his mother walked into the Rhine, and his father soon became quite an important person; but life's far from cozy in the kind of stately homes they grew up in. It's cold, and there's usually not much to eat.

ERNST GROBSCH: Like last night at Kapspeter's: not even the food was good, and it wasn't even plentiful—altogether a pretty poor show.

EVA PLINT: Yes. The soup wasn't even hot; and the fish was too dry and there wasn't enough. And the pudding was like glue. Yes, you're right. Forget it.

ERNST GROBSCH, *mildly*: No, I won't forget it. I might forget the lousy food, but not the rest. Sometimes I think you cling to the title and that's the reason why you won't get a divorce—because if you did . . .

EVA PLINT: Yes, I've got to admit I do cling to the title, and thanks to the title I have a very nice father-in-law.

ERNST GROBSCH: And you have a very nice father as well; you're well off for fathers. My father died when I was twelve, of cirrhosis of the liver, and my mother died of a broken heart. Yes, that's what it's known as: her heart was broken by our poverty and our curses, by grief and fear, and so I can't even provide you with a mother-in-law.

EVA PLINT: Now you're going to have some more soup, and I'm going to massage you again. Then you'll sleep, and so will I. I'm very tired. I'm so glad I'm with you, and staying with you.

ERNST GROBSCH: Was it because you were sorry for me that you went home with me the first time and stayed the night?

EVA PLINT: No; I wasn't sorry for you then, but I was last night. I wanted to know you—not just to get to know you superficially but to really know you. It almost broke my heart when I first went with you to that room of yours, that dog kennel of a room. Nothing but papers all over the place, a few bits of sausage, and mustard stains on the tablecloth. It's dreadful what conditions you all live in here—hardly any of you has anything like a real *home*. It's like a cross between a dog kennel and a furnished room, but not a home. I've only really known you since last night; before that I was just fond of you. I'll cry a bit over Jesús: he was so unlike the Germans, so charming.

ERNST GROBSCH: And hard, Eva—as hard as nails. The women from those countries are so keen on German men.

EVA PLINT: There's one thing I don't understand about this whole Plukanski-Blaukrämer affair. If Blaukrämer's going to succeed Plukanski, they must both belong to the same party.

ERNST GROBSCH: They do—didn't you know?

EVA PLINT: I've never been all that interested in the political parties, but you're right: it's obvious. And so you're in the same party as Blaukrämer, are you?

ERNST GROBSCH, *laughing out loud*: My God, how clever you are! What ruthless logic! Yes, I'm in Blaukrämer's party. Just one more thing, Eva: if ever you do go away, don't join *them*.

EVA PLINT: Join whom?

ERNST GROBSCH: It's better to go to Cuba than to join *them*.

EVA PLINT: I'm not going anywhere—I'm staying here, with you. (*Puts out the light.*)

Chapter 6

Soliloquy of Ernst Grobsch

Whenever I drive over to see this man Plukanski I have to get a firm grip on myself to avoid being overcome by fury and losing control of the steering, which could mean driving into tree or a streetlamp or crashing into another car. Maybe one day I'll strangle him. He's such a nonentity. He isn't even a hypocrite; he's just himself—a nothing. They call him Apple Cheeks—and it's true, his skin really is incredibly telegenic. A makeup artist once whispered to me, "*He* doesn't need makeup—he's permanently made up." He always looks like a ripe apple that's about to fall or be picked any moment—so appetizing, so salable, with the thick blond hair that's now turned to silver. Even now, when he's going on fifty-five, he still looks like a boy you'd like to have played football with. He can even put on a roguish smile, and he has dimples too. Nobody's yet worked out precisely how many votes he's worth, but one thing's certain—it's plenty. And public opinion surveys reveal that most people think he's a nobleman who's dropped his title out of democratic modesty. Yet the truth is that he's just like me, one of the few real proles in our ranks. His father was a drunken coal miner and his mother a local beauty of dubious repute, who succeeded in devising a rare combination of indolence and ambition and now manages to convey, by veiled hints and knowing smiles, that Apple

Cheeks, Hans Günter Plukanski, was the issue of an early liaison with a baron, who was brokenhearted because he couldn't marry her, after which she married Plukanski the coal miner, so that her love child would be born in wedlock. Plukanski was in fact born five months after her marriage to Jürgen Plukanski. I've researched all this because I was once given the task of composing his campaign address. I visited the hypocritical old bitch several times at an expensive old-people's home, where she was every inch a lady, with her English tea service, her pretty furniture, and her genuine rocks; she had created for herself an aura of unapproachability, which made every conversation seem an act of condescension on her part. After all, she was no longer just plain Frau Plukanski from the mining village of Klissenheim, but "the minister's mother." However, I was able to discover that she had once worked as a laundress in a stately home owned by the Häck-Pavignys, and it's quite possible that at some stage one of the young barons got his leg over her on top of a stack of laundry. I visited her several times when I was having to cobble Plukanski's campaign address together. She didn't mind my mentioning that she had been employed at the castle, though she took grave exception to the phrase "in service" and insisted on the formulation "in a responsible position." I accepted that; after all, doing the washing in a large noble household is something that calls for responsibility. Nor do I have anything against girls who take service in castles. My own mother worked part-time as a cleaner and washerwoman all her life, because *my* father was a drunk too. Even when Apple Cheeks was nearing forty his mother thought nothing of saying to me, "I always saw Hans Günter as a bishop, bending down benevolently to talk to confirmation candidates." Her Polish-sounding name worried her a lot, she said; it always had, because there was nothing Slav about her and Hans Günter. At times she'd thought of changing it to Plockhardt. Her maiden name was Müllmer, she said, and she mumbled something about her people being "in grain"—a family tradition, she said. It wasn't a total lie; her grandfather had worked in a flour mill and her father had been a baker's assistant, so actually both of them had in a sense been "in grain." I have to admit that I didn't take to either her or her son. They both had the same blue eyes, but these eyes had a slimy lasciviousness about them that's hard to describe. The way she spoke about her husband was not exactly contemptuous, though there were hints of contempt. "He was talented," she said, "but he simply couldn't cope with the temptations that unemployment brought with it."

That was her way of putting what might have been expressed another way: he drank himself to death on the cheapest hooch available, some kind of turnip spirit brewed by himself and some of his mates, who were also out of work. There were photographs of him, a good-looking guy, tall, fair-haired, and with an astonishing resemblance to Apple Cheeks himself, who seemed to have inherited nothing from his mother but his slimy blue eyes. Of course, the old man had been in trouble a number of times, but that didn't have to go into Apple Cheeks's biography, and so I decided on the wording: "P's father was one of the many victims of the economic crisis." It was difficult to work out where the old lady got her fancy airs from. Possibly being in service at the castle prompted a desire to appear "refined." She always seemed to speak on tiptoe, as it were. What I learned about Apple Cheeks at Klissenheim wasn't very edifying. The village priest had given him Latin lessons and sent him first to the high school and then to the seminary, and there were actually pictures of him as a boy wearing a kind of cassock and looking for all the world like a very young von Ketteler. In the end we didn't use any of these pictures in the campaign literature. Denominational elements are tricky things to handle in political campaigning and can easily misfire. Plukanski might have come across as "one of ours," but he might equally well have been seen as a "lapsed Catholic." Either way it would have brought us votes from two different quarters, but it would also have cost us votes in both. Renegades are not popular, even with those who are renegades themselves, and the votes we were trying to bring in were after all pro-church votes. It was much the same with the photographs showing him as a dashing young officer cadet. We mulled it over for a long time: in such circles people aren't all that pro-military, yet at the same time they're proud of "our boys," and whether they want to or not, they all, without exception, march to the war memorial on remembrance days, singing marching songs, and lay their wreaths. You can't deprive them of such atavistic rituals and you can't talk them out of them. So in the end we put one of these pictures in, and it proved effective all over the country— everywhere, that is, where he was not known personally, where there were no recollections of him and his family.

When it came to my principal aim—which was to get hold of some stories about his youthful escapades—I drew a blank. Schoolboy pranks go down well, provided they don't involve incendiarism, but this was precisely what I found—one or two cases of arson, which were never wholly cleared up and in which he came under suspicion. In desperation I *invented* an escapade—about him climbing onto the church roof, removing the weather vane, and hiding it in the cellar of the presbytery, of all places, where it was found by an astonished housekeeper. An escapade like that goes over well—it shows youthful exuberance, physical daring, wit, and an underlying sense of fun.

What I actually found was of barely any use. I met his old teacher on his daily walk to the cemetery, and although the old gentleman confided to me that he was an atheist—

though I wasn't to spread that around the village—he led me to the grave of one Father Pleyel, who had been the parish priest. Standing by the grave, he said, "He broke that man's heart. It really broke his heart when the boy was expelled from the seminary. He was expelled for two reasons: first for exhibitionism, though they could easily have cured him of that—after all, they'll take anybody." "Anybody?" I asked. "Yes, anybody," he insisted. "But in the second place it was because smart little Hennes—that's what they used to call him—was somehow stupid, unintelligent in a way that even they didn't know how to handle. You see, there wasn't the slightest trace of any spiritual dimension in his makeup, a dimension that you find even in the feebleminded. Call it grief, pain, anxiety, despair, longing, or what you will—it's something everyone has, whether he's the local squire or a coal miner. Our little Hennes was just vacuous. He could learn by heart anything that was put in front of him—quite fantastic—but if I spoke to him about it and asked him *what* it was that he was reciting, he would look at me as though he didn't know what I meant. I never knew whether to give him top marks or bottom marks. Unfortunately I gave him top marks, and so he went on to be taught by the priest, then to the seminary, and from there to the army. But this man here," he said, pointing to Father Pleyel's grave, "this pious, upright man . . . he broke his heart, not just as a person but as a phenomenon." The village of Klissenheim turned out in the end to be too much of a dump, with its clinker cottages and garages wedged between them.

There was nothing there that I could use for my campaign address. Was I to write: "He broke a pious old clergyman's heart . . . was thrown out of the seminary for exhibitionism . . . lacks any spiritual dimension"? Then I tried an angle that's of immense importance for publicity purposes—sport. The ideal thing would have been a youthful photograph of him in football gear—with a beaming smile on his face and the ball at his feet—spearheading his team's attack; or as the goalkeeper, making a magnificent save. Some indication of the sportsmanly idealism that was around at the time, the amateur spirit that people took for granted, would have made such a picture a real scoop. But those of his school friends whom I managed to track down just grinned when I asked them about his sporting activities. One of them said simply, "He didn't bring disgrace on Klissenheim." And another said, "He's really gone a long way—but vote for him? No, I'm not going to vote for him. And he never played football. We didn't have any money for motorbikes . . . and bicycles, well, perhaps he did have one. He did do something for us when the Yanks released him from the POW camp. He spoke good English and helped as an interpreter when the rebuilding program got under way. He had good connections, I've got to admit—but vote for *him*? No way. Not even if he *is* in the party I'd like to vote for."

A photograph of him with a bicycle would have been almost as good as one of him as a footballer, but the only sporty picture I got hold of, from an elderly aunt of his, showed him with a bicycle at the age of about fifteen, wearing a rucksack. However, that was something. The caption we used was "Cycling in the country was a passion of his from an early age." And we forced him, at the age of forty-five, to sit on a brand-new bike and adopt a jaunty pose. After all, there was a bicycle factory in his constituency. We took a photo of him and added the caption: "And still is." There was something they all kept resolutely quiet about in the village, though I could never discover what it was. He only managed to poll twenty-eight percent there, though we were able to plug his real services in the rebuilding program without the least resort to dishonesty: "He tirelessly used his knowledge of English, as well as the knowledge of mining he had acquired as a prisoner of war, for the benefit of his beloved village." And in the local mining offices I managed to unearth a photograph of him, his face covered with coal dust; all we needed now were a few life-size pictures of him patting children on the head, smiling at old ladies, and walking his dog. That went down well too, except in his own village, where I came across hardly anything but grins.

I straightened out the crooked bits in his life story by writing: "Painful diversions alienated him at times from the Church he loved, to which he returned later with increased ardor. He was a brave soldier, but was soon horrified by the war aims of a misguided government." Of course, I'd rather have said "a Fascist government," or "a criminal government," but that was strictly ruled out. There were a few stories I heard involving girls; these were recounted without any smirks; in fact, with a certain amount of bitterness. Even I was surprised by them, as I'd always rather assumed he was gay. All this was summed up in the sentence: "No wonder he broke so many hearts."

There are mysterious laws according to which stories about women can benefit one politician and work to the detriment of another. There must be completely irrational and mythical motives behind this, which we've not yet succeeded in analyzing. Chundt and Plukanski, for instance, represent the type of politicians who benefit, but those on the left never do. This may be connected with the moral pretensions projected by the left wing, whereas the right wing gains votes through its open indifference to morality. In this sense Plukanski was clearly right-wing. And finally an aristocratic angle came into the story: he married a Countess Auel, a countrywoman with a pleasant personality and simple good looks, who owned a small but well-run estate: fruit plantations, trout breeding, and—what was more important when it came to photographs—dog breeding. There were some splendid pictures to be had here, showing him on the castle terrace, a radiant, apple-cheeked Laocoön encircled by his dogs. And then they had children, who in due course cut quite a figure in their high-class country outfits. There was quite a lot of mileage here: "Worker's son marries countess. What unites them is their shared Christian heritage."

Meanwhile, for the last twelve years he hasn't known what his wife's bedroom looks like. She now has her children by a lover, and her husband is quite happy to acknowledge them as his own. Only the eighteen-year-old daughter, Ruth, and the sixteen-year-old son, Huldreich, are actually his; eleven-year-old Ethelbert and nine-year-old Mechthild are the issue of other loins. But this doesn't spoil the scenario. At election time he visits his wife, has himself photographed with her, sits pensively on the terrace, deep in conversation with her lover—a pleasant man, an agronomist by profession—and occasionally gets on a horse. On one occasion he even rolled up his sleeves and took hold of a pitchfork.

Even so he never lives anywhere but here, at what passes for a modest address—in an old part of town where every other house is smartly furnished and those in between are run-down. The run-down houses are inhabited by Turkish immigrants, students, communes and dropouts, the smart ones by doctors, lawyers, and covert millionaires—with enormous apartments that are more spacious than many a small castle. At any rate it's not an exclusive residential area, and the cars parked in the street are battered and painted in bright colors. Plukanski doesn't drive himself; he has an official car with a driver, and sometimes he actually gets on his bicycle and rides around the block, stopping for coffee at the counter of some anti-establishment coffee shop. It's up to me to make sure that the photographers are informed in good time. He'll call me up and say,

"Bicycle hour tomorrow from ten to eleven." All the same, he lives in the middle of his constituency, where he polls a regular fifty-four to fifty-six percent; and when he goes into one of the cafés he gets people to tell him about the "concerns of the young." He's good at this, and he knows how to give interviews—from the bicycle track—about everything from nuclear energy to the pill and tax reform. He always knows how to switch on the tapes I've prepared for him. He knows where to locate the right button in the welter of clichés. He's an adept at that: he's superbly programmed for every eventuality. I've even drilled him in how to produce an embarrassed stammer, the odd "ah," "oh," "er," and "hm," so that it doesn't all come across too pat.

The one thing he can't do is write speeches; if he has a speech to make he goes all limp and becomes apathetic and depressive, and then I have to go over and pump him up. I write the whole speech for him, right down to the very last word, working in a few impromptu passages to give an impression of spontaneity; he then has to put these across as though they really were impromptu, by pausing briefly or stopping to clear his throat, although in fact these bits are planned just as precisely as the other parts of the speech. I simply insert the letters "IMP" in brackets and underline the passage in red: this is the cue for him to run his hand through his hair or fiddle nervously with his nose, or else he can put his hand behind his ear or simply stare thoughtfully ahead, as though searching for words. I structure the speech under headings, work in logical transitions, and then rehearse the whole thing with him, IMPs and all. I make him read it to me three or four times, until his resonant baritone has the ring of conviction. The one thing he does have is a good voice, which I don't. With my squeaky tenor even the cleverest speech would be wafted away on the breeze; I wouldn't be able to hold a single listener for more

than three minutes. He, on the other hand—precisely because he's indifferent to the meaning or content of what
he's saying—can sound off like Mario del Monaco. In his
incredible way he's empty, hollow—and that's what produces the sound, the boom, the drum roll. I sometimes call
him "the best drum in the West."

There's already something senile about the helplessness
and bewilderment on his face when he has an attack of
what I call "the droops," and at such times I secretly hope
he's about to have a stroke. Unfortunately the doctors' di-
agnoses don't give much ground for such a hope. Again
and again I'm consumed by a single desire—to scratch at
his apple cheeks until I've found out what kind of worms
are eating him up inside. He has taste—he probably gets
that from his mother, who picked it up from the Häck-
Pavignys, and because I've no taste myself, this furnishes
an additional motive for my anger and resentment.

He received me with a radiant smile; dressed in a rust-
colored silk gown with a white cravat, he was more apple-
cheeked than ever, his silver hair both soft and thick. There
really is something benedictory about his gestures, and so
I can quite easily picture him as a bishop. For a moment I
was afraid he was going to embrace me. According to our
latest information he's bisexual, and whenever I'm inclined
to wonder whether he really is devoid of all human feelings, I have to concede that he has some: he's turned on by
sex and money. There was an open fire in the hearth, and
in that inimitable voice of his, which I envy him so much—
at once so soft and so resonant—he said to me, "My dear
Grobsch, what would I do without you?" Nothing, I
thought. Without me you'd be nothing.

An attractive girl got up from the sofa; I say a girl, but
she could easily have been a slightly padded-out boy. He
introduced her to me. "This is Lore," he said. "I have no
secrets from her." She was really pretty, slim and blond,

and I wondered how I could play the old trick by which you discover whether someone is male or female. It involves throwing an apple or a ball into the person's lap. If it's a woman, she spreads her legs; if it's a man, he clamps them together. At least this holds good in western climes, where women habitually wear skirts and men wear pants. I looked into her eyes, and she smiled, as if to say, "Don't worry—I really am a woman."

I sat down, and Lore poured me some champagne. For the last ten years I've visited his apartment at least four times a month—which adds up to nearly five hundred visits—and he still hasn't got it into his head that champagne makes me sleepy; and the same goes for coffee. When I have to work I need tea and mineral water, and sometimes beer positively peps me up. My proletarian organs don't respond properly to champagne. I'm a victim of my lousy digestion, which has been ruined by an excessive intake of cheap sausages and cheap potato salad. And I had to start working too early in order to get myself through high school and to the university.

For the five hundredth time I declined the champagne, more or less politely, and for the five hundredth time Plukanski clapped his hand to his forehead, as though suddenly remembering. Lore took the champagne away and brought me some beer, and we got down to work: a thirteen-minute speech about the potential and the dangers of cable television. The party had realized that it wasn't a good thing for *all* its leading members to declare themselves unreservedly in favor of the new medium, and so it was decided that one critical voice should make itself heard. This voice was to be his, and I had accordingly composed an appropriate text for him. As usual, I first let him read through the typescript, and since he was standing up, I stood up too and walked around the room, admiring the various antiques and art treasures. Even I can appreciate the beauty and the value of some of them—for instance, the decorative open-work paneling backed by orange-colored velvet, which probably came from a harem. And the Chinese porn panels are so sophisticated that I sometimes get sexually aroused by them, quite involuntarily. This time I caught myself casting lascivious glances at Lore, and she momentarily pushed her loose silk dress to one side so that I could see for myself: she really had a woman's bosom. At that moment Apple Cheeks raised his hand and said, "Grobsch, you've surpassed yourself yet again."

To think of all the speeches I've concocted for him in the last ten years! There was even one about shoes, but there were also speeches about education, the churches, disasters, and trees. And sociology, psychology, advertising and law—subjects that I'd studied and knew something about—and all this I spiced with a few theological principles. "Cable soup, cable vegetables, cable roast, cable pudding, cable salad, cable stew, strangulation cables, cables for being strangled like Laocoön, cable promotion, cables as promotional strangulation . . ." All this acquired resonance when spoken by him, was made resonant by his voice. He was standing up, holding the typescript in one hand. From his lips it all sounded convincing, the product of conviction, and the more confident his intonation became, the more convinced he became that the words he was speaking were not mine but his. It was his opinion, his conception. He accepted it, adopted it, appropriated it. And indeed these attributes of his—his voice, his gestures and his looks, plus his ability to appropriate other people's ideas and formulations and insights—were what made him indispensable to the party.

As he paced back and forth he even became an intellectual, while still retaining the common touch, and all my intellectual garbage became comprehensible when relayed through his lips. And I realized why he had gone through all his previous researchers and speech writers so fast—faster than he had me—and rewarded them with good jobs: they'd all become mayors, theater directors, bank managers, and diplomats. He'd gotten rid of them for repeatedly insisting, too blatantly and single-mindedly, on what was in fact their intellectual property. They'd demonstrated their intellectual superiority. This was a thing I never did: whatever I wrote for him was his property and his alone, and he was proud of it. The one thing that tickled me was the idea of someday stuffing a speech down his throat that would make him look a fool, before I finally throttled him—some elegantly formulated apologia for total Marxism, some subtle dithyrambic defense of anarchy. He cut such a majestic figure, pacing to and fro, Apple Cheeks with the lion's mane, the gestures now minimally suggestive, now sweepingly expressive; there was a majesty, too, in the way he stood and delivered his speech, his very own speech, and the way he enunciated it: ". . . the betrayal of the Glad Tidings, proclaimed from the cable inferno."

I had been instructed—not by him but by someone higher up—always to work in a few religious or metaphysical notions "at appropriate points," which he could then thunder out like some seventeenth-century preacher calling for repentance. This time it was "the poisoning of the word of God."

I could have ruined a much better speech. I began to wonder how he'd pay me off. I'd be no good as an ambassador: without Eva I'd be utterly lost, and as she wasn't my lawful wedded wife I couldn't take her with me, except possibly as head of protocol. I'd never learn how to tell the difference between a lobster cocktail and an ordinary fish course—I might even whisper to the hostess, "The herring was fabulous!" I'd be even less suited to the chairmanship of a bank, because I'd spend too much of my time brooding on where the money was going and why it was coming

back a hundredfold. Oh, Beethoven! Oh, those genuine
dower chests, Georgian or Edwardian or whatever! And all
paid for with that heavenly stuff that flows in like milk and
honey from the lands of the blessed Marcos or the blessed
Pinochet, or even from the land of the sainted Brezhnev—
that divine substance made of blood, toil, tears, and shit.
And when I thought of Kapspeter, even Plukanski dwin-
dled into one of those common crooks who are brought
into politics to eat shit. Kapspeter bathed in dragon's blood
every day, and no lime leaf landed between the delicate
white shoulder blades of his venerable frame. What had
become of all the money and the hair, all the gold from
each and every gold tooth they'd knocked out? Who collected the proceeds of the soap they'd made from the bodies, of the hair they'd used to make mattresses? Where were
they, the gentlemen with the refined faces, with the delicate
hands that were just made for playing the spinet? What
bank accounts did it pass through? Oh, what angel was it,
which of you angels was it, that touched me on the shoulder and charged me with this metaphysical electricity which
makes me shudder, despite my well-known cynicism and
powers of analysis, my ability to take things apart and reas-
semble them—me, whom neither Chundt nor Blaukrämer,
neither Halberkamm nor Bingerle, could ever impress? Who
was it who imbued me with this powerful charge of rest-
lessness, which only Eva's soup and oil of lavender can
assuage?

I cry whenever I listen to Beethoven. I know that it's bad
taste, that it's not done, but I can't help it. Only yesterday,
at Kapspeter's, I managed to hold back the tears, telling
myself, "You mustn't cry in front of these people—not in
front of *them*!" I'd rather have cried at Plukanski's. Chervil
soup, with a little milk, a dash of honey and sherry, and
very tender, finely chopped meat . . . How shall I live without you, Eva—without you and your soups, which I can't

eat in front of the TV because unfortunately they make my glasses steam up! Oh, Eva, don't go away; drop your Cuban friend. He's not a nice, harmless guy; he's a tough boy with the charm of a macho Communist. You'd be stuck there in Cuba and never be able to get out. No, he's not a nice, harmless boy: he does deals for Fidel and dreams about Che. He'd rather be here than back in Cuba, where he's stifled by bureaucracy. I can understand that you want to be with him: he still has some of that glorious recklessness and revolutionary fervor that have taken hold of us all at some time or other; yes, taken hold of us—or of me, at any rate. But don't imagine that you could have a fling with him. Stay with me, and if you positively have to go to Cuba, wait till I can go with you. What you need is a cynic, somebody with powers of analysis, a lawyer, a sociologist; you need a politician, someone who's active in politics. Stay with me; you don't have to marry me; and then, when I'm finally rewarded for my loyal and discreet services, I'll ask for a directorship, the only job apart from banking that carries any real power. And it would look good for me to be married to a countess—even if she weren't a countess by birth—with her girlish modesty and impeccable taste. And then—at last—I'll be able to become *active* in politics.

I'm still here; I hope I'll be here forever: this is my country, the country that made me and that I helped to make. And if Kapspeter gets his daughter to invite me—*gets* her to invite me, Eva—out of curiosity and condescension, compounded with a modicum of disgust and disdain, then I shall at least get invited. Do you think I'd invite him? Okay, everybody have a good laugh! Do you realize, Eva, that I'm in the one party you never thought I'd be in? It's the one party where I belong, precisely because I've pissed on the pictures of the Sacred Heart.

Apple Cheeks constantly tries to evade the final and all-important stage of our rehearsal sessions, the stage I've always forced on him and always have to force on him—namely, going into his study, being left all alone with himself and his voice, and recording all that crap on tape, so that we can listen to it together once more—objectively, so to speak. He listens to himself and I listen to him, this time through the loudspeaker. I can't let him get away with not doing this: it's the last and crucial test, checking the rhythm, the intonation, the credibility of the IMPs, and it only works when he's thoroughly sickened by his own speech. And then, when the time comes for him to deliver it, he can spew it out properly; he's got to know and be made to feel that politics is a hard game, that it's dirty and necessary—and makes you vomit.

He constantly tries to get out of it, but I have a way of looking at him and directing him into the next room with a movement of my head; he can never put up any resistance, and on this occasion, too, he slunk out, like a dog that would have liked to bite but decided to wag its tail instead. And so I was left alone with Lore, who came and sat next to me and switched to beer herself. She asked me about my career. I kept quiet about my proletarian background and gave her a quick rundown on my schooling, my time at the university, and my political work as a member of the federal parliament and various parliamentary committees. Nothing about my father, an industrial cripple who had his legs mutilated by a conveyor belt and was then pensioned off with a pittance because he had allegedly been guilty of negligence. Nothing about my mother, a local beauty with a lot of guts who was determined to "make something of all of us." A backyard in Wuppertal—the smell of garbage, rats scurrying all over, and the gray washing on the clotheslines, everlastingly dripping . . . Should I have confided all this to her as she sat there dressed all in silk? A Catholic mother, and a Protestant father from East Prussia, who made a point of saying nothing and didn't even believe in socialism—who limped over to visit his mates and be told all about Kropotkin. Living in two rooms, with the lavatory and the water tap half a flight below. And what they would now call my "initial sexual experiences"—in the corridor, where we had to show the girls "what we had," and they showed us what they had. We'd grope one another until they squealed with delight, discovering the source of cheap thrills. And then the girls wanted to have it "for real," and so we gave it to them for real.

Was I supposed to tell all this to Lore, dressed all in silk and making it more and more obvious that she was a woman? Should I confess to her that it was always a trauma with me that I could never do it lying down, only standing up—that all I could manage was the proletarian knee-trembler? It was Eva who taught me, very patiently and tenderly, and sometimes with tears in her eyes, how to make love lying down. How wonderful it was to lie down—and to be able to stay lying down! Back home we wouldn't have known where to lie. My clever Eva, who blushes at the slightest hint of smut, was the one who taught me how to do it lying down—not just in bed but in the woods or the fields in summer. And before that I couldn't do it lying down even in the park, where it would have been possible; I could only do it against a tree or the back of a park bench. There was a time when I thought people who did it lying down were perverted. And we pissed on pictures of the saints and still went to our first communion. We had clothes donated to us by charitable ladies. They also brought us homemade cakes, little bunches of flowers, and cold meats—but never cash, because we didn't know how to "handle" money. No, we didn't know, because we never had any. And naturally I got help with my education—scholarships—because of course I was "so talented," but I also had to work, carrying loads, chopping wood, helping with removals and garbage disposal; I had to breathe the sickening fumes of the chemical factory, and sometimes I cursed my talent when I was studying in the evening—with the lights turned down because my brother and sister were asleep in the corner. Latin or Adorno, Hegel, and Hölderlin. I cursed my old man when he got pissed yet again, but I still bought him schnapps when he didn't have any, out of *solidarity*—in spite of Adorno and Hegel and Hölderlin. And naturally I joined the party of the charitable ladies, not the other one. In their party I could get on faster, which is what I wanted. I wanted to get on, and it would have been too much of a slog if I'd joined the other bunch. So I joined the party of the charitable ladies who refused to give us cash because we didn't know how to handle it. Naturally I joined the Church, if only to please my mother, and that didn't impede my progress either. And I still go to church, even though I can't stand the sight of a priest.

And sometimes I even go to the bank and draw money out, lots of money, though I shudder to think where it comes from, and I still don't know how to "handle" it. I don't enjoy handling it, because I have no taste. To handle money properly you've got to have taste, and I have none. Even Eva hasn't been able to teach me taste; maybe you have to be born with it or to have had a different upbringing. Plukanski's mother has taste, and so has he, and so have Eva and Krengel and Kapspeter. Where do you learn it? How horrified Eva was when she first visited me in my office at the parliament! She thought everything was either "ghastly" or "atrocious." She called it a doghouse, and ever since then one of our favorite but agonizing topics of conversation has been the connection between taste and character—why it is that the majority of people with good taste have bad characters and the majority of people with bad taste have good characters. I couldn't buy a chair or choose a wallpaper, and if I were buying crockery I'd automatically go for late-forties kitsch, which fortunately is no longer available. And sometimes, when I'm invited to some very smart diplomatic dinner, I secretly drive to the nearest food stand and have curried sausage with chips and mayonnaise to fill myself up, because I can't wait for Eva to serve me her wonderful soup.

Suddenly it dawned on me. I don't know whether I *smelled* it or whether I saw it in her eyes: Lore was one of us. And she told me what I hadn't told her: things about her proletarian past—in Cologne, not Wuppertal, and almost a generation later. Not a backyard but a project for problem families, in the early fifties. And she knew all about screwing on the cellar steps and about the cheap thrills. She knew the charitable ladies who brought donations in kind because people couldn't handle money. And her father was a drunk too, though not a cripple; "one who had charm—and they're the worst." She, too, had learned to throw up at the chemical factory; she, too, used to buy her father schnapps, though she hated his drinking; she, too, wanted to come up in the world, as quickly as possible, before she was killed by work. And she'd decided it was better to become Plukanski's companion than to rely on the charitable ladies, who might give her a pair of stockings or a bar of soap, or even discreetly slip her a packet of pills so that if she "went off the rails" she wouldn't get herself pregnant into the bargain. Oh, Lore, one can't have two women: it's harder to realize the perpetual bourgeois dream of the eternal triangle than to square the circle. One can't have two women: it has to be either one—or a few dozen, as in Chundt's case. Otherwise I'd take you away with me, because you've backed the wrong man, whose rise won't go on much longer. And how will you come up in the world then? What have you learned? Moderately good at school, worked in a chemical factory, a spell of prostitution. Honey, I should have smelled it—we're the same breed.

She shouldn't have done it—she shouldn't have got up and put a tape on. Not Beethoven. I was already twenty-five, just about to take my doctor's degree, when a girl-friend took me to a concert. Until then I'd only sung tunes to myself, gone to dances, and listened to warped records. And when I heard Beethoven for the first time I couldn't help crying—I just couldn't help it. I had to cry, and it was no good seeking an intellectual refuge in the hydrochloric acid of party cynicism. Nothing helped. I haven't the fog-giest notion about music: I never listened at school because I was always too tired. But Beethoven I know and recog-nize. How? Where did Lore get to know him? Hell, she was crying too, and I gave her a kiss.

And there he was, when we finally remembered him and began to wonder where he'd been all the time . . . there he was, Hennes from Klissenheim, lying sprawled across the desk in his study, gasping for breath. We were scared, seeing how pale he'd become: no longer any trace of his rosy cheeks. The telephone receiver was swinging on its cord, and from the tape recorder his voice was still boom-ing out: "Cable transmission stifles the voice of God—suf-focates it." He wasn't suffocated, but the pallid face, which had always been so ruddy, was the face of a stranger who nonetheless seemed somehow familiar. Lore rushed up to him, kissed his pale cheek, and screamed, "You were al-ways good to me—you were always good!" She was ac-tually crying, and under her makeup I could see her proletarian cellar-step skin—it had the same greenish pallor as mine. I switched off the dreadful tape recorder, picked up the dangling receiver, and said "Hello." I heard Blau-krämer's familiar vinegary voice: "Haven't you got it yet? You're finished. The Poles have managed to do what we never could."

Lore took the receiver from my hand. "Hospital or police?" she asked anxiously. "Hospital," I said. I didn't know whether it was sympathy, fear, or plain horror that I felt when I saw him lying there, unrecognizable because of his pallor, yet somehow familiar: Hennes from Klissenheim, who'd grown old but hadn't made it after all.

Chapter 7

Elisabeth Blaukrämer's room at the Kuhlbollen Spa Hotel, a large room with a writing desk, telephone, television, and two large windows with a view across the fields to the woods. On the walls are prints by Klee, Chagall, Hundertwasser, and Picasso. There are flowers on the bedside table and the desk. The whole room is furnished and decorated in yellows and browns, with various intervening shades of beige. The ceiling has an old-fashioned gold border. In the foreground, to the left of the desk, is a kind of dining table, surrounded by a couch and two chairs, all matching. Frau Blaukrämer is sitting on the couch. Opposite her is Dr. Dumpler, a woman in her mid thirties. Dr. Dumpler's profession is not at once apparent. Both women are respectably dressed. On the table are a teapot, cups, and a dish of pastries.

DR. DUMPLER: If you were to recognize that you had falsified your recollections, making some of them more beautiful and others—let us say—more ugly than the original experiences, you would have no reason to feel ashamed. Most people beautify some of their memories and exaggerate the causes of their traumas. When the traumas have arisen in later life, they are often transferred to the patient's childhood or youth, to parents and teachers, while other memories of an unpleasant nature acquire a pleasant gloss. In some cases the parents can be *shown* to have been loving and caring, though in retrospect they are transformed into monsters. In the same way, erotic experiences that at the time were pleasant become unpleasant, and vice versa. Men who in reality were seduced by women come to be seen as heartless seducers. In your case both things have happened: a very unpleasant experience has been embellished and given an ideological coloring. We have entirely reliable statements—some of them sworn statements, for the most part in writing—about the death of your father, your brother, and the Plotzek family. Your mother, your late sister, and Tine Plotzek (who is still alive and is now Frau Ermeck) have sworn that your father was shot by the Russians and then hanged like your brother; so was the Plotzek family. Yet you persist in maintaining that these were cases of murder and suicide. (Smiles.) You must have a curious mechanism inside you for justifying the Russians, a mechanism connected with the other experience you underwent at the time, which you persist in romanticizing.

ELISABETH BLAUKRÄMER, *calmly:* I know, my mother and sister maintained that I was raped by Dimitri and that I had a romantic attachment to Eberhard Plotzek, who was seventeen. It was all in keeping with the time-honored Scottish or English pattern—young noblewoman falls in love with stableboy. However, there was nothing romantic about my relations with Eberhard: he was forever putting his hand up my skirt, and I was forever slapping his face. I didn't want to tell on him, and he knew it. He wanted to take me by force. And Dimitri . . . (Smiles.) I didn't actually rape him, but I practically forced him to kiss me and tell me he loved me—he was so incredibly shy. He was always bringing us sugar or tea, and now and then a bar of chocolate, even bacon. He was pathetically shy, and what's more, he had that respect for the lousy nobility which seems to be ingrained in all Russians. He was billeted on us with his boss, who was a colonel. *(Dr. Dumpler tries to interrupt her, but she stands up and begins to speak louder and more vehemently.)* My father and my brother and the Plotzeks executed by the Russians? Not on your life! That fits in only too well with the refugee story. It was a case of murder and suicide. First they shot our last two horses—the floor of the stable was thick with blood, lots of blood, and they even strung up little Erich, who had water on the brain. The Russians weren't even going to be allowed to have a little hydrocephalic child. I heard and saw it all. *(Points to the border on the ceiling.)* That's where they were hanging, up there, from the roof beam—the Plotzeks' two children, my father, my brother, and Plotzek himself. "As for the women," they said, "they're all whores anyway." They shot and strung up everybody, and then they hanged themselves next to them.

Yes, I suppose that could be called a trauma. And then everything happened very fast. We had to leave, and my mother had only one thought in her head: couldn't we take the horse flesh with us. The only thing she ever thought of was eating. There may have been some rapings and shootings and hangings later; maybe, but *I* wasn't raped. *(Speaking more quietly)* He looked seventeen, but in fact he was twenty-two. An interpreter. Yes, we were in love, and we became lovers, but then he was too sensitive to go on bringing us bacon. The combination of bacon and love didn't appeal to his romantic soul, so from then on he only brought tea and sugar, and my mother asked me why there was now no more bacon— you understand?—why there was *now* no more bacon. She knew everything and had no objections. She wanted her bacon, to fry it and mix it with the vegetables and put it on her bread, and my little sister made faces and wanted milk and cocoa. As for me, I wasn't as sensitive as Dimitri. *(Dr. Dumpler again tries to interrupt, but Elisabeth*

Blaukrämer raises her hand to silence her.) No, wait! Dimitri told me a lot, far too much, about the interrogations he attended as an interpreter—all about murders and fires and destruction, and about the interrogations where his services weren't required, where Russians were interrogated about looting and rape. We loved each other, if you know what that means; we took refuge in each other. And my mother wanted bacon—and she wasn't averse to butter either. And Dimitri still respected her, because after all she was a baroness. Then he was arrested, and of course there was no more bacon or butter or milk or tea or cocoa, no more flour to make bread. And Dimitri's colonel was arrested too, and so it was time to leave the east and cross over to the west. And it was also time to think up an appropriate story.

DR. DUMPLER: And you went along with it.

ELISABETH BLAUKRÄMER: Yes, I did; I went around telling the whole cock-and-bull story.

DR. DUMPLER: So it was all invented: as you saw it, you were lying about something that may nevertheless have been true.

ELISABETH BLAUKRÄMER: Yes, I was lying. I tried to find out about Dimitri, but it was no good: I could discover nothing, nothing at all.

DR. DUMPLER: You were also active in the German-Soviet friendship organization, weren't you?

ELISABETH BLAUKRÄMER: Yes, I was. And I wanted to stay in the east. Oh, if only I'd stayed! *(Sits down, exhausted, and begins to weep.)*

DR. DUMPLER: You were prepared to remain voluntarily in the Eastern Zone?

ELISABETH BLAUKRÄMER: Yes, but my mother thought it would be better here—reparations, housing, money. And above all we had relatives who were under an obligation to take us in. First of all we were put in the transit camp.

DR. DUMPLER: That's when your confusion must have begun. Please understand that we want to help you and cure you, to help you to be happy again. These two events which you've described in a way that is so at variance with the facts are after all the basis, the core of your future destiny. Your mother and your late sister were unanimous in their testimony: that it was a case of rape—and murder.

ELISABETH BLAUKRÄMER: In other words, they were unanimous in lying. . . .

DR. DUMPLER: And you agree that you yourself lied.

ELISABETH BLAUKRÄMER, *agitated:* We wanted to get out of the refugee camp; we'd been there long enough. Then Blaukrämer came with a party delegation and made me a proposal of marriage, giving me a day to make up my mind. My mother said, "Take him, take him—and then we won't have to go and live with that mean cousin of mine, Plodenhöver. Take him, for heaven's sake, and if necessary we'll become Catholic." *(Speaking quietly)* So I accepted. . . . I was told that Dimitri had disappeared without a trace.

DR. DUMPLER: So you still had contacts in the Eastern Zone?

ELISABETH BLAUKRÄMER: Yes, Dimitri's friend Ivan came across. It was dangerous for him, but he came over and advised me to clear out, to get as far west as possible. *(Quietly)* So I took Blaukrämer. I'm to blame for that, not him.

DR. DUMPLER: So your marriage to Dr. Blaukrämer was based on a lie, then?

ELISABETH BLAUKRÄMER: Yes, of course. *(Coldly)* On both sides. He wasn't in love with me; he was attracted by the fine-sounding aristocratic name. He knew everything: I told him all about Dimitri and me. He knew everything, including the fact that I hadn't been raped. He was actually the one who raped me. And he tried everything he could to get a church divorce.

DR. DUMPLER: You mean an annulment—there's no such thing as a church divorce.

ELISABETH BLAUKRÄMER: Okay, an annulment if you like. I've never understood what the difference is supposed to be.

DR. DUMPLER, *severely:* It's a legal distinction. There's no such thing as a church divorce.

ELISABETH BLAUKRÄMER: Okay, a legal distinction, but the main reason was that I didn't want children after I'd seen so many children hanging up there *(again pointing to the ceiling)*—German children. *(Quietly)* You can see from the divorce papers—or rather the annulment papers—

DR. DUMPLER: We can't consult the church documentation; we have no access to it.

ELISABETH BLAUKRÄMER: Of course not; but it's all there as I've described it to you. *(Calmly)* Everything. And of course, I shouldn't have married Blaukrämer; I deceived him, and he deceived himself. I'm not accusing anybody, I'm only complaining that if ... if ... But there's nothing to complain about. Now I'm in my mid fifties, and the only things that were real were Dimitri and the people hanging from the beam in our stable, and the floor thick with the horses' blood. . . .

DR. DUMPLER: You have a vivid imagination. You should keep it in check.

ELISABETH BLAUKRÄMER: I don't have a scrap of imagination. Maybe that's my misfortune; maybe that's the sickness you should be curing me of. I have no imagination, only a memory. Why don't you give me imagination—and happiness?

DR. DUMPLER: And then later certain things—how shall I put it?—found their way into your memory, things that can be based only on imagination, and it's these that make it hard to believe you when you talk about your basic experiences.

ELISABETH BLAUKRÄMER: Such as?

DR. DUMPLER: You talk about documents disappearing, about a bishop making improper advances, about Dr. Chundt coming into your room, with the connivance of your husband, Dr. Blaukrämer.

ELISABETH BLAUKRÄMER: I saw it, I actually experienced it, just as I saw those people hanging from the beam. I probably shouldn't have mentioned the thing about the bishop. They got him drunk—it's a favorite game of theirs, especially with priests. I wasn't even annoyed with him, poor man; I was sorry for him. I should have kept quiet. But when Chundt came into my room with that leer on his face and I heard Blaukrämer laughing outside . . .

DR. DUMPLER: These are nothing but sexual fantasies. And after your first experience of love had ended so bitterly— let's just suppose for a moment that it was true—after the rather unpleasant experiences with the Plotzek boy—let's suppose that that was also true—you must understand that after all this we suspect an imaginative pattern that corresponds to psychological experience. And fire—the fire in which the Plottger documents are supposed to have been burned—fire is also a basic sexual symbol.

ELISABETH BLAUKRÄMER: You can also reverse the argument. *(Dr. Dumpler looks at her inquiringly.)* Blaukrämer couldn't *have* me, he never had me, and so he sent these two men to my room—the bishop, whose beer they'd secretly laced with loads of schnapps, and Chundt. Neither of them got me, because I belong to Dimitri and always will. And as for the fire . . . I wasn't at all keen to go on that hunting trip with them, and there they were, standing around the fire, stoned out of their minds,

and throwing documents into it. I can't prove anything—not a thing. But I did see it.

DR. DUMPLER: If you knew what some of our other guests
claim to have seen and heard and experienced!

ELISABETH BLAUKRÄMER: Yes, the fat woman, Frau
Schwetz, and little Frau Bebber. Frau Schwetz goes to
the safe three times a day to count her money: her husband has given her 250,000 marks to leave him in peace,
because divorce is out of the question. Two thousand five
hundred hundred-mark bills—fifty packets of five thousand—and then she counts them a second time because
she can only make it 249,500. What did he give her the
money for? And the little Bebber woman is forever taking showers, all day long. Sooner or later her skin'll come
off with all that showering. And she's constantly crying
out for Jesus. I used to know them both. In those days
Frau Schwetz didn't count money, and the last thing Frau
Bebber would have done was cry out for Jesus. She was
keen on dancing, tennis, the odd flirtation, and clothes.
Such an innocent little thing, a really nice little blonde.
Why does she now cry out for Jesus? Why does she have
to spend all her time taking showers? And washing her
clothes? She's always got piles of clean clothes ready. And
I knew both their husbands, Schwetz and Bebber. What
did Schwetz give her so much money for? What has that
to do with imagination? (Speaking louder, almost threaten-
ingly) Why do I have to shout? Why? Dimitri's been dead
for the last forty years, and I haven't enough imagination
to imagine him as a sixty-two-year-old translating
Hölderlin into Russian. That's not how I see him, and I
can't cry out for him: I saw him when he was young,
and I'm not young anymore.

DR. DUMPLER: All the same, for a long time you led a
peaceful life with Dr. Blaukrämer at Huhlsbolzenheim.

ELISABETH BLAUKRÄMER: Yes, and there were times when I even enjoyed it—coffee mornings, parties, fairs. I even went to the fire brigade ball, where everyone wanted to dance with me, and of course to the patronal festival. All for the sake of the party: it probably brought the votes in, though the party wasn't short of votes. But Blaukrämer used to say that a good turn-on produced a good turnout. And although I didn't have to, I became a Catholic. Blaukrämer used to say that the pretty Protestant girl from the Prussian nobility was an attraction—it was so exotic. But I was taken with Catholicism, and so I converted. And I didn't mind about Blaukrämer's womanizing; it meant that he left me alone. He wanted children—and I wondered how a man like that could want children. I didn't: I could still see my brother and the Plotzek children hanging up there from the roof beam. I could see them all the time. I tried having lovers, but it didn't work; I drank, and read Stevenson. None of my lovers made me happy. I was happy for short spells, when we were living by the Rhine. I would sit by myself in the conservatory and slowly get drunk—alone with the Rhine, and the worse for drink. I could sit there for hours. The only company I could endure was Erika Wubler's. She kept quiet and drank with me as the Rhine flowed past. I'm sorry I told the story about what happened with the bishop. I had spells of happiness by the Rhine, but you've deprived me of the Rhine. I'm not allowed to be seen there any longer.

DR. DUMPLER: I should think not! So you take back the story about the bishop: it wasn't true?

ELISABETH BLAUKRÄMER: I take it back, not because it wasn't true but because he wasn't himself when he came to my room. He wasn't in his right mind—they'd made him thoroughly drunk. But I don't take back what I said about Chundt.

DR. DUMPLER: Your position became acute—intolerable, in fact—when you thought you'd recognized Plonius.

ELISABETH BLAUKRÄMER: Yes, Plietsch, who now calls himself Plonius. The Bloodhound. I saw him one day in Chundt's trophy room. When I came in, I had the impression that he was about to get up and greet me. But then he remained seated; they probably restrained him. I knew him: he'd been at our place a few times, to go hunting and then to have drinks by the fire. The Bloodhound! A handsome man, a dashing officer with perfect manners; I even used to dance with him in the old days. He's hardly changed—the past forty years have left hardly a trace. Of course, his hair's gone white, and his face has become slightly wrinkled. He's well preserved, and his voice . . . his voice . . . He was the one, after all, who gave the order that people were to kill themselves and their children if the Russians ever came. And the Russians came, and people did kill themselves and their children. That was Plietsch, who was known as the Bloodhound and was actually proud of his nickname. I think he was one of the youngest generals at that time. Dashing, perfect manners, always kissed a lady's hand, and so on. It occurred to me later that they'd probably taken me there specially to see whether anyone could recognize him. I recognized him. I went deathly pale and ran out of the room screaming, literally screaming. I screamed all night and ran through the village screaming.

DR. DUMPLER, *as calmly as Elisabeth Blaukrämer:* If it isn't imagination, it's a classic case of confusion or persecution mania linked with your first basic experience. Plietsch is dead—his death is officially attested, even by the Russians. You *can't* have seen Plietsch; you saw Plonius, who may bear a certain resemblance to Plietsch, perhaps even a striking resemblance.

ELISABETH BLAUKRÄMER: And what about his voice, and

those eyes of his—the steely blue eyes of the master race—and the scar on his neck?

DR. DUMPLER: The scar on his neck?

ELISABETH BLAUKRÄMER: I noticed it years ago when I was dancing with him: a white patch on his neck just behind the ear, no bigger than a bean—I saw it while we were dancing. And I'm not supposed to scream when I see the Bloodhound sitting there large as life, with Chundt and Blaukrämer and Halberkamm? I'd never screamed before: I'd always taken everything as it came, everything. I used to drink a little, read my Stevenson, go for walks, and dutifully contribute to the party spirit. But Plietsch—no, that was too much!

DR. DUMPLER: Plietsch is dead, and Plonius has been rehabilitated. Nobody denies that he was implicated in various things, but he's been rehabilitated. He isn't Plietsch. You're not doing yourself any good by this constant self-delusion *(Sighs.)* After all, it was all more than forty years ago. Your marriage was annulled years ago. You're a mature woman of fifty-five, physically fit, and you want to live your life; and so you shall. Haven't you any . . . I mean can't you find any consolation in religion?

ELISABETH BLAUKRÄMER: You mean I ought to cry out for Jesus too? *(Shakes her head.)* No, that's something I can't do. I believed in Jesus as a child and a young girl. I still believed in him when we were at Huhlsbolzenheim, and Blaukrämer was my crucifixion—that's the truth—but they drove Jesus out of me, positively drove him away, and I let them. To see them all kneeling in the chapel after all the orgies, all the boozing and the lewd behavior! They would kneel there, covering their faces with their hands, filled with remorse, and so pious—truly pious. Even Blaukrämer is a pious man, there's no denying it, and Chundt is halfway to being a mystic. That nice bishop would say the mass. He was a man I might even have loved—perhaps I was wrong not to let him into my room. A very sensitive man. No, it was down there in the chapel that Jesus finally left me, never to return. And then Plietsch! Oh no!

DR. DUMPLER: If only I knew what you wanted and could give it to you . . .

ELISABETH BLAUKRÄMER: There's nothing I need. I can swim, play tennis, go for walks, and there's plenty of exquisite food. Every day we're offered three different menus, and downstairs in the bar there are gigolos who'd dance with me if I wanted, but I don't dance anymore. And in the evening the baby deer come across the fields from the woods.

DR. DUMPLER: Why do you say "baby deer" and not simply "deer"? It's not very nice, you know, to make ironic comments on the beauties of nature. Or to use the word "gigolo" to describe our selfless colleagues, who are quite simply professionally trained hosts. You're completely free to do what you like. Your car's outside, and you have the key in your bag. Dr. Blaukrämer isn't stingy with money. You can take your meals in your room or downstairs in the dining room. Our library is at your disposal, and the music room. You have television and radio, and medical attention when you need it. But you don't need it; organically you're perfectly healthy.

ELISABETH BLAUKRÄMER: And if I were to drive off, say to the Rhine, would I be back here voluntarily the next day?

DR. DUMPLER: Yes, and the same would apply if you went to Huhlsbolzenheim. Everywhere you go you disturb the peace with all your horror stories, all that talk about Plietsch. You cause disturbance, hatred, and hostility, bringing out all those obscene details, and telling those ludicrous stories about vanished documents. Committing a public nuisance isn't a private offense—it's covered by the criminal law, and you ought to be thankful that you're here.

ELISABETH BLAUKRÄMER: And not in prison, you mean, where I really belong?

DR. DUMPLER, *putting her hand on Elisabeth Blaukrämer's arm:* Why . . . why are you so bent on destruction?

ELISABETH BLAUKRÄMER, *calmly:* For a reason you've so far failed to discover: because *I* am destroyed. I ought to have stayed in Bleibnitz and worked as a stable girl for the Russians. I ought to have cleared out and gone to the west with Dimitri, not with my mother. I loved him. I shouldn't have married Blaukrämer. I should have—should have—should have . . . but I didn't. And then this lousy aristocratic name that inspires excessive respect in everybody . . . My mother's a horrible woman. And my sister—well, you know. . . .

DR. DUMPLER: Your sister committed suicide a week ago.

ELISABETH BLAUKRÄMER: Because she lived with my mother. You don't know Blaukrämer, you don't know either Halberkamm or Chundt. . . . He's been made a minister at last. *(Laughs.)* I heard it on the radio.

DR. DUMPLER: Dr. Chundt belongs to the same fraternity as my husband; he's a charming, retiring man.

ELISABETH BLAUKRÄMER: They're all fraternity members. Even that nice man Wubler belongs to a fraternity. Do you actually know your own husband, fraternity brother Dumpler?

DR. DUMPLER: I really must protest!

ELISABETH BLAUKRÄMER: Why, have I insulted you? Hasn't Chundt tried to—how should I put it?—to ingratiate himself with you? Why are you blushing? Why are you so indignant? They're all pious men, the fraternity members, truly pious, and they cover their faces with their hands in remorse, confess their sins, and go to communion. Where do I belong in a scene like that—where?

With my memories that I can't blot out or get into perspective. It's you who are excessively credulous: you believe the evidence of your eyes, you trust in what you've been told. Your view of me is as logical as it is stupid. It's even partly correct, but only partly—and that's what makes you so blind. I can see what you can't see: I can see German children swinging up there—I can see them whipping Dimitri. Am I hysterical? Yes. Do I tell lies? Yes. Am I sick? Yes. Suffering? Yes. So why shouldn't I refer to your deer as "baby deer"? I'm sure there's somebody over there in the wood who injects them with Valium before they take their walk in the dusk. They trot so gracefully and sniff around so sensitively, the dear little Bambis. What I'd like most is to sit somewhere I'm not allowed to go—by the Rhine. And now you can clear out. Clear out! Out with you: go back to your fraternity members!

Elisabeth Blaukrämer goes across to the window. Dr. Dumpler leaves in horror.

ELISABETH BLAUKRÄMER: The baby deer are a bit earlier today; they're so sweet and shy, yet so trusting. Perhaps they're getting heroin injections now—they certainly get something mixed in with their food. Pohl, the game warden, admitted as much. He grinned when I asked him what it was. And I don't need imagination—which I don't have anyway—to know that the sweet little creatures are being manipulated. I need only to press a button to get top-quality Vivaldi or Chopin. Not long ago I bumped into the little Bebber woman in the hall, and when I stopped her and said, "What, are you a patient here too, Edith?" she became quite angry. Although she's normally a gentle, rather lackluster little thing, her eyes really began to flash, and she said, "I'm a guest here, not a patient. I'm going to take a shower." She just left me standing there, though she's usually so polite. We're guests, not patients. They attach great importance to that. My tea is brought to me by a smart girl dressed in white who looks like a nurse but doesn't like being called one. Recently she held forth to me about the different qualities of tea and explained the six stages between flowery orange pekoe and congou—it was quite a lecture. And flowers, flowers all the time, flowers everywhere. Even God is here, in every denominational variety—Catholic, Protestant, even Russian Orthodox. And it took me a long time to realize that the question as to whether my father committed murder or suicide was really a question about his colonel's pension: if it was a case of murder the legal position was clear-cut, but if it was suicide it was dubious. My little brother would now be going on sixty, and he'd probably be a colonel too—he could ride and he could shoot! Just one shot, and the crow would fall out of the tree or off the telephone cable. And my father would now be about ninety. He wasn't all that bad, though he allowed that man Plietsch to poison his mind and egg him on to do bad things. And although we're guests here, most of our expenses are met by the health plan—we're health insurance guests. Blaukrämer isn't as generous as they pretend he is, and his second wife, Trude, hasn't any children either—she probably wants children, but she hasn't any. I never dared to try and find out whether I could have children. I never felt the presence of an unborn life inside me—I'd seen too many who'd come to term hanging from the roof beam. We don't want for anything here. There's nothing we can't have. We can even have love if we want it; that doesn't appeal to me, but it does to the younger women. Nice young men who are polite and tender; or if they prefer, they can have wild, starry-eyed students or rough-and-ready soldiers. And now my sister Christine has passed away. How could she have endured life with my mother for a whole forty years? I don't bear her any grudge for perjuring herself about my being raped; it fitted in well with our story: young noblewoman falls victim to rape. In any case we always had a good laugh when we had to swear to something on oath: we raised our hands and said impassively, "So help me God." At first sight Blaukrämer didn't make a bad impression. First he turned up with his fellow parliamentarians, then in the evening he came back alone. The moment he knocked on the door and came into the room, I knew things were getting serious. He's so intelligent, and he can be very direct, and he was good-looking—tall and dark, with arched eyebrows. The only thing that didn't appeal to me was his mouth—and his hands! I didn't look at his hands; if I had, I'd have turned him down. He had his hand on the door handle when he said, "Elisabeth von Bleibnitz, will you be my wife? I'll come back tomorrow." And then he left. My mother began whining, "Take him, please take him, and then we'll soon be in the west. He's good-looking, he has a university education, he's an attorney, he has influence, and he'll deal with our reparations claim. Please, Lisbeth! Then we won't have to go and stay with those awful Plodenhövers." And so I took him, without ever looking at his hands. The pension and the reparations were settled in no time, and I moved in with Blaukrämer's parents, as his wife. His father ran an inn and was also an attorney. His family was well-to-do—what I think is called solid middle class. In the back room there were consultations and negotiations about forthcoming cases; statements to be made by witnesses were agreed upon—even in criminal cases—and sometimes there was even a judge present. It was a huge joke—a genuine peasant comedy. But it wasn't in keeping with the comedies I'd already experienced. At least there was no shortage of bacon. And I got caught up in the local traditions—

brass bands, incense, dancing, and beer. Nobody pulled
the wool over my eyes, but I became involved. (*There is
a loud knocking at the door.*) Yes, who is it?

*Eberhard Kolde enters. He is thirty, well built, with a smart hair-
cut, and dressed in a white shirt, white trousers, and white shoes.
He gives the superficial impression of being a medical man, but one
senses that he is not.*

ELISABETH BLAUKRÄMER: I didn't order anything.

EBERHARD KOLDE: I'm not a waiter. I'm—

ELISABETH BLAUKRÄMER *interrupts him, laughing:* I can
imagine what you are, but I won't say it: perhaps it's not
true, and I wouldn't like to insult you.

EBERHARD KOLDE: I'm a professional therapist, and there's
nothing insulting about being called that.

ELISABETH BLAUKRÄMER: A therapist for a certain female
complaint, I take it. That's not a complaint I suffer from.
You're a nice boy, and I'm in my mid fifties—I take it
I'm allowed to use that description. You've no doubt
been chosen to bring harmony into my life—to make me
happy, let's say.

EBERHARD KOLDE: I'm familiar with your problems: I was
allowed to inform myself about them. I'm afraid you be-
little my therapeutic work in a way that doesn't corre-
spond with my ambitions, my training, or my ability.
We could talk to each other, about Stevenson, say, or
about Modigliani, whom I know you also admire.

ELISABETH BLAUKRÄMER: And about Proust, or Kafka?

EBERHARD KOLDE: Of course, we could talk about them
too—about the contrasts between them and the features
they have in common. Both had, let us say, anancastic
tendencies. But we can also go for walks, play tennis,
dance. You're so fond of dancing.

ELISABETH BLAUKRÄMER: I *was* fond of dancing—past
tense, my dear boy.

EBERHARD KOLDE: Then we could have a conversation in a café, or a bar—a friendly, relaxed chat.

ELISABETH BLAUKRÄMER: But I'm so unrelaxed. A little tenderness too, perhaps?

EBERHARD KOLDE: Yes, but with one proviso: you mustn't fall in love with me. I reserve my real persona for my private life, where I have a wife and two children.

ELISABETH BLAUKRÄMER: So you're a kind of medicine they give people?

EBERHARD KOLDE: "Medium" would be a better word.

ELISABETH BLAUKRÄMER, *extremely calm and relaxed:* What might be called a middleman, an intermediary or a go-between. Interesting. You're not by any chance a professional host—what's sometimes called an *animateur*?

EBERHARD KOLDE: That means someone who animates, and *anima* means "soul." Yes, I like to animate people—in the sense of reaching out to their souls. Unfortunately the term has acquired such vulgar connotations that I hesitate to use it. But to speak of an affinity of souls would be too pretentious.

ELISABETH BLAUKRÄMER: And to speak of an affinity of bodies would be too crude, would it? Do you suffer from some complaint?

EBERHARD KOLDE: No.

ELISABETH BLAUKRÄMER: You're not ill?

EBERHARD KOLDE: No.

ELISABETH BLAUKRÄMER: You're completely balanced and normal?

EBERHARD KOLDE: Yes, and I'd like to share my normality with you and bring your life back into balance. You see . . .

ELISABETH BLAUKRÄMER: Are we talking of harmony?

EBERHARD KOLDE: Yes. You see, I . . .

ELISABETH BLAUKRÄMER *goes to the window again:* It's beginning to get dark. I must draw the curtains. *(Draws the curtains and examines the curtain cords.)* First-class material. *(To Eberhard Kolde)* Please go now. Don't be angry, but I don't require your services. I don't need Stevenson, Proust, Kafka and Modigliani. Let me make a suggestion: let your real persona come out, the nice husband of a young wife, the nice father of two no doubt lovely children, and while you're on duty let yourself fall in love with little Frau Bebber—then make love to her off duty: take the risk of getting into a state of imbalance. I'm completely balanced and at peace with myself. Now go. There's one Bible quotation that nobody ever uses: "Blessed are the barren, and the wombs that never bear, and the paps which never gave suck." Someone should send it to the Pope.

Laughter, then silence. It is as though there were no longer anyone in the room. Eberhard Kolde leaves. Elisabeth Blaukrämer disappears behind the heavy curtains. Unidentifiable noises. Elisabeth Blaukrämer is heard shouting: God bless you, Minister. *Erika Wubler appears in the doorway, carrying a large bouquet of flowers. She calls softly:* Elisabeth, Elisabeth—the young man said you were here, in your room. *Erika Wubler goes to the window, draws the curtains, and finds Elisabeth Blaukrämer hanging from the curtain rod. She screams, throws the flowers on the floor, and rushes out into the corridor.*

Chapter 8

The garden in front of Blaukrämer's villa. The lawn is transected by a path leading to the house and bordered to left and right by other paths, lined with lamps. Ten to fifteen couples are walking around the lawn with glasses in their hands, meeting in the middle and then separating to left and right in the manner of a polonaise. A certain amount of snickering is to be heard, as well as the repeated question: Your grand's still okay, I hope? *or the remark:* To think that she had to choose today to do it! *Another version of the latter remark is:* I didn't know curtain cords could be so strong. *One couple at a time, beginning with Chundt and Blaukrämer, detaches itself from the rest and moves into the fore-ground. Throughout the scene Katharina Richter and Lore Schmitz circulate with trays, offering the guests canapés and drinks.*

PAUL CHUNDT, *testily and nervously:* You ought to have can-celed the reception.

FRITZ BLAUKRÄMER: But I heard the news only two hours ago. The preparations were already under way—drinks, buffet, waiters. It would have been virtually impossible to contact anybody, and some people would have turned up anyway.

PAUL CHUNDT: It would have been quite enough to put a notice on the door saying: "Owing to a bereavement the reception has unfortunately been canceled." You just have no sense of dignity. After all, she was married to you for almost twenty years. A lot of people knew her, and most of them liked her. It'll make a very bad impression around here. Imagine the headlines: "On the day his ex kills herself, Blaukrämer gives a reception at which his latest steals the show." Don't forget—you're feared but you're not liked.

FRITZ BLAUKRÄMER: I thought you and your friends had most of the press in your pockets. You could stop headlines like that from appearing. Hermann Wubler could fix it for me.

PAUL CHUNDT: *Most* of the press is not the same as *all* the press, and Hermann wouldn't stop a headline like that from appearing. Don't forget the threat you made to Erika, and Erika found Elisabeth in the very place where you wanted to send *her.*

FRITZ BLAUKRÄMER: I'm sure she hanged herself after hearing that I'd been appointed minister. *(Gloomily)* That would be quite in keeping with her malicious nature— and her sense of drama.

PAUL CHUNDT: She's dead, and in some mysterious way the dead are always right, so nothing you can say will do any good. And of all people it had to be Erika who found her. It was absurd to send that stupid stud up to her room: that wasn't what she wanted.

FRITZ BLAUKRÄMER: So you know what she wanted, do you? You probably knew that when *you* went up to her room . . .

PAUL CHUNDT, *still in a gloomy mood:* Yes, I wanted to get to know her, to love her. *(Contemptuously)* But why should I discuss it with you? I've never thought of myself on such occasions, only of the person I was going to see. I've never wanted to endanger anyone's life. I've never wanted blood—never.

FRITZ BLAUKRÄMER: No, you've never *wanted* it, but you've sometimes gotten it all the same. What you wanted was your own undisputed empire. You've probably no idea what a trail of embittered, disillusioned, and half-demented people you've left behind you.

PAUL CHUNDT: Everyone does that, everyone who's successful, even if he's only the mayor of some hick town with a thousand inhabitants. It's all very well for you to laugh, but I grieve for Elisabeth, and I don't want to have to grieve for Erika as well. *(Looks around.)* She isn't here—and neither is Hermann. Will you be going to the funeral, at least?

FRITZ BLAUKRÄMER: I don't know. Elisabeth couldn't have been saved, believe me.

PAUL CHUNDT: I thought she could be cured; I thought she could pick up the pieces and have some sort of life, with some nice lover. I never thought *this* would happen. I liked her. She was tough and fierce, and she never gave in. I feel bad about the practical jokes we sometimes played on her.

FRITZ BLAUKRÄMER: It's a bit late for remorse. At the time, you . . .

PAUL CHUNDT: Christ, I fancied her—okay, I wanted to have her. There's nothing insulting in that. Perhaps there was in the way I went about it, but not in my wanting her. No woman's insulted if a man wants her or finds her desirable—she'll always let him know how far he can go. You never felt any desire for Elisabeth: all you wanted was this exotic Protestant baroness, the disturbed child with the greedy mother. You're not very skillful in your choice of women. Remember—we won't be able to engineer a second annulment.

FRITZ BLAUKRÄMER, *indignantly:* I've no intention of parting from Trude.

PAUL CHUNDT: Elisabeth had style. Her receptions were unique; some were unforgettable. But here *(points in various directions)* there's caviar by the ton, champagne by the gallon, and the motleyest collection of guests: that literary buffoon Tucheler, for instance, who chatters away about Proust to everybody—literally everybody—in that brainless way of his. And all those antiques! Where antiques are concerned you have to have taste—you can't just buy any old junk and plonk it all over the place. And I'm not sure that a minister's wife should go around displaying her admittedly exquisite bosom to everybody—literally everybody. Hell, you had enough women; did you absolutely have to remarry—and what's more, in church, with all the ecclesiastical pomp and circumstance? Of course, we needed the clergy as window dressing, and window dressers. We need them to provide the right ambience—for the army, for armaments, and for the economy—but we've overdone it, we've overexploited them to such an extent that they're now superfluous to our needs and will soon prove an embarrassment. At any rate they don't bring in the votes anymore. But you had to have a bishop to splice you and Trude.

FRITZ BLAUKRÄMER, *with mounting indignation:* Don't you think you sometimes go too far? Trude has a good background.

PAUL CHUNDT: I always go too far. One has to, or one can't go any farther—you've been around long enough to know that. We went too far when we gave you a ministry. I never guessed it would go to your head—to both your heads. You're the last person I'd have expected that to happen to. Look at Erika—a salesgirl from a miserable little village shoe shop, who nevertheless has more taste than the Queen of England with her ludicrous hats. And my own wife, Grete, who's so quiet and sensible—she runs the business side and I take care of the politics. But look at Trude! *(About to explode)* And you'd better keep quiet: I now have a few photos in my dossier. You weren't even in the SS, you weren't just a little officer cadet: you were in charge of a machine-gun unit and far worse than many SS types. The photos show you ordering the men to fire on the poor swine who were trying to escape from a concentration camp—pathetic human wrecks dressed in rags, who wanted to make it to the American lines. And you—

FRITZ BLAUKRÄMER, *coldly:* You're getting old and don't realize that that sort of thing does no one any harm nowadays. I was eighteen at the time and I was doing my duty. I'd been ordered to do it. And you—*you*'ve done everything possible to make sure that things like that can't be used against people. *(Quietly)* Remember Plonius *(even more quietly)* and the scar on his neck, which no one can now identify. And no one would be able to recognize me on those badly exposed photographs. . . .

PAUL CHUNDT, *in surprise:* You've seen them?

FRITZ BLAUKRÄMER: Yes, they were offered to me—the negatives—but they weren't worth a penny to me. And in any case, there's nothing disgraceful about being a dashing eighteen-year-old who does his duty. *(Quietly)* Don't forget the scar . . .

PAUL CHUNDT: Don't worry, I won't forget it. And yet . . . you won't believe me, but I'd rather she were still alive, even though she did know about the scar. I've never wanted anybody dead; I've never wanted blood. You'll find nothing in my dossier, nothing.

FRITZ BLAUKRÄMER, *eying him coldly:* Don't you think you might be deceiving yourself? Do you know who might have collected evidence about you? Do you know what Bingerle has in his safe? I don't. And what about Plottger's wife . . . and Antwerp?

PAUL CHUNDT: You drove Plottger's wife to her death with your cynical talk when she asked about documents that you and your people had burned. You ought to have known that she was part gypsy and that the story of her parents was burned with the documents on the gypsies. And in Antwerp you drove the poor little creature mad and forced her to have a back-street abortion that went wrong. I'd have acknowledged the child, as I've acknowledged others, and the Klossow files are nine hundred feet deep. Oh God, and to send that brainless lover boy up to poor Elisabeth's room! I don't understand Erna Dumpler: that wasn't what she needed, what was missing in her life.

FRITZ BLAUKRÄMER: You no doubt know exactly what she needed, what was missing in her life.

PAUL CHUNDT, *looking at him in surprise:* There's a strange word for it, my dear Fritz, and if my memory serves me correctly, that word is "love." You ought to have left her the memory of that Russian boy who was in love with her and meant so much to her. You ought to have left her the memory of her father and brother—the Nazi baron who hanged himself and her brother in the stable—but at all costs you had to have a noblewoman who'd been raped and whose father had been shot by the Russians. You should have left her with her grief and her memories. She'd have been a tremendous wife, but you got that horrible old bitch of a mother to aid and abet you. . . .

FRITZ BLAUKRÄMER: There was no way of saving her: she went from one house to another, from one café to another, telling horror stories about you and me. Wherever she turned up she caused nothing but scandals. We had to get rid of her.

PAUL CHUNDT: But not to where she is now—in a coffin. *(Agitated)* I don't want people to die—I want them to live. Anything but that!

FRITZ BLAUKRÄMER: Anything but that, you say. But they

have to fall into line, don't they? And don't forget about another death that took place today—Plukanski's. They couldn't save him in the end. I heard about his death when the party was already under way.

PAUL CHUNDT *shakes his head:* No, I don't feel guilty about *him*. I'd have gone on supporting him for a time in spite of that Polish story. He was invaluable in his way. Plukanski's not *my* victim. There were others involved there. You for sure—*(quietly)* but let's not forget the other one: haven't you found any trace of *him*?

FRITZ BLAUKRÄMER: No trace at all. We'll have to wait till he surfaces somewhere.

PAUL CHUNDT: And what about the little count?

FRITZ BLAUKRÄMER: He was there on the dot, but Bingerle had got away two hours earlier. Somebody must have put through a call to Stützling. Can you guess who?

PAUL CHUNDT: I don't want to guess at present; before long I'll know. What we have to do now is to get ready to act. Do you think the Swiss police . . . ?

FRITZ BLAUKRÄMER: One can see how old you're getting by the way you overrate your own importance. No, the Swiss police won't help us: they've got nothing on Bingerle. He was in custody for questioning and has been released. It was you who pressed for his release, just as you've been at pains to see that nobody should be accused of offenses committed during the war. I advised against releasing him. We had him where we wanted him and could work on his nerves. He could just as easily be in Italy or France by now—he could be hundreds of miles away.

PAUL CHUNDT: Then there's only one thing to do, Fritz: keep our nerve and take immediate counteraction, now, before he turns up somewhere. All the newspapers that are on our side—which means most of them—could publish a report: "Document swindler at large, probably in the service of a foreign power." The Russians won't be explicitly mentioned, but everyone will know they are meant. Then an additional line, saying: "A man who does anything for money"—which is actually true.

FRITZ BLAUKRÄMER: You're deceiving yourself again. Bingerle is no longer just after money: he's after your head. Don't underestimate him.

PAUL CHUNDT: He won't get my head. You must inform Heulbuck at once, and all the pure in heart—who don't know anything and don't want to know anything. We must take steps, inform the embassies, supply material to all the press agencies, all the editors in chief. *(Quietly)* On no account must it get out that *he* could have been saved. It'd be bad enough for us, but we're dirty anyway. The pure must remain pure.

FRITZ BLAUKRÄMER: I've already informed the purest of the pure. He really didn't know anything and was horrified when I indicated that Bingerle's revelations might turn out to be true and provable.

PAUL CHUNDT: He doesn't have to know the truth—we don't need to tell him. Remember—the truth always sounds incredible: truth is the true fiction. Don't forget that everything Elisabeth told people was true, and that was why nobody believed her. Show me where the telephone is. . . . *(Exeunt to the right.)*

Wubler and Eva Plint move into the foreground. Eva is wearing a bright green dress with a daisy brooch of rock crystal.

HERMANN WUBLER: I've only come here briefly, to see you. Erika can't stand it here, since . . . But perhaps you don't know yet . . .

EVA PLINT: Yes, I do. And he's giving a grand party. We're supposed to be celebrating his appointment as minister, but it's almost as though we were celebrating something else. *(With a shudder)* I don't understand how that poor woman could hang herself. She should have walked into the Rhine or climbed to the top of a mountain.

HERMANN WUBLER, *pointing to Eva's dress:* I've never seen anything so becoming on a woman.

EVA PLINT: Not even on Erika?

HERMANN WUBLER: For forty years I've never known anything but happiness with Erika. Now she's lying at home, crying her eyes out and praying. She said she wanted to be alone. She won't get over what she saw, and I'm afraid she'll do something to our host when she sees him.

EVA PLINT: What about the other one, his boss—won't she do something to him as well?

HERMANN WUBLER: No; curiously enough she won't. He has a kind of animal energy that's not evil as such but only when it has to be. And even then he's reluctant to take action, though he takes it all the same. But this man! *(Points to the villa.)* I hear that your . . . that Ernst Grobsch isn't well. Did the Plukanski affair come as such a shock to him?

EVA PLINT: Yes; in the end he almost took a liking to the man when he saw him lying there, gasping for life. Frau Blaukrämer's death was also—well, let's say a shock. I put him back to bed with lots of tea and soup—and Proust. It's time he read some Proust instead of always reading Brecht. I was very scared when I heard about her death. I'm told they tried to destroy her memories—and her grief for someone she loved. Ernst clings to his memories too. He's very ill.

HERMANN WUBLER: What's the doctors' diagnosis?

EVA PLINT: He's made his own diagnosis. He says he's suffering from a metaphysical rigor. Maybe he'll switch parties after all. What drove him to join your party was something he calls the dialectic of hatred.

HERMANN WUBLER: A good diagnosis; it could apply to

Erika too. She's reading her old prayerbook, the one she was given at her first communion, fifty years ago. See you soon, then. *(Takes her hand.)*

EVA PLINT, *holding on to his hand:* Where are you going?

HERMANN WUBLER: First she wants to go to Rome. After that we'll have another drink at the bar, at August Krechen's. *(Shrugs his shoulders and leaves. His place is taken by Karl.)*

EVA PLINT: You here? Were you invited or . . . ?

KARL VON KREYL: I'm actually still on Blaukrämer's guest list. *(Quietly and gravely)* Caviar, champagne, and chitchat, while she's lying there in her coffin.

EVA PLINT: I'm scared.

KARL VON KREYL: What of or who for?

EVA PLINT: Of myself and for Ernst. He even understands what you did all that time ago, and I'm beginning to understand too. It scares me. *(Quietly)* What happened last night? It wasn't you, I hope.

KARL VON KREYL: No, it wasn't me. And I don't intend to do it ever again. And forget about the divorce, Eva—it's not important. Katharina doesn't want it; she doesn't want to marry me. I wish you had a child. Why don't you have one, by Grobsch?

EVA PLINT: Funny how neither of us has ever had one. It probably wasn't to be. Ernst doesn't want children. He's been so gloomy, so pessimistic, ever since he had to see Plukanski fade out—yes, just fade out. He's trying to rediscover the hatred he used to feel, but he can't. I was shocked when he told me that he even hated the Church, considering that he goes to church every Sunday, even more religiously than I do.

KARL VON KREYL: Try to understand him. The Church has served its purpose—in this country at least. It's been sucked dry by Chundt and the rest of them—even by Erftler-Blum. They hardly need it anymore. How can

Grobsch go on hating it? One can only feel sadness. Even my father was sad after the memorial service for Erftler-Blum—though at one time he couldn't have too many high masses. This time he was completely downcast: I've never seen him in such a state before. I don't know what's happened to him.

EVA PLINT: Could it be a metaphysical rigor, perhaps?

KARL VON KREYL, *in surprise:* What makes you say that? It sounds . . . it sounds like a perfect diagnosis. Where did you get it from?

EVA PLINT: From Ernst, and I had it confirmed by Wubler in the case of Erika. A new disease: I wonder who knows a cure for it.

KARL VON KREYL: Who indeed! I must go—I can't stand it here. *(Quietly)* It was just as well you left me. And yet . . . only death can part us. *(Embraces Eva, then leaves. Eva is now joined by Adelheid Kapspeter.)*

ADELHEID KAPSPETER: It was nice at our place the other evening, wasn't it? *(Eva does not answer.)* We thought that Grobsch of yours was really quite intelligent.

EVA PLINT, *politely but icily:* How nice that you thought he was nice—intelligent, even. By the way, his name is Ernst, and although he *is* "that Grobsch of mine," as you put it, and likely to remain so, I'd have thought that to you he should be "Herr Grobsch" or "Ernst Grobsch."

ADELHEID KAPSPETER: Oh, how touchy we are!

EVA PLINT: Yes, we are. That's because we have feelings. Incidentally, Ernst heard you whisper to me, "Daddy didn't find it easy inviting that Grobsch of yours." That Grobsch of mine has very acute hearing, and I blame myself for not having got up and left at once.

ADELHEID KAPSPETER, *bursting into tears:* I didn't mean it like that. It was—

EVA PLINT, *taking hold of her arm:* You've got a lot to learn, Adelheid. Perhaps I might even find time to teach you.

You've got to learn to be angry, to be stupid, to be hard when you think you have to be, but the one thing you mustn't be is condescending. You can call *him (she points in the direction in which Karl has just left)* a cranky count—decadent, if you like—because he wears a kind of armor that's called nobility. It would pain him, but not deeply. As for me, it'd be okay by me if you called me an old boiling fowl who was spoiled by a *nouveau riche* father. It would pain me, but not greatly. I have an armor that's called pride, and it's lined with money. But *(with sudden vehemence)* Ernst has no armor; he's not even protected by his intellectual arrogance. He's been rubbed raw—he hardly has any skin left. He's worked hard ever since he could walk—he still works like someone demented—and he has none of the aesthetic armor known as taste. He's sick with misery. Yet I'm grateful for it: that stupid remark of yours wounded him so deeply that he's started to reflect. And if you could tell me why your father found it so difficult to invite him . . .

ADELHEID KAPSPETER, *still weeping:* He's said to be left-wing.

EVA PLINT: He actually *is* left-wing, but he's a member of the German Federal Parliament, and until yesterday he was adviser to a minister.

ADELHEID KAPSPETER, *no longer weeping:* So you think I'm stupid, do you?

EVA PLINT: No, just utterly insensitive, in spite of your music and all the unquestionably tasteful *objets d'art* you have in your house. If someone gets too close to you for comfort, you talk about your sensitivity—other people are touchy, but you're sensitive. *(Speaking very seriously)* I learned something last night after the musicale at your place. I learned that when you're dealing with someone like Ernst, someone from the working class who actually has the effrontery to be a left-winger, you expect him to be insensitive. In the same way, when certain populations are dying by the thousands, you say that they simply have a different attitude toward death. *(More quietly)* What I've learned is a bitter pill for me to swallow, because I also pride myself on my taste. It's painful to realize that taste means nothing, nothing at all; it's all got to do with how things taste to you. You must try to understand me. You like the taste of Beethoven; Ernst doesn't—he cries when he hears him. *(Takes Adelheid's arm, and they go off. Their places are taken by Krengel and Karl von Kreyl.)*

KRENGEL: Do you remember me? My name's Krengel. I'm a banker, a friend of your father's.

KARL VON KREYL: Yes, vaguely; I remember vaguely. It must have been at my father's place. Actually I was just about to leave. Your daughter was there too; I thought she was nice. Is she here?

KRENGEL, *urgently, very seriously:* Please spare me just a minute. At that time you were a promising young civil servant, and I persuaded you to consider a diplomatic career. *(Urgent and very serious)* We needed young, progressive people in those days.

KARL VON KREYL: Well, I'm no longer young, and I was a bit too progressive in the way I handled the embassy's money.

KRENGEL: I know. It was a bit foolish: not quite what they call youthful folly, but quite pardonable since you—how shall I put it?—were on quite close terms with the lady in question, and in any case you acted out of altruism, despite your temporary liaison with her, and you took a certain risk. We need people who are prepared to take risks.

KARL VON KREYL: You're not saying that you'd like to see me retrospectively rehabilitated, are you?

KRENGEL: As for your private folly—you know what I'm referring to—I don't think anybody recognized the spiritual dimension involved in it, the ritual, almost liturgical dimension. *(Kreyl stares at him in astonishment.)* And as for the financial irregularities in the service, they could have been overlooked: you simply overstepped the limits of your competence. It involved a man's life, didn't it? And you acted with spontaneous humanity. Your boss could have given his approval retrospectively. But at the time, after your ritual act, there were people around who didn't understand you and were ill disposed toward you. My directors often have to make snap decisions that may appear controversial or even questionable. I authorize them retrospectively, even when I disapprove of them. You paid for an air ticket to Cuba for a young lady whose charm we were able to admire on the photographs, and you supplied her with a little additional cash. Now, from the political aspect, your action wasn't altogether neutral, but I—er *(pauses in embarrassment)*—I actually wanted to invite you to do to my piano what you did to your own grand. I still have mine: I'm the last banker but one who still owns a valuable piano, and before it falls victim to this sinister guest who's haunting the place, I'd like to put it at your disposal, so that you can perform one of your works of art—for a fee, of course—on a special occasion.

KARL VON KREYL, *mistrustfully:* I don't dismantle pianos, like the sinister guest you refer to. I once chopped up a piano. Do you want yours dismantled or chopped up? I must admit that the fee would come in handy.

KRENGEL: Dismantling was what I had in mind. Having it chopped up would be a bit too barbaric for my taste. There's no need to discuss the fee. You can have a blank check, and apart from my personal auditor, no one will know how much you've drawn. Even I don't want to know. A musical instrument, a precious piano that Bach almost certainly played on . . . taking such an instrument

apart *(with genuine emotion)* I see as an act of supreme spirituality, a kind of divine protest against the delusions
produced by music—against luxury, hunger, and thirst,
against war and all forms of misery and all forms of ma-
terialism. You asked about my daughter. You said you
liked her and asked whether she was here. No, she's not
here, and when I suggested a concert a moment ago, what
I had in mind was a farewell concert—for Hilde, my
daughter. *(Pauses for a few moments.)* I've done everything
for her and with her that one can do with one's children
when one loves them. And I do love her. School, then
the university—where she took a doctorate in agricul-
tural science, then later in economics. She accompanied
me to receptions, parties, and balls, and after my wife
died she used to organize dinners and receptions at home,
just like the lady of the house. She was always there when
I invited my friends and business associates. Do you
know what my wife died of? Anxiety, imagination, and
apathy . . . She couldn't bear the sight of money—it made
her think of the gold that was removed from the teeth of
the people who were murdered. . . . And where could she
possibly go without seeing money? I saw Hilde as my
successor—we're an old family bank—but it's months
since she stopped going to receptions and balls and so
on. When I offered her a position, first as my assistant
and then as my representative, do you know what she
said? She said, "I'd rather die in Nicaragua than live
here." So now she's leaving for Nicaragua. We've discussed the matter for months; I've spent whole nights
talking to her, hardly ever quarreling—you see, we like
each other—but time and again, after we'd gone through
all the arguments, her answer was the same: "No, Daddy,
I'd rather die in Nicaragua than live here. It's a decision
that arises from my *studies*; my feelings on the subject
only came later."

KARL VON KREYL: I don't know whether to feel sorry for you or to congratulate you. In these circumstances I wouldn't take on the task, and I certainly wouldn't accept a fee. Also, I doubt whether your daughter would really appreciate the symbolic destruction of a valuable object as a farewell gift.

KRENGEL: But I want to show her that I love her, not just that I sympathize with her. She'll get money from me anyway. I can't claim to understand her, but I feel respect for her, not just love and sympathy. *(Apathetically)* I want to *show* her that, to demonstrate it to her, and I thought you . . .

KARL VON KREYL, *seriously:* Hearing you talk like that, I think it would be better if you dismantled the piano yourself. You shouldn't chop it up—and I'd be quite incapable of dismantling it anyway. What I suggest is this: you invite people to a musicale and have a program printed. All the guests turn up, dressed formally as if for a wedding, and you then proceed to strip down your own piano while the pianist who's supposed to give the concert hammers the printed music—Beethoven, Chopin, Mozart, or whatever—to the wall. You could even put him (or her) at a bare table and get him (or her) to hammer the music onto it. That would be a real demonstration if, after the concert, you informed the guests of your daughter's decision.

KRENGEL: But I'm not an artist!

KARL VON KREYL: Nor am I; I'm a lawyer. If you need practical instructions, get a piano maker to explain the—how shall I say?—the surgical details to you: I mean the basic construction of a piano. Nothing must be splintered, you understand—everything must be done cleanly and precisely. Probably all you'll need is a screwdriver and a cold chisel.

KRENGEL: A cold chisel—what's that?

KARL VON KREYL: It's a tool rather like a crowbar. *(With an explanatory movement)* Dentists sometimes use something of the sort. It's sometimes simply called a lever. It's important not to dislodge any of the lacquer—that's what's called showing respect for the material. Many parts of a piano are not screwed together but have mortise-and-tenon joints, and these have to be taken apart with great care.

KRENGEL: Do you have a cold chisel?

KARL VON KREYL: No; I only chopped my piano up: I went to work with a common or garden ax. Incidentally, I could imagine that if the man you call the sinister guest were to hear of what you're planning, it might persuade him to desist from his irresponsible activity. *(In a cordial tone)* You really ought to do it yourself, Herr Krengel, with your own hands. It could have a liberating effect, reducing the tensions; it could be understood as a metaphysical signal, as an antimaterialistic gesture—getting away from the material aspects of music, raising it to a higher plane of abstraction, freeing it from the ear, as it were. I'd explain that to your daughter if I were you.

KRENGEL: Interesting. Can I count on your advice? It's an interesting idea. So you yourself have never operated with a—with a cold chisel, as you call it?

KARL VON KREYL: No, the only tool I used was an ax. The sinister guest is more advanced than I am. He must have made a precise study of the structure of grand pianos. He doesn't seem to have much spontaneity. He plans and carries out his actions with careful deliberation. That bespeaks a cool intellect.

KRENGEL: Do you admire him?

KARL VON KREYL: No; I'm just trying to imagine what motivates him.

KRENGEL: And he deliberately picks on big bankers, you think?

KARL VON KREYL: Yes, there must be some connection there that nobody has recognized—though your daughter may have. Anyhow, I wasn't a big banker. Some connection between music, grand pianos—and money, money as material defined in metaphysical terms, recycled into what it is made from: tears, toil, sweat, and blood. *(Thoughtfully)* That should also find expression in your performance. It might even provide a definition of your daughter's motives.

KRENGEL: Could I count on your involvement as a kind of artistic director?

KARL VON KREYL: Yes.

KRENGEL: Come on, let's both have another drink. *(More quietly)* It's a bit vulgar here, don't you think? Too much caviar, champagne, and naked bosoms. *(Exeunt to right, holding glasses and continuing to converse.)*

Blaukrämer and Halberkamm, both in a state of excitement, step into the foreground.

FRITZ BLAUKRÄMER, *agitated:* I didn't invite him. He gatecrashed the party. What are we to do with him? The Sponge, I mean.

HALBERKAMM: The Sponge must be treated with the utmost courtesy: he's more important than the ambassador, more important than the foreign minister. He can help us find Bingerle and get Count Erle zu Berben out of a fix. And besides, don't forget the Heaven Hint shares, which can be obtained only through him.

FRITZ BLAUKRÄMER: I know. What worries me are his requirements where women are concerned. He always wants decent women—no tarts, hostesses, call girls, or photographers' models. They have to be married and respectable—and also pretty.

HALBERKAMM: And he obviously doesn't understand that

as soon as they get involved with him they cease to be respectable.

FRITZ BLAUKRÄMER: He understands, all right—that's what he intends. He wants to make them unrespectable. He must have had painful experiences with respectable women. What's more, they have to be pretty and not under thirty-five. He wants them mature and respectable. On the last occasion we tried to palm off a young girl on him. God, was he furious!

HALBERKAMM: Let him pick one up for himself. He must realize that we can't do it for him.

FRITZ BLAUKRÄMER: At this moment he's chatting up that Eva woman, Grobsch's girlfriend. She's just his type—around forty, respectable, though quite coquettish. When he learns that she's a countess he'll go crazy and proposition her, and then there'll be a scandal we can ill afford.

HALBERKAMM: She'll slap his face, and then when he gets to know that there's been something between her and a Cuban there'll be a political angle. And we can't offer him the little Blömer woman, because he's already had her and so she's no longer respectable. No, your Trude really is pretty, and the very fact that she's a minister's wife makes her respectable *(grins)* and probably more attractive to him than the mistress of a left-wing conservative politician.

FRITZ BLAUKRÄMER, *angrily:* Now *I* should slap *your* face— but I won't do it in public.

HALBERKAMM: Just let's get him away from that countess—she'll cause trouble! Just push Trude between them. Come on, invite him to stay the night in your guest apartment; otherwise he'll go for the waitresses, one of whom is highly respectable. I'm not so sure about the other—she was Plukanski's last companion. *(Exeunt.)*

The Sponge and Trude Blaukrämer step forward.

TRUDE BLAUKRÄMER: I hope you won't be offended if I tell you you're a flatterer—but a charming one.

THE SPONGE, *not without some charm:* My dear lady, the charm of German women is constantly underrated—constantly. Spanish women, you know, are at one and the same time prudish and lascivious. English women can be delightful, but with them one never knows precisely where the borderline is between real dignity and sudden vulgarity. The charm of French women always seems rehearsed, even when it is natural. You, dear lady, are a German woman. It took me a long time to discover the postwar German woman: her wit, her elegance, and her—please forgive me—her emancipated, republican sensuality. The new Germany gave birth to a new German womanhood—who would have believed that possible? I hope your husband will spend a lot of time abroad, if only so that I can enjoy the pleasure of your company. Your free and open personality will be of great benefit to him as a politician.

TRUDE BLAUKRÄMER: You're going to be our guest for a few days. I hope I shall have many opportunities of hearing your opinion on our antiques.

THE SPONGE: They all appear to me to be genuine, though they are not always correctly disposed. Fortunately you are not one of them.

TRUDE BLAUKRÄMER, *smiling as she leaves:* You'd be surprised if you knew what an antique I am.

THE SPONGE: In order to establish that, one needs an expert opinion—and I'm an expert, and serious too.

Chapter 9

The scene empties. Remaining in the foreground are Katharina Richter; beside her, Karl von Kreyl; and to her left, Tucheler. The two men are sitting on the lawn as Lore serves them coffee. Katharina takes the money from the pocket of her apron, counts it, and puts it in the large purse hanging from her shoulder. She takes off her apron and throws it behind her.

KARL VON KREYL, *to Lore:* How much have you made?

LORE: Thirty-one marks twenty.

KATHARINA RICHTER: Seventy-five guests . . . I've made twenty-four marks sixty in tips and Lore's made a bit more—thirty-one twenty. That's fifty-five eighty altogether—less than one mark per guest. And from Karl alone *(she points to him)* I got five, and from *him (points to Tucheler)* I got two. I'm not complaining; an average of nearly a mark a head isn't bad—it's been worse. Incidentally, I won't be getting any more tips: I've lost my job because I slapped that guy's face—the one they call the Sponge. When you're waitressing you have to listen to so much crap and put up with such a lot. There's hardly anything more stupid than drunks: you listen to them, pay attention to them, and then you immediately forget what it was they said. I always tell myself it's like going to the john—just get it out of your system! The surprising thing is that the more intelligent they are when they're sober, the more stupid they become when they're drunk. Having suppressed their sentimentality and aborted their emotions for so long, they then spew up their guts. Their consciousness constantly plays tricks on them: they're intelligent enough to recognize their complexes, and then they spew them up in public and come out with the sort of crap they give to hookers. Any number of hookers have said to me: "The worst thing is having to listen to them; the rest of it makes you throw up, but the drivel they talk!" Naturally there are some drunks who are nice and quiet and sit there calmly nursing their troubles, hardly speaking at all: you call them a taxi, help them in, and off they go home.

I studied psychology for my sins—with him *(points to Tucheler)*. A clever man, an educated man in fact, a psychologist of literature—Proust and Brecht, the Mann brothers and Hofmannsthal. He likes talking, lecturing, and making speeches. He's a critic of culture, and he's disappointed because nobody here is interested in what he has to say, only in who he is. That's why he's sitting there looking so woebegone. He's made a name for himself, and he's naturally proud of it, but he'd like people to listen to him on his subject, which is literature, and he still won't admit what I've tried to din into him so often—that the people here are only interested in politics and business, and that he's merely part of the scenery, like the token bishop or general they invite. I feel genuinely sorry for him, but he simply does it all wrong. What people come here for is the odd nibble, not great mouthfuls, yet every conversation they have with him becomes a disquisition; he starts out from a distance, makes a zigzag approach to the subject, and finally jumps across a ditch that's less than two feet wide. You have to be careful to interrupt him in good time, otherwise he'll treat you to a complete lecture on Thomas Mann—usually one you've read somewhere before. He has only one function here, but he's no more aware of it than the token bishop who wants to preach a sermon on morality. The generals know what role they're expected to play—to display the gold on their uniforms, and if possible a bit of red too, and to smile. The bishops still imagine that they're being honored and respected as representatives of the Church, but all that matters is their purple collars. In a scene so devoid of culture, Tucheler naturally seems like a bird of paradise, and when he has some poetess in tow, he's particularly welcome. I like him, this narrow-chested clergyman's son. As a professor he's fantastic—but there's a growing sadness behind those spectacles of his. I'll probably do my doctorate under him—on the role of money in the works of Balzac and Dostoevsky. It's a subject that links up with banking, even with the third world.

There he is, sitting alone now that he's been deserted by his poetess—she's made off with some handsome colonel. There he sits in his creased suit, with his bourgeois tie, having wasted his intellectual sweetness on the desert air. But how can he possibly want to persuade Grete Chundt to reject Sartre, when no one has ever tried to persuade her to accept him? All she knows about Sartre is that he had dirty fingernails. The only topics that interest her are the market for prewar properties and her children. And Blaukrämer's latest has never been in any danger of perceiving the metaphysical dimension in Faulkner, let alone of being overwhelmed by it; she's only interested in china, parrots, and antiques, and not even remotely in Gorky, whom he tried to persuade her against. Her eyes lit up when he mentioned the Moscow antique shops where you can apparently still find china from the Czarist era, and she immediately asked him if one could find a sauceboat there that had belonged to Catherine II. I'm sure that some embassy clerk—perhaps even the ambassador himself, considering the position Blaukrämer now occupies—will be given instructions to search for china; a telex may even be on its

way already. And when Tucheler tries to inform Blaukrämer about the spirituality of contemporary ballet, Blaukrämer doesn't even hide his boredom, because his mind is on
arms shipments to Guatemala. Perhaps Krengel, the banker,
would be a better conversational partner: his eyes lit up at
the mention of Beckett. The bankers are altogether the most
sensitive of the lot; that nice man Krengel was just offering
me a job in one of his banks when Blaukrämer threw me
out and announced that he would spread the word around
that I was useless and impossible. My experiences with
bankers have been wholly favorable: they seldom get drunk,
and when they do they do so quietly; they are discreet and
polite; and among themselves they don't talk shop as much
as politicians—they can talk for hours about art. Altogether
they're the most cultured of the lot, and in my opinion,
Karl *(addressing herself to him)*, you ought to accept Krengel's
offer, if only because we need the money. The whole trouble arises from the fact that I slapped that man's face—the
one they call the Sponge—so that his cigarette fell out of
his mouth and burned his patent-leather shoes until there
was a dreadful smell, and his champagne glass broke, and
apart from that, his spectacles got dislodged, so that for a
few moments he looked pretty dumb. If somebody starts
fumbling my clothes I lash out, even if he's a prime minister, since I'm incurably sensitive about such things and
liable to get ugly, and since I belong only to him *(points to
Karl)*, my one and only, to him and to my son. And if I
ever became a call girl—if I *had* to become one—I'd send
my clients a visiting card with my consulting hours and the
words "Driveling prohibited." And then *(bends down and
strokes Karl's hair) he* lost his cool and let fly too, with the
result that the Sponge's spectacles fell on the floor and
broke. For a time he groped around like a blind man, and
now they're looking for an optician, because he hasn't got

his second pair on him, and without glasses he can't see Blaukrämer's wife's bosom.

So now we're expelled from court. Our services are no longer required. Perhaps they still need *him (points to Tucheler)*. I just wonder whether he'll go on making himself available, since he surely ought to know that vanity is a by-product of stupidity. He's analyzed the whole of world literature in order to prove that this is so. He knows all about the great and wise men who come a cropper when they yield to vanity. He'd be better advised to address a gathering of bankers about Beckett; they'd listen—they'd be interested. Now we'd better get him home and help him over his hangover with a cup of coffee.

It used to be exciting here sometimes, when the guests had gone home and a few people were left sitting on the lawn on a summer night. You saw people you knew from television; they seemed shrunken when seen at close quarters. Especially the nights when Halberkamm and Grobsch spewed up their proletarian origins to each other. Halberkamm's mother was a showman's widow who used to go from village to village with her chairoplane. Halberkamm had to turn the handle and take the money, and in the evening his mother used to beat him to get him to hand over the fifty-pfennig pieces he'd tried to keep for himself. Turning the handle, taking the money, feeling the autumn rain falling in Upper Franconian villages, buying the leftover wine from the waiters who'd gone around collecting it from all the jugs, carafes, and bottles, and cadging leftover food from the kitchens of the local inns. And Grobsch would go on for the umpteenth time about his tenement in Wuppertal, and about his crippled father, and they would argue about whether the rural proletariat was worse than the urban variety. They never asked me, the illegitimate daughter of an illegitimate waitress, what it was like to sleep in filthy attics, waiting for my mother to come home. I didn't go hungry or freeze—I was always warmly wrapped up—and I was glad when she finally did come home. She'd tip out all of her takings onto the tiny table to count them, and then let me sort out the coins into one-pfennig, two-pfennig, five-pfennig, and ten-pfennig pieces. Occasionally there were some silver coins; these we would immediately fish out and put aside—for my stockings, and later for my books and my clothes. *We* couldn't run around in frayed jeans and patched shirts—that's a luxury reserved for bankers' daughters, who drive barefoot and can afford to have straggly hair because everyone knows who they are. And *she (pointing to Lore)* now lives with us. I'll make something of her. She was recommended by Eva. We'll send her to school and see that she comes up in the world: she's got to learn what the others no longer want to learn. I won't rest till she's done her doctorate too—she won't be allowed to forget anything. And now let's go home—coffee, tea, fresh bread, butter, and eggs! *(Pulls Karl and Tucheler to their feet. Tucheler takes Lore's arm.)* You know, you two, you wouldn't make a bad couple.

Chapter 10

The veranda of the Wublers' house as in Chapter 1, lit only by a standard lamp in the corner. Now and then one sees the flash of headlights on the right bank of the Rhine. Erika Wubler, wearing her bathrobe and wrapped in blankets, lies on a couch. Beside her, in an armchair, sits Hermann Wubler.

HERMANN WUBLER: Wouldn't you be better in bed?

ERIKA WUBLER, *weakly:* No; please let me stay here. I'm afraid of the curtains in my room. I'm afraid if I draw them back I'll see someone hanging there. Oh, Hermann, I'll always see her hanging there, her face so angry and distorted, and her tongue hanging out. I can still remember her coming to see us at Huhlsbolzenheim—young, witty, sharp-tongued, and a bit unbalanced. She was hardly twenty, and she found comfort in religion and folklore. She never said a word about being raped. *(With a shudder)* Sometimes she'd start talking about the people she'd seen hanged—her father and her brother—with their tongues hanging out.

HERMANN WUBLER, *quietly:* I had it checked out. There wasn't a single lie in the whole story—it was all true, just as she told it. Everything fitted in, even the affair with the Soviet lieutenant. I heard about it from a Russian who'd been in Berlin at the time.

ERIKA WUBLER: I'm afraid that Bingerle will be found

hanging behind a curtain somewhere or other. I'm having the curtains taken down in all the rooms.

HERMANN WUBLER: You don't need to have any anxiety about Bingerle—not that kind of anxiety.

ERIKA WUBLER: Switzerland is a small country.

HERMANN WUBLER: He's not in Switzerland. *(Very quietly)* He's somewhere where nobody's looking for him.

ERIKA WUBLER: Do you know where?

HERMANN WUBLER: He'll pocket his pride, heave to, then moor quietly in some harbor and disappear. *(Turning to Erika)* He's crazy, but without knowing it you did Chundt a great service by calling Stützling. Yes, he's crazy; now it's Chundt who's a jump ahead, not Bingerle. They'll be gunning for him from all sides before he can fire a single shot. Don't forget the newspapers and the other media that do Chundt's bidding; even the most cynical journalists will join in. You've no idea what staunch patriotic hearts they all have—as sensitive as rose petals in the Mediterranean wind. Bingerle will be branded as a fraud, a forger, and a traitor even before he surfaces. Even the best documents won't do him any good. Who's going to examine them? And believe me *(takes hold of Erika's hand)*—believe me, it's better for it to happen that way: all he really wanted was money, and he'll get it. All his prating about truth did truth no good; he's just a rogue, thank God, not a hero, and least of all a martyr. The one truth he had to sell will be believed by nobody, however many commissions of inquiry are set up. Idealists may flock to his support, but it won't do any good, because it will be transparently clear that basically he was motivated by money. My guess is that we won't hear any more of him and that there'll be no commission of inquiry—he's too disreputable. Don't worry: he's got nothing to fear from outside. I don't know about his private fears. I just don't know: I could never make him out.

ERIKA WUBLER: He was hungry, like the rest of you, and never really had enough to eat. He wolfed everything down: soup, fried eggs, and bread, then later houses, real estate, shares—and probably women too; I don't know. But he was never satisfied—in fact, he's insatiable. If I were in your place I wouldn't be so unconcerned.

HERMANN WUBLER: In this particular matter, which he hoped would be his big coup, he'll have to declare himself satisfied. Maybe his insatiability will manifest itself elsewhere—perhaps even on our side.

ERIKA WUBLER: Do you think Chundt is likely to take him on again?

HERMANN WUBLER: Yes, of course. You wanted to help Bingerle, and in the end you helped Chundt. It's quite possible that Bingerle will appear on the horizon carrying the white flag. He's lost this battle, but maybe he'll win the next one. There's one thing you didn't take into account: Chundt is also insatiable, and Bingerle is important to him because he has a certain flair: he has a good nose, an almost perfect nose, for other people's sore points. He'd be the man to scuttle Blaukrämer . . . say in a year's time.

ERIKA WUBLER: You were at his reception. He gives a party on the very day when his wife is discovered dead with her tongue hanging out—and you go to it, just to see *her*. Did you see her?

HERMANN WUBLER: Yes, I'm happy to say I did. Next to you, she's the least frivolous woman I know. She's beyond the reach of any desire I might feel for her. I enjoy her company, and (as you understand) she holds out the promise of a different life here, a new life. I want her to stay here, and apart from that *(laughs)* I have a deal going with her husband.

ERIKA WUBLER: That property by the Rhine, you mean. You won't get that. And it would be a shame if you did—it's so beautiful as a ruin, so beautiful in its decay.

HERMANN WUBLER: You talk like her, and I understand you both. I naturally have to act on my client's instructions and on Kapspeter's instructions and do everything I can to get hold of the property, yet I'll be glad if I don't. I hope the boy will have a long life and stay tough. In his position I'd weaken if I were offered so much money for a monument to shame, where in the evening you can hear toads croaking—everything decaying and covered with moss. She's right: monuments should be expensive; and yet *I* couldn't resist the money. Could you?

ERIKA WUBLER: Don't lead me into hypothetical temptation. The property doesn't belong to me, and just supposing it did belong to me, here and now, I'd say, "No, you're not having it." I can imagine it being replaced by a piece of pretentious chocolate-box architecture with a view of the place where the dragon's blood was shed. I have enough to eat, I'm not freezing, I have an apartment . . . No; in these circumstances I'd rather let the toads go on croaking for the sake of a few million. She's right, your friend Eva: real monuments are expensive, and monuments to shame should be especially expensive. And the man who built it, whose sons and grandsons were born in it—he was also a banker, and the bankers should preserve this particular monument. Just imagine: the bulldozers move in, and in one day the whole site is cleared, a hundred years of memories. No; you wouldn't get it from me, even if I were poorer than I am. It would be like selling my parents' graves for a mess of pottage.

HERMANN WUBLER, *with a sigh:* I know people who gave their wedding rings for a piece of bread.

ERIKA WUBLER: I know people who felt no shame or pricks of conscience about stealing and bending down to pick up cigarette butts. There's one of them sitting next to me.

HERMANN WUBLER: Yes, yes—I haven't forgotten. Maybe that was the wrong way to begin—to go into politics so hungry, with somebody who realized how hungry I was and who had never known hunger himself: with Chundt. Nobody ever went hungry on his father's big farm, and he himself was an army paymaster in charge of a big supply depot in Italy—that's something I've just found out. Those who were hungry and greedy crawled to him, and he gave them handouts, and he even felt some sympathy for them: he saw their tongues hanging out and their hands trembling and wasn't stingy. *(Speaking more quietly)* Maybe he didn't even despise them: he discovered the power of the hungry, their enormous energy, their insatiability, which can be harnessed to politics. And yet he does have a heart.

ERIKA WUBLER: Three deaths in one day: Elisabeth's, Plukanski's ... and there's talk of some young woman bleeding to death in Antwerp as the result of an abortion.

HERMANN WUBLER: You can't blame him for Plukanski's death. He'd have kept him on, because he was popular and well liked—something Blaukrämer can never be. And Elisabeth wasn't a victim of his either. As for the young woman in Antwerp, that's not been clarified; probably he'll use her to get rid of Blaukrämer.

ERIKA WUBLER: Through Bingerle, you mean?

HERMANN WUBLER: Probably. In two weeks at the most we'll be seeing the white flag, but *(hesitates)* we've got to face up to something unpleasant: we'll probably have to dismiss that girl Katharina.

ERIKA WUBLER: Because she slapped the Sponge's face and Karl joined in and hit him? That's the only good news I've heard lately. And you'd better get one thing clear:

we're keeping the girl. I like her, and apart from that she needs the money.

HERMANN WUBLER: I don't know . . . I thought you wanted to leave here.

ERIKA WUBLER: To go where? Back home? I couldn't bear it there anymore. Things are even lousier and more corrupt there—even cases of suicide are hushed up. No; no more fairs and church festivals and ladies' charity guilds for me! No, perhaps we should go to Rome, but even now I know that I'd soon want to be back by the Rhine— yes, the Rhine. It really flows, down there. *(Points toward the river.)* And Karl's here, and your Eva, whom I hereby declare to be my Eva too. And then there's that sharp-tongued monster Grobsch. And perhaps one day I'll get around to playing my piano again. I haven't touched it since what happened at Kapspeter's; I just haven't been able to. It's as though there were a spell on it. The one thing I don't want to do is go back home . . . perhaps a trip to Rome, and then back here. And the girl—Katharina—stays with us.

HERMANN WUBLER: I don't know whether we'll be able to keep her on. You know what the Sponge is like. He doesn't mind whatever happens to him—except being made to look a fool in public. He'll destroy anyone who's made a fool of him publicly, and both of them laid into him on Blaukrämer's terrace—both Katharina and Karl.

ERIKA WUBLER: On one occasion I taught him a sharp lesson too.

HERMANN WUBLER: But that wasn't in public; and he's never forgiven you—or me.

ERIKA WUBLER: I'm keeping Katharina. What designs can he have on us? What can he do to us?

HERMANN WUBLER: Nothing directly. He'll brood for a long time and then strike at some spot or in some area you hadn't thought of; if necessary he'll resort to slander

that you can't counter. He was the only one who pub-
licized my affair with the Golpen girl—remember? It was
lapped up by everyone who disliked my normally correct
behavior. He was the one who fished up the photograph
of that Cuban girl who had an affair with Karl and got
embassy money from him. He's sure to come up with
something.

ERIKA WUBLER: But what?

HERMANN WUBLER: How would I know? First he'll go
for Karl, then for Katharina's conviction for theft, the
demonstrations she's taken part in, the stones she's
thrown. He'll get somebody to put an unpleasant gloss
on my relations with Eva and your relations with Karl.

ERIKA WUBLER: Did you say "get somebody"?

HERMANN WUBLER: He has his own people who research
that sort of thing.

ERIKA WUBLER: He'll do that even if we dismiss Katharina.
(Sighs.) Let him do it, then; he'll do it in any case if it
suits him. So let's keep Katharina. After all, she's never
been in trouble—except for these minor matters.

HERMANN WUBLER: I'm not so sure about Karl.

ERIKA WUBLER: You think . . . ?

HERMANN WUBLER: Nobody knows how he earns his
money, and he does earn some, not only from me. He's
involved in some mysterious business or other.

ERIKA WUBLER: And even you can't find out what it is?

HERMANN WUBLER: No, even I can't find out. He has
buddies in every branch of the service who look after
him and see that he isn't compromised.

ERIKA WUBLER: Let's be thankful for his buddies and just
bide our time. You still haven't told me about the high
mass.

HERMANN WUBLER: You managed it, Erika. *(Erika looks at
him questioningly.)* As always, it was a beautiful occasion.
Chundt served, and a strange feeling came over me when

they all went to take communion. That was your doing. It wasn't that I felt any less sinful than the others—it wasn't that—nor that I felt more of a Christian; it wasn't that either. *(Stands up.)* What disturbed me was the thought that possibly *we* weren't the true Christians— you and I and Karl and Eva—but the others. *(Stops in front of the couch.)* As I was watching the cardinal, listening to him and taking him in, it struck me that in reality *they* were the ones who always decided what Christianity should be—all the time, everywhere—and that the rest of us were wrong: you, and to a lesser extent myself, and all the rest, including the tortured and embittered Grobsch. This thought preyed on my mind and turned my stomach; it was almost unendurable, and however beautiful the service was, I couldn't wait for it to end. That's what you managed to do, Erika: I feel dizzy when I think of it. Naturally your absence was noticed, but it didn't cause a scandal. They announced that you were sick, although that was not what you wanted. It caused more regret than annoyance. And of course the television and radio were there, with Grüff and Bleiler, as you predicted. The sermon was unendurable, and the cardinal's face seemed like a mask. Oh, Erika, that's what you managed to achieve, and I don't know whether it was such a good thing. I get frightened when I think of my parents, of my childhood, of my time at school and college, of all we had going for us, as they say, after the war. That's what you managed to achieve. Just don't ask me what you achieved.

ERIKA WUBLER, *seizing his hand:* I also had God-fearing parents and a religious upbringing, and at school I was taught by pious nuns, whom I always think of with gratitude. They even tried to explain to me about the delights and dangers of the senses. Of course, there's no comfort to be had there any longer—that's all over. And not one voice was raised—not even a cardinal's—against the bombs and the rockets. Not one. You didn't protest either. And now you're surprised that you've been deprived of this one consolation, the sublime beauty of a church service, which at one time couldn't be spoiled for you even by a sanctimonious sermon.

It's not just my doing, Hermann. You and your friends are to blame—though I played along too—by always being eager to use the Church as window dressing. I could see what it would all come to when I was photographed with bishops at conferences, and when Erftler-Blum appeared on film with nuns and priests. I never felt entirely happy about it, though I felt happy enough. It affects me too—it affects me very much, in fact—and I knew what I was doing this morning when I stayed at home. It affects you more deeply, because in your innocence you believed that the two things could be kept apart. And now you have to destroy absolutely everything—we all have to. Now we have to run like mad after every unmarried mother-to-be as though she had Christ in her womb. They already had, even before you started running after them, when you still despised and condemned them. Katharina made that clear to me this morning: her mother was an unmarried mother, and so is she. This sudden canonization of unmarried mothers appears to them as a mockery, and it *is* a mockery. You were all blind, as blind as bats, when you welcomed the arrival of the rockets. You yourself joined in the jubilation. I didn't, and I don't take any credit for that. You cleared everything out of the house, and now you're surprised that it's unoccupied and unfurnished.

A "mask"—that was the word you used. A good description, and now comes the unmasking. It pains me that a girl like Katharina should shudder at the very mention of the Church—it really pains me. But then I picture her as an elderly woman kneeling with her son beside Karl, in a quietness that can't be unmasked, that needs no unmasking. *He* exists after all, the one who wrote in the sand. Why did it all have to be so blatant, so contrived? I still don't think you're right: I don't think they have the truth and we are in error. I don't believe it: he exists.

My mother went to church twice a day whenever she could, and she was happy when she could magic a few scraps of egg into the soup we had for supper. My father would curse when the wholesalers came to present the bills and collect the money, and my mother would ask him not to. They were both severe, almost hard, but the baron would be sitting in his private pew, close to the altar, and sometimes he would nod to us. I learned later that he was the one who ran the wholesale business that had a stranglehold on my father, dictating his prices and conditions of payment—he was the one who later greeted me with such gracious condescension at receptions. My father called him a penny-pincher who knew no mercy and who never gave a discount or allowed credit.

And my brother joined the army because that was the only way to get enough to eat. He wouldn't listen to what my father said about Hitler; he didn't give a damn about politics. He was keen on the cheap French red wine and the chickens, and I hope he had a girl as well. What he had to do in the army was nothing like as hard as working for the farmer who grazed cows and grew a bit of barley on his meager acres. He was a happy boy, or at least he became a happy boy when he joined the army, thanks to the red wine, the chickens, and I hope a girl. And then he was killed. . . . He could never understand how some of the men could be dissatisfied with army food. He was killed; he fell at Avranches. What does that mean, Hermann—"he fell"?

HERMANN WUBLER: I don't know much about that. I spent my time in various company offices. I had a clear, legible hand, I'd been to college for a few semesters. I was a coward—I had no desire to be a hero. I always stayed well away from the front, but naturally I heard various stories. To "fall," Erika, means to yell and curse, sometimes to pray too. As you know, when things got serious I deserted.

ERIKA WUBLER: And that was braver than if you'd stayed. You didn't have to become a POW, because Chundt vouched for you. He protected you from a very early stage: he needed you.

HERMANN WUBLER: He also liked me. He actually liked me; the others he only needed—Blaukrämer, Halberkamm, and Bingerle. He liked me, and I wonder whether it wasn't his liking for me that caused him to go after you—in order to put you to the test. You passed the test, but I was afraid, even though I knew you. He went after almost everything in a skirt. He often got his face slapped, but he was never vindictive. What makes him dangerous is the animal energy with which he pursues his aims.

Chundt enters the veranda very quietly. They start when they see him.

PAUL CHUNDT, *laughing:* It seems that another Bible quotation wouldn't be out of place: "Fear not, it is I." You're probably talking about me—I had a distinct impression I heard my name. I ought to ask which one of you did it—that is, if I didn't know it was Erika.

ERIKA WUBLER: Yes. I knew Stützling when he was a hungry student and a refugee. He sometimes came to our place to prepare for his exams with Hermann. He was eighteen at the time, a trembling refugee who was constantly freezing and used to warm his hands by my oven before he had his soup. Sometimes he even got fried eggs—

PAUL CHUNDT: Provided by me. *(Laughs.)*

ERIKA WUBLER: It was pathetic to see how lost he was, surrounded by black market dealings. Yes, I telephoned him without telling Hermann, though he knew I was going to. And then I got dressed and ordered a taxi and went . . . well, you know where I went.

PAUL CHUNDT, *looking depressed:* Yes, I know. The very thought of it makes me want to throw myself over the balustrade. *(Goes to the balustrade.)* How high up are we?

HERMANN WUBLER: About twenty feet—quite high enough. But you're not going to do it, any more than I am. We're all innocent. We didn't want it to happen, right? We didn't want Plottger's wife to kill herself; we didn't want whatever it was that happened in Antwerp and what happened to Elisabeth Blaukrämer. We didn't even want Plukanski to die. Only Blaukrämer . . . we wanted him, and the even more notorious Halberkamm . . . and Bingerle.

PAUL CHUNDT, *still standing by the balustrade:* How about pushing me over and then jumping after me? A double suicide. Everyone would believe it was genuine, considering the flood of rumors that are going to swamp us. *(Silent, grave, looking pensively out into the darkness and down the Rhine. He begins to weep, sobbing audibly.)*

HERMANN WUBLER: I find it hard to resist your tears.

PAUL CHUNDT: You've never understood me, either of you. Yes, I wanted both money and power, but never blood—I saw enough of that in the war. I was responsible for supplying twelve field hospitals. I saw the men who'd been wounded and crippled or who'd cracked up. I saw it all. And in the camp, the Americans offered me various political jobs because I gave anti-Fascist lessons. And you, Hermann, were the first person I took under my wing. You were the one who knew how to behave correctly, the intelligent one, the planner, the irreplaceable deskman. And I ask you now: who is more guilty—the chief of the general staff or the general who has to conduct the battle? You, with your maps and your little flags—you were the strategist who built up our organization. Blaukrämer was the former Nazi whom I needed because he was open to blackmail. And Halberkamm was anti-Nazi. Both of them were too young to have the one or the other held against them. And Bingerle—he was the hungry little stray dog who'd do anything for a scrap of sausage. And now . . . *(Sobs.)*

HERMANN WUBLER: It's really quite out of character for you to whine like this. Only yesterday the Sponge congratulated you on your ten thousand Heaven Hint shares, which had appreciated by thirty percent, and you responded with a grin—that was after Elisabeth Blaukrämer had died, after Plukanski had bitten the dust, and after what had happened in Antwerp . . . whatever did happen there.

PAUL CHUNDT: You forget one fundamental point: I'm a human being; I have a wife whom I really love, two daughters I'm devoted to, and four grandchildren. It's only because of them that I don't throw myself over the balustrade—not because of you, who sit here by the Rhine, prophesying doom. *(Quietly)* I'm not a murderer, even if I *am* partly responsible for one or two deaths. I don't have Plukanski on my conscience—or Elisabeth Blaukrämer. And as for what happened in Antwerp, I hope you'll both judge me fairly when you hear what . . . when you hear who . . . You'll see that it's a hellishly tricky and complicated story. I was horrified by Angelika Plottger's death. Yes, I have to admit it, it didn't sadden me to hear that my shares had risen in value. I'm a fairly simple character who thinks of his family. . . . Oh, what use are your reproaches to me? *(Turns around and faces them both.)* Believe me, what I'd like to do more than anything else is put an end to it all.

HERMANN WUBLER: All the same, you made sure Blaukrämer became a minister. He governs, and you control him—that's your old principle.

PAUL CHUNDT, *wearily:* That's how it used to be. Now he's begun to show his teeth—and to show me my limitations. Your innocence gives me the creeps. Did you imagine, when you were at the end of a telephone, at your desk, at conferences, sitting there quietly, knowing what you were after, that you'd come out of it all with clean hands? Do you intend to go on sitting on the balcony with Erika, deploring the wickedness of the world, writing your memoirs, perhaps, and having whispered conversations—platonic, of course—on park benches with your enchanting Eva or going back to playing duets with her? No longer operating with four or five telephones—like playing piano arrangements for four hands? Bringing a blameless life to a blameless close, going to mass in the morning and telling your beads in the evening? You? You're not out of it yet: you've spun a web that extends into all the countries of Europe and overseas. You with your maps and your plans! You stick a pin in every place you've conquered. But you don't know whether someone out there—in Bolivia or Spain or wherever else you've spread your net—has been found with a knife in his belly or a bullet in his back just because *you* stuck a pin somewhere and sparked off legal actions, jealousy, and greed. Naturally you never wanted all that to happen, nor will you ever hear about it, but *you* made it happen—by opening an office, by supplying money without any of us knowing what use would be made of it. It may have been used to buy weapons, or it may have disappeared in brothels or gambling joints. It may even have been used for the purpose it was intended for—for the greater glory of God, or simply for the glory of Germany. Or it may just have been pissed away on booze. The odd check, the odd letter, the odd telephone call . . . You've no idea what you're starting, what you've started.

One telephone call from you, Erika, and good old Stützling paid you back handsomely for the fried eggs—which were provided by me. *(Laughs.)* And all you achieved was to protect Bingerle from the somewhat violent attentions of Count Erle zu Berben. Incidentally, as Hermann will doubtless explain to you, from our point of view that turned out to be by far the best solution: it means we can call the shots. And the press, my dear Hermann . . . Who was it who came up with the brilliant and breathtakingly simple idea of getting control of the press, and later of television—an idea that even I didn't think of? Who had the idea, ages ago, that these pathetic provincial rags might one day have a significant role to play? Who was it who first imagined that those brainless flickering pictures that appear on the box every evening might one day become so important? Who could it have been? Who was it? Our clever little deskman: he foresaw what I was incapable of foreseeing. Let's hope that Bingerle is alive and trembling; all we wanted to do was get him to safety. There he is, all by himself, safe but trembling, thanks to someone's nostalgic memories of a few fried eggs and a few cigarettes.

But do you know what else you achieved, Erika? *(Erika looks at him in alarm.)* You *almost* caused a fatal accident, my dear. Berben was naturally anxious to catch him and drove off at high speed, and a motorcyclist rode into him head-on. He flew right over Berben's car, but fortunately sustained minimal injuries. According to our plan everything would have been done differently, rather less dramatically and with less bloodshed. *(Quietly and with some emotion)* I'm glad, for your sake, that it didn't turn out worse.

ERIKA WUBLER: You've succeeded in making me feel scared of making any move, any telephone call, even if it's just to order some wine . . .

PAUL CHUNDT: Yes, and they send a delivery boy on a bicycle or a moped and he has a fatal accident on the way. Nobody knows what they're triggering even if they're only inviting Auntie over for coffee. I'm not just saying this to involve you in the guilt—I'm afraid of *myself. (Speaking more quietly)* They could all have been alive still: Angelika Plottger, Elisabeth—we were too clumsy, and she was in his way. Even Plukanski could have gone on living, surrounded by his dreadful kitsch. I don't need to topple his successor. He'll be suffocated by his new post because he's not prepared to give up any of his other offices: member of the provincial assembly, regional councillor, local government administrator, member of the dam operators' association, supervisor of the regional savings bank, the health insurance company, and the hospitals board—and, in addition to all this, member of the party. *(Laughs.)* He'll suffocate because he won't be able to get enough power. Do you really want to leave me alone with *them,* Hermann?

HERMANN WUBLER: And what about you? Will you ever get enough? *(Stands up and straightens the blanket around Erika. Speaking more firmly)* You do all in your power to make him a minister so that he'll suffocate? I've never pleaded my innocence. I didn't always know what I was starting up, but I always knew what I was doing—and not just at my desk. I dumped the Klossow files in the lake with my own hands; with these very hands I burned the Plottger files—a fishing excursion and a hunting fire, with Halberkamm doing his Indian dance around it.

But, Paul, as Erika told me this morning, I've done enough. She said that before she saw Elisabeth dead, her face contorted and her tongue hanging out. You can no more saddle her with the guilt for the injured motorcyclist than with the responsibility for Berben's wrecked car. It was you who initiated these operations, you who planned Bingerle's kidnapping, and if you hadn't, Erika wouldn't have had to make that call. And what might have happened if it had all gone according to your plan? If Bingerle had defended himself, pulled a gun, say? You have to balance what did happen against what could have happened. And just think what could have happened if Bingerle had defended himself—which he probably would have done. Your friend Berben would have been lying dead in the gutter, along with Bingerle.

Just stop all this—don't get Erika into a state of panic. I find myself of two minds every morning when my driver asks me which way to go—left along the Humboldtstrasse or right along the Wilhelmstrasse? Every morning I have these doubts because I ask myself: what might happen somewhere or other because I've made this or that decision? We can't live without deciding between alternative actions. Every time I eat a piece of bread I'm depriving somebody else of it, somebody I don't know. The milk I drink I owe to fodder that might otherwise have produced bread, porridge, or pancakes. Not even the wine we drink belongs to us: it requires fertilizers that could otherwise be used to grow grain. And if I pick up my telephone—one of the four—and dial a number to bawl somebody out—somebody who's deserved it—I don't know whether he'll go home and beat up his wife and children that evening as a result or get into his car in a rage and cause an accident. We're condemned to act: I know what I do, but I don't know what I'm triggering. Perhaps the only one who does know is that mysterious character who goes around silently and serenely, at dead of night, dismantling bankers' grand pianos and stacking the parts neatly in front of their fireplaces like so much firewood.

PAUL CHUNDT: Probably he's the same man whose girlfriend you've taken into your house, against my advice. You'll probably have to say good-bye to that energetic young lady.

ERIKA WUBLER: No, we won't. She's clever and efficient, and what's more she needs the money. I won't get rid of her.

PAUL CHUNDT: Slapping the Sponge's face in public—that's a risk no one's ever taken before. Erika, you've probably no idea what that man can do. He—he— *(Stops involuntarily for a moment.)* I'm a fairy-tale prince or a poor orphan boy compared with him.

HERMANN WUBLER: He's gotten his prey, and perhaps he'll be less ferocious in the morning, because by then he'll have made his conquest. He's even got his spectacles again. I know what he can do: he can cancel the Bolker-Huhm-Brisatzke order, which means a turnover of just about a billion marks. But he won't do that, because his commission's safe and he doesn't know whether he can get it anywhere else. He can even have Bingerle traced and encourage him to spill the beans. He can cook our goose, as the saying goes. Elsewhere he's managed to start rebellions.

ERIKA WUBLER: And you think he'll do that because he made an unsuccessful pass at a girl: that he'll ruin firms, start press campaigns, perhaps even hire terrorists, because a sensible, energetic young woman slapped his face—and was supported by her boyfriend? For no other reason?

PAUL CHUNDT: That's one reason. Where women are con-

cerned he's vain and sensitive. But what is more important to him is that people should do his bidding. He can't
stand disobedience. I advise you to get rid of the girl. I'll
tell you one thing: even Kapspeter, who makes plenty of
people tremble, is scared of him.

HERMANN WUBLER: Fortunately his attention was di-
verted away from Eva. I think I'd have strangled him if
he'd touched her. When I think what Grobsch would
have done . . . He'd have laid into him even more firmly
than Karl. Halberkamm reacted very cleverly and offered
him Blaukrämer's second wife as bait—obviously with
success. We shouldn't get too worried; he won't shine
his torch into every corner where the girl still works.

PAUL CHUNDT: This isn't just any corner—this isn't the
corner bar, where she can happily go on serving beer and
sausages. From you, Hermann, he expects loyalty. He
might even have enjoyed having his ears boxed by a
countess. He could have told people: I once had my ears
boxed by a countess. But by a waitress? I'm warning
you: I'd find it very hard to help you against *him*.

ERIKA WUBLER: Listening to you, one begins to have serious doubts. It all sounds so reasonable, so humane—as
if you were genuinely worried about us.

PAUL CHUNDT, *highly offended:* It sounds? It sounds? I really
am worried about you. And if I've made passes at you
. . . is it an insult if I find a woman desirable?

ERIKA WUBLER: Her husband might find it so, mightn't
he?

PAUL CHUNDT: No, he wouldn't either, because it would
confirm to him how desirable his wife was, and if she
remained resolute, as Erika did . . . I tell you, there are
women, including married women, who are insulted if
you don't try to make it with them; there are even husbands who find it offensive if no one makes passes at

their wives. I get really worried about you innocents, living in the midst of the world, amid all the hurly-burly, yet not knowing what game's being played.

HERMANN WUBLER: I'm not the sort of man you've just described. We're keeping Katharina on; don't *you* threaten us before the Sponge has. Don't tell me what he's capable of. What you're capable of I already know. Now go and leave us alone: Erika's ill, she's scared, and she's tired.

PAUL CHUNDT, *sadly:* You've never thrown me out before, not even at four in the morning. This is the first time *(pauses for a moment)* . . . the first time. How many times I've found consolation at your kitchen table . . . ! *(Exit.)*

HERMANN WUBLER: Come to bed now; it's getting chilly.

ERIKA WUBLER: Not until you've taken the curtains down. Be careful as you climb the ladder. *(Exit Wubler.)* Time and again he's allayed my suspicions when he's standing or sitting there talking: it all sounds so natural and convincing. Time and time again.

Chapter 11

A large room in the Wublers' house, comfortably but not ostentatiously furnished. Erika Wubler is lying on a sofa next to the grand piano as Katharina Richter opens the door to admit Heinrich von Kreyl.

HEINRICH VON KREYL, *going up to Erika and kissing her hand:* I'm sorry I had to call the meeting here. I wanted you to be present, and as you couldn't leave the house . . .

ERIKA WUBLER: That's all right. I like having visitors, and everyone you've invited is welcome.

HEINRICH VON KREYL: I've come earlier than the others because I'd like to discuss a very personal and delicate matter with you, which has perturbed and perplexed me since yesterday. *(Sits down on a chair next to the sofa and begins to speak, awkwardly and hesitantly.)* I—I don't know quite how to begin. I'm somewhat embarrassed. . . . We were brought up not to speak about such matters—I mean religious matters. We took it all for granted—though naturally there was criticism and mockery and *(shrugs his shoulders)*—well, you know. I've spent a long time wondering whom I could talk to about it, whom I could try to explain it to. You're the only person I could think of. I hardly know you; I've only met you a few times, years ago at my son's house, and then at receptions, and naturally I know Hermann Wubler through the party. But after everything I've heard about you, I

thought . . . *(Stands up, agitated, and begins to pace the room.)*
Please don't laugh—but no, if I were afraid of your
laughing I wouldn't have come. Please forgive me. I . . .
for as long as I can remember I've enjoyed going to
church. Nobody ever needed to make me go. Although
it was a duty, I never thought of it as such, and during
the war and afterwards it was an even greater comfort—
and a real need. But since yesterday . . .

ERIKA WUBLER: Since yesterday there's been a change in
Hermann too. He was really disturbed, like you . . .

HEINRICH VON KREYL: And you—you didn't go at all,
though I'm told you weren't ill at the time.

ERIKA WUBLER: I'd been eavesdropping again during a
meeting they had here—you already know who . . . I
didn't sleep a wink all night for thinking about the dead,
about my brother and my parents and the forty years that
have passed since the war—and about all the solemn
services I'd attended, sitting in the front row, I might
almost say in the front rank, making sure I was seen—a
kind of second lady, you might say, sometimes standing
in for the first lady. I used to enjoy it, just like you; I
always enjoyed going to church, and most of all to even-
song. But yesterday I was afraid to play my usual rep-
resentational role, precisely because I was supposed to sit
in the place of honor, as they say. I was afraid that the
same thing would happen to me as happened to you and
Hermann. My nerves wouldn't have stood it—I'd probably have started to scream or something.

HEINRICH VON KREYL: I could hardly stick it out to the
end, and yet I didn't arrive until the sermon was almost
over. I didn't even sit at the front, where a place had
been reserved for me; I stood at the back, which I preferred in any case. Then suddenly—or perhaps it wasn't
so suddenly—I had the sensation that the church was
empty . . . and that I was empty too. The security people

outside turned away some young people who wanted to come in. They might have filled the church, but they were scared off. All those who didn't have invitations were turned away, even regular members of the congregation. I was allowed in—I had my ticket. I ask you, my dear Erika Wubler, what kind of a mass is that?

ERIKA WUBLER: A security mass, my dear Count, a security mass. There were probably one or two security officers among the servers. . . . Was Number Three there too?

HEINRICH VON KREYL: Number Three . . . who's that?

ERIKA WUBLER: Come a bit closer. I can only whisper the name, very quietly. (*Heinrich von Kreyl moves closer and holds his ear to her mouth as she whispers.*)

HEINRICH VON KREYL: No, I didn't *see* him. I can't believe he's around.

ERIKA WUBLER: You can take it from me that he is.

HEINRICH VON KREYL: Is he . . . I mean is he a Catholic?

ERIKA WUBLER: Why shouldn't he be? And he's quite decorative—good-looking—and even if he's not a Catholic, why shouldn't he go to a memorial service? It's a state occasion, so to speak: there'd be nothing to stop the Soviet ambassador from attending. (*More quietly*) I know why you're so anxious: *he* wasn't present, the one you were looking for. They've driven him away; he was absent even during the consecration. Not because they're all so sinful, so utterly corrupt—there's nothing new about that. It was because they don't *feel* themselves to be sinful. They take bribes, they rejoice at the arrival of the rockets, they worship death—none of that is new. What *is* new is that they're not aware of any guilt, let alone sin. And those who would have anointed his feet commit suicide and stick their tongues out at them as they die. They have no hearts, and they talk constantly about being dispassionate, about the force of circumstance, about objectivity. And the precious oil that could

have been used to anoint his feet—they've put it on the
market, dealt in it on the stock exchange. Dried-up bishops and desiccated cardinals have driven him away and
now celebrate security masses from which those who
might turn them into real masses are excluded. There's
no place there for us, my dear Count, either inside or
outside.

HEINRICH VON KREYL: So where is there a place for us?
(Despairingly) I can't live like this. I'm afraid I'm going
mad. Perhaps I already am.

ERIKA WUBLER: You ask where? Perhaps where your wife
went, Karl's mother, of whom I've heard so much. If I've
understood correctly, she walked into the Rhine when
Erftler-Blum and his party turned up at your place. What
did she see in his face and the faces of his cronies, in—
when was it?—1951, I think, when Karl was five, right?
(Heinrich von Kreyl nods.) At that time Hermann was still
a regional councillor and we were enjoying life: we had
a big house, always well heated, and were never short of
food. I was thirty-one at the time and still keen on dancing, and I looked forward to the high masses. What was
it that happened?

HEINRICH VON KREYL: Sometimes I had the impression,
even then, that the church services were more in line
with the party than the party itself. *(Pensively.)* It was not
just a sense of uneasiness. No, I shouldn't have been angry, I should have tried to understand, when Karl refused
to join the army and chose instead to feed the mentally
handicapped, when he stopped going to church, and
when he hacked his grand piano to pieces. I should have
. . . should have . . . And now I have this emptiness inside
me which not even grief can fill. And, my dear Erika, it's
not just the emptiness produced by all the pomp and circumstance *(shakes his head),* not just the emptiness of these
ostentatious security masses, as you call them. I can't find

what I'm looking for anywhere else either. Today I went to church, to a quiet low mass. I told myself I'd be able to find it again where there were only five or six—at the most eight—people sitting together and where the mass was said by a tired, overworked priest. I couldn't find it there either, even where no show was being put on. And today, today especially, I'm so much in need of it. Something awful has happened: I'm facing a decision that I'm incapable of making alone. I can't make it myself, and that's why I've come. I've been offered Heulbuck's job. *(Looks at Erika anxiously.)* He wants to retire.

ERIKA WUBLER: Chundt is behind it, my dear Count. Oh God, oh God, oh holy Number Four. Naturally it's an idea that could only have occurred to *him.* It could also have been dear old Hermann, who wants to save the state. *(Sits up and looks searchingly at Heinrich von Kreyl. As she goes on speaking, Karl and Katharina enter, then Eva and Grobsch, and finally Lore Schmitz.)* Estimated height five feet eight or nine, a bit above average, white hair, a face that has been refined by thirty years of grieving for his wife, an unblemished record, not a penny he owns acquired by illegal means, a count, and a Catholic into the bargain. Or is there some stain on your character that we don't know about? If so, you must reveal it before Chundt can use it against you. *(The newly arrived guests sit down, except for Karl and Katharina, who lean against the grand piano.)*

HEINRICH VON KREYL: The trouble is that I really can't think of anything to reproach myself with, and that frightens me. Perhaps *he* could be held against me *(pointing to Karl),* but he's thirty-eight and answerable for his own follies. I love him, even though the grandson *she's* borne him *(points to Katharina)* doesn't bear my name. My wealth grew out of the soil and fell from the sky like pennies from heaven. The unproductive fields, many of

which we'd owned for centuries and leased to poor tenant farmers ... it wasn't anything I did, it wasn't my
good management that suddenly made them so valuable
when power stations, army barracks, apartment blocks,
and shopping centers were built on them. They turned
our land into real estate. I feel guilty without *being* guilty,
and the only vice I have costs nothing—grief over Martha's death, over the way of the world, over the way
things are. I'm not sad about my son, who turned his
back on everything I valued—the West, the Church, and
tradition. The important thing is that he hasn't turned his
back on the law, or on the One I can no longer find. I'm
empty, like someone who's had everything driven out of
him, and I'm afraid of all the things that might come
flooding in to fill the vacuum. And now, Erika, I'll ask
you first: should I or shouldn't I? I still have six hours
in which to decide.

ERIKA WUBLER: Who's the alternative candidate?

HEINRICH VON KREYL: Dimpler. I gather that he'd accept
without hesitation, but I'm the first choice.

ERIKA WUBLER: Oh, what devils they are! Dimpler—such
a nice gentle person, who knows how to smile and smirk,
a dear little conjurer who's both dynamic and likable.
He's everything: a good dancer and *genuinely* pious. He
might easily have invented the notion of compromise:
when he asks for a hundred, he knows precisely that he'll
only get forty-two, and then they give him forty-three
and a half and he's euphoric, because he doesn't know
they'd have given him forty-eight, that they were even
expecting to have to, and that *they* are the ones who have
reason to congratulate themselves. Dimpler! What an
idea! No, my dear Count, let Dimpler have precedence.
He's young, only forty-eight, dynamic, Catholic
(laughs)—nice, really nice; charming, even. Chundt is a
villain who know's he's one; Dimpler's one too, but he

doesn't know. *(Shakes her head.)* They'd make a fantastic pair of illusionists. . . .

HEINRICH VON KREYL, *turning to Lore, who is seated on a chair:* And you, my dear child. Eva, my daughter-in-law, asked me to bring you in, though I don't know what you're supposed to advise me on. Do you know Heulbuck?

LORE SCHMITZ: Yes. He's likable enough, but *(shrugs her shoulders)* even if I didn't find him likable, he means nothing to me.

HEINRICH VON KREYL: And if I were to be his successor?

LORE SCHMITZ *smiles:* You're even more likable, and maybe there'd be some advantage in it for me, since you happen to be Karl's father, and I'm living at his place.

HEINRICH VON KREYL: I won't be able to provide you with any advantages. Nor will Karl, and he wouldn't want any. Don't you think of anything but your own advantage?

LORE SCHMITZ, *hesitantly:* I've also got friends I'm fond of, and I have feelings. I wouldn't have stayed with Plukanski forever, but he was good to me—he gave me money and clothes—and I was able to give something to my parents, and on one occasion he helped me protect my brother from being severely punished. Attempted bank robbery: he committed the worst offense it's possible to commit—getting caught. Plukanski found him an expensive attorney, and my brother got off lightly—he even got probation.

HEINRICH VON KREYL *listens in astonishment:* Is that all that matters—not getting caught? Isn't it a question of . . . *(Stops.)*

LORE SCHMITZ: Law and order, you mean? No, that's not what it's about. It's about having what other people have, and to get that you have to do things that you mustn't be caught doing. I also read the paper, Count, and I watch television and listen to the radio. And if somebody who didn't really need to do anything crooked gets caught— I mean somebody who has millions—and I read about them having serious heart disease one day and then appearing in court bronzed and beaming—innocent and beaming—and I *see* them standing in court just as they appear before committees—beaming, gracious, and laughing—am *I* of all people supposed to keep to the law and worry about order? I've never done anything crooked—I've never stolen the slightest thing—for fear of being caught. *We* can't appear in court, beaming with triumph: we're condemned even before sentence has been passed.

I grew up in the crummy corridors of a housing project for disadvantaged families, and then I worked in a chemical factory, in the department where you begin to throw up early in the morning. When I was seventeen, I was sent on the streets. That was where I met Plukanski, who took me in. Okay, he was—how do you put it?— well, corrupt, I guess, but in a way I can't explain, he was fond of me. Corrupt? What does being corrupt mean? Plukanski even sent me to courses, so that I got decent educational qualifications. He had me driven there in his official car. That was probably—how would you put it?— not quite correct. He wanted to leave me something in his will, but now he's died, and it'll all go to that disgusting old lady of his, and to his wife, who actually seems quite nice. Law and order? *(Laughs.)* The only things that matter are love and loyalty—not faith. I'd do anything for my kid brother, even if he turned out to be a murderer. Law and order, Count, is something we can't afford; even those who *can* afford it don't bother to. And so, whether it's Heulbuck or you who has the job—I find you both likable, but if there are no advantages, it's all the same to me. It doesn't really interest me, any more than who becomes Pope or whatever in this whole setup. First I want to learn something—I want to work and study. Then maybe I'll be able to afford to think seriously about law and order. I can afford them at present because *they (pointing to Karl and Katharina)* are nice to me and I'm fond of them. I read, and I keep my eyes and ears open, and every report or testimonial I ever got ended with the words "She is not stupid." I'll be good as long as I can afford to be.

KARL VON KREYL, *who has listened open-mouthed, shakes his head:* Tell me, my dear child, aren't you a Catholic?

LORE SCHMITZ: Yes, I am. And there's one request I have to make: please don't call me "my dear child." That's what they all used to call me—the teachers, the priests, the church welfare officer, the social worker, the charitable ladies who brought us parcels and who gave me the pill when I was fourteen because they knew we led what they called an irregular life. There came a time when I began to hate them, one of them in particular, who's been on television. She probably belonged to the same party as you . . . a pretty woman, smartly turned out, not all that young anymore, but elegant. And once, when I told her I'd like to be as elegant and well groomed as she was, she was horrified and said, "That's not what Jesus intended." Another of them even wanted to put me into a convent. Please don't ever call me "dear child" again. My Christian name is Lore, and I don't mind if you use it. But please don't talk to me about religion. Religion's for the people who smile in court—the people who own hundred of thousands, or millions.

HEINRICH VON KREYL, *having listened in horror, shakes his head and turns timidly to Grobsch:* And what do you say, Herr Grobsch? Should I or shouldn't I?

ERNST GROBSCH: You must, if you want my answer—you must. This is the only state we have; there's no other, and certainly none better. This is the state that made us and that we made. Heulbuck, I understand, has retired because he could no longer endure all the filth. You must endure the filth and try to reduce it. My childhood and youth were not quite as bad as Lore's, but they weren't much better either. Like her, I loathe everything connected with the Church, yet I go to church every Sunday. Okay, it's crazy. I'm crazy, but the craziest thing of all is that now, when I sometimes feel the need to go to church, I shall stop going. I'm a climber who wanted to get on, and to this end the Church was indispensable. I hated Plukanski. I want to see a state in which Lore here would recognize that it's a good thing—yes, a good thing—to obey the laws, even if others insolently disobey them with impunity. To make it clear that they are *our* laws and not theirs. Heulbuck couldn't stand the mess, all the filth that comes up from the old sewers. But you, Count—you must put up with the stench. Don't yield to Dimpler: he's not even corrupt; he's just got a damned sensitive nose. He's like the master of the galley slaves who has to hold a bottle of perfume to his nose to disguise the frightful smell of sweat and shit and urine coming from below. The only thing that worries me is that I can't see any blemish in you.

HEINRICH VON KREYL: My wife left us; I couldn't stop her.

ERNST GROBSCH: Then you must remove everything that drove your wife to suicide, everything that she saw in the faces of Erftler-Blum and his cronies, everything that you can see in Dimpler's face—the smirking self-confidence that you also see in the faces of the people Lore reads about in the papers, people whom she sees and hears and who don't encourage her to take any law seriously. Perhaps you should have given your wife the assurance that I expect to hear from you—that our present masters will not remain our masters forever. So my vote is an unreserved yes: you must take it on.

Heinrich von Kreyl turns silently to Eva.

EVA PLINT: I'm beginning to understand what politics are about. I've never understood: I thought they were an inconsequential game that people played for its own sake. I was never frivolous, but I may have been thoughtless. This evening I've begun to understand that Ernst, this Grobsch of mine, precisely because he's a cynic, really thinks he can do something. Now, I can do without Heulbuck, but you're my father-in-law. Tell me: how do *you* propose to get rid of Chundt and Blaukrämer—and the Sponge, who is a greater threat to us all than the rest of them put together . . . What kind of power does the Sponge actually wield?

KARL VON KREYL: We may have gotten rid of the Sponge. He was shot at by Blaukrämer's bodyguards, in the early morning light, as he was making his way to visit Blaukrämer's latest. It's still not clear why he didn't go in through the gate, which would have been open. Perhaps he had romantic notions about stealing through the shrubbery in the pale light of dawn to a woman he was obviously genuinely in love with. The whole thing's obscure. The one thing that's certain is that he went the back way through the park. He was challenged several times; they even shone a floodlight on him, but he carried on even when they threatened to shoot. I don't know, but I have the impression that he wanted to put himself at risk. You know how bodyguards and security men feel: they get tired of always hanging around and become extremely edgy; there was a case recently when one of them shot his own comrade in the leg out of sheer nerves. And so he went on creeping through the park for eighty, almost a hundred yards, toward Blaukrämer's villa. It's possible they didn't know who he was. It's also possible that one of them did recognize him and fired all the same. The Sponge has never been too popular.

ERNST GROBSCH: How do you know all this?

KARL VON KREYL *smiles:* I have my informants. It probably won't be announced until this evening, so I ask you all to exercise discretion. I just didn't want Eva to be afraid of somebody she may no longer need to be afraid of. He may of course survive.

HEINRICH VON KREYL: But why would someone like the Sponge put himself in such danger?

KARL VON KREYL: Because he's lovesick.

ERNST GROBSCH: The Sponge lovesick?

KARL VON KREYL: Why not? Why shouldn't the Sponge have a romantic streak?

EVA PLINT: Okay, perhaps we'll be rid of him. It wouldn't make me all that sad, though I suppose it should. But who was it who freed us from him—who? The police, a policeman—and by mistake! We'd never have gotten rid of him by political means. *(The others look at her in astonishment, especially Grobsch.)* Yes, Grobsch, I've learned a thing or two. Do you want to rely on Chundt or Blaukrämer or whoever being *accidentally* shot by the police? Could you even wish such a thing to happen? No, Father-in-law, you mustn't become Heulbuck's successor. You'd only be an altarpiece. You'd be—you'd be a sort of rood screen behind which all kinds of terrible things went on in secret. Now let's hear from you, Katharina. . . .

KATHARINA RICHTER: I won't take refuge in the fact that I'm a waitress and that it would be indiscreet of me to refer to the circumstances under which I've seen and gotten to know you all. Now, my dear adopted Father-in-law, whenever I've seen you in my capacity as a waitress you've been quiet and serious, sometimes rather sad, and you've always left before the real boozing began—and never without giving us a decent tip. But speaking in my other capacity, I'd say you've got to do it. I didn't have a miserable childhood; I was always warm and had enough to eat. I wanted to get on in the world, and I've succeeded. I wasn't unfamiliar with law and order. My mother took pride in never having anything to reproach herself with, as she put it, and she really did see plenty of corruption and shady dealing. I only once put my hand in the till and helped myself to what was due me. They called it theft, but I still maintain that I was entitled to what I took. My father was a nice man, but he was poor—a poor count who would have liked to adopt me and marry my mother. And she'd have married him if he hadn't been a count. I think that was unfair *(laughs),* because counts are human beings too, and yet *I* don't want to marry *this* count. *(Points to Karl.)* That's really the only thing that might make me hesitate—your title. It could be dangerous, because it could cover all those who arouse such notions but don't justify them. You are who you are—a man who could bring law and order closer to me than they are now.

KARL VON KREYL *steps forward from the grand piano and embraces his father:* In both my capacities, as a son and as a citizen, I have to say that you shouldn't take the job. As a citizen I have this to say: you look too good, you *are* too good, and your title is positively dangerous—a democratic count, of all things! *(Shakes his head.)* No state can be so good or become so good as to deserve to have you as an advertisement. And as a son I'll say this: you won't be able to endure it. You're seventy, remember, and you're neither a good speaker nor a good actor. Every speech you made would be a torment, and you'd have to lie.

HEINRICH VON KREYL *smiles:* You're forgetting that thing on my car that you could have without any effort.

KARL VON KREYL *smiles:* You know that I'd be duty-bound
to acquire it by illegal means; in that particular area I'm
contractually obliged to act illegally, and you know how
seriously I take my obligations. No, let Dimpler do it:
he's just the man for the job—he's cunning, yet not a
villain. *(More softly)* You'd have to receive Plonius, and
be polite to him—don't forget that—and not only him.
You'd . . . I don't know what you'd do.

HEINRICH VON KREYL, *to Erika:* Where shall I go? Are you
going to walk into the Rhine?

ERIKA WUBLER: No, I'm going to sit beside it. It's the only
place I can call home. *(More quietly)* Be patient with yourself *(more quietly still)* and with *him. (She stands up, puts on
her dressing gown, and goes to the piano. She sits down at it,
raises her hands to play, then drops them again.)* I can't. There's
a spell on this instrument. Who's going to break the spell?
(Looks at Karl.) Are you?

KARL VON KREYL: No, I can't. I can't play the piano anymore, and I can hardly bear to hear anyone else play.

ERIKA WUBLER *looks around at Heinrich von Kreyl:* Can you
play?

HEINRICH VON KREYL: No, I never learned.

ERIKA WUBLER: Isn't there anyone here who can break the
spell? Eva . . . ? *(Eva shakes her head. Grobsch does so too.)*

LORE SCHMITZ *steps forward:* What spell? I can tickle the
ivories a bit, if that'll do.

ERIKA WUBLER: Have you had lessons?

LORE SCHMITZ: Not proper lessons. But I once worked in
a bar, and there was a girl there who could play, and
there was an old piano. She taught me a bit. Shall I? I'm
afraid it won't be the sort of music you're used to. Shall
I? *(Erika nods. Lore sits down at the piano and plays a senti-
mental song, but stops when Bingerle suddenly appears. Bingerle
is about sixty, of medium height, with a friendly face. He is
carrying a small attaché case. Erika and Heinrich von Kreyl both*

freeze when they see him. Putting the attaché case down on the grand piano, he goes over to Erika and tries to kiss her hand, but she pulls it back and shakes her head.)

BINGERLE: I wanted to thank you, Erika, not just for the soup, the bread, the fried eggs, and the cigarettes—which I can still taste forty years later—but also for what you did for me through Stützling. It didn't work out the way you thought it would: freedom has turned out to be anything but free. I was more than just a prisoner in the little boardinghouse on the Swiss border. I was bombed out by press, radio, and television, and so I put my hands up and surrendered. I showed remorse and confessed my errors. Your mistake, Erika, was to assume that your noble intentions were matched by noble motives on my part. I've never had any. But thanks all the same.

ERIKA WUBLER: And so now you've come here on Chundt's behalf, I suppose.

BINGERLE: Yes. *(Takes the attaché case from the piano and hands it to Karl von Kreyl.)* You can probably guess what's in here, can't you.

KARL VON KREYL: Yes, probably the *corpora delicti* of my deniable activities. And the receipts too, I assume?

BINGERLE: All the receipts are there, but not all the *corpora delicti*—only ten of them. The first ones really were for the Russian: he took them with him, or more precisely they disappeared with him. The last ten were only ostensibly for him. *(To Heinrich von Kreyl)* So that disposes of everything connected with your son that might be used against you. Of course, you know the request that Herr Chundt links to this present?

HEINRICH VON KREYL: You can take the case away with you. I don't accept presents from Chundt. I don't feel responsible for anything Karl has done. There are a few other obscure episodes in Karl's past *(shakes his head)*, but that's not what prevents me from accepting the job.

KARL VON KREYL, *taking the attaché case:* I'll take it, and I'll keep it. And as for the other obscure episodes—there's no charge, no evidence, and no confession. Incidentally, I'm going to accept Krengel's offer. That means that everything is declared to be a work of art, and art is free, Father.

HEINRICH VON KREYL: Before I die of laughter, my dear Karl, let's get it straight: art is free so long as it gets its materials free or through patrons. Your materials were expensive and weren't given freely. It's a good thing there's no evidence and no charge—but let's drop the subject. And now at last I'd like to have a good laugh, preferably with you, Erika, because you and I are the only ones who know who Bingerle is.

KARL VON KREYL: I know who he is.

HEINRICH VON KREYL: So will you join in our laughter?

KARL VON KREYL: No; normally I'd enjoy a good laugh, but not this time. I don't find it a laughing matter.

HEINRICH VON KREYL: What about you, Erika?

ERIKA WUBLER: No. *(Raises her hand to her heart and sighs.)* No, I can't laugh either, as long as I don't know whether you're going to do it or not.

HEINRICH VON KREYL: I'm not going to—I'd have thought that was obvious, and if you want to know whom I found most convincing, it was the young lady over there *(points to Lore),* whom I won't call "my dear child" again. *She* convinced me. Dimpler will do it, and may the Sponge have mercy on you all—may the Sponge hear your prayer! *(He bursts into insane laughter and leaves the room. Everyone looks on in horror. Karl takes the attaché case and hurries after him.)*

Chapter 12

KRENGEL, *standing in a large, empty room containing only his grand piano, holding an ax in his right hand and a cigarette in his left:*

The concert will not take place, the creative demonstration is canceled, and I wouldn't mind smashing the thing to pieces. But what good would that do? *(Puts down the ax.)* Hilde has left. I took her to the airport. She kissed and hugged me and told me how much she loved me—and how sorry she was for me. What she didn't know and will probably never learn is this *(he takes an airline ticket from his pocket and throws it onto the piano next to the ax)*: I'd booked a seat for myself next to her, then changed my mind at the last moment. What business would I have in Cuba or Nicaragua? Come to that, I don't know what business I have here either. Kapspeter's finally succeeded: I've surrendered, and he's taking over the bank, as he's taken over so many others. When the banking system was being Aryanized, he often got them for a tenth of their real value. Legally, of course. What he didn't have until now was an old family bank with a good background and a decent history. Ours. Now he's got it. Way back, when Jewish assets were being confiscated, I took flight—into the army. We handed everything over to the government commissioner, and I became the paymaster. We weren't dispossessed, just put under a sequestration order, and somewhere, somehow he was always involved—though always in the background. He was involved in everything: church, state, and banking. A pious man with an almost irresistible charm. It was probably because of his charm and his irresistibility, plus his meticulous insistence on observing legality in the conduct of illegal dealings, that Switzerland was prepared to accept their gold. Booty is always legal when it's taken by the victor. I made big mistakes: I wanted no more to do with gold after my dear wife Anna refused to accept gold jewelry from me. She said: "Do you know for sure that it's not from the gold teeth of the people who were murdered, or from what was taken from them before they were murdered?" Since that time I've kept my hands off gold—and off Heaven Hint shares, which the Sponge actually offered me.

Since Heulbuck retired and was replaced by Dimpler, they've been slowly but surely driving me to ruin. Rumors. Rumors are lethal to a bank like ours; there were whisperings about insolvency, and as more and more customers withdrew their assets we did come very close to insolvency. Kapspeter helped me out. He helped me out two or three times—which was kind and generous of him—until, I presume, the Sponge forbade it and threatened him. In the end it was imperative to save the customers' assets, and they're safe with Kapspeter; I myself could no longer guarantee their safety. The firm remains, and I'm even on the board of directors, drawing a director's salary. An American once said: "It's safer to buy a bank than to rob one." That's the accepted method, and I'm not up to it. The safest and totally legal way of robbing a bank is to buy it up after you've forced it into a corner. That's the new-style Aryanization. I'm glad my customers now have the security I could no longer offer them. *(Picks up the ax.)* No. *(Puts it down again.)* At any rate, I now understand Karl: he wanted to strike a blow at the heart of money, but *(shakes his head)* money has no heart; money is invulnerable. Our bank will flourish again under Kapspeter's management. He'll speculate in gold and take as many Heaven Hint shares as he can get his hands on. And any banks that come his way; he won't Aryanize them—he'll Europeanize them, Americanize them. He's a genius. I still can't help thinking about the gold from the gold fillings. On what exchange do they deal in it? With such preoccupations I was a poor banker, but not a bad father, and I had a good wife, whom I loved dearly and who hated parties after she'd seen the pictures of the gas chambers. Right to the end of her life she refused to go under a shower. She always said, "How do I know what will come out, and who put it there?" No, she wasn't crazy, but one day she went to bed and never got up again, and to this day I don't know whether it was suicide. She was healthy enough physically, even mentally. Kapspeter advised me to send her to Kuhlbollen, where he said they would expel her fixation about gold fillings and her fear of showers. But I didn't want her to have anything expelled from her. There were better candidates for expulsion: Schirrmacher, Rickler, and Hochlehner should have been expelled—and Kapspeter too. When reparations began—what one might call the process of de-Aryanization—he discovered that he was also an attorney; and again he was involved, and again it was all legal and aboveboard. And now the man who calls himself Plonius is also back in circulation. We knew him by a different name, and in a different capacity; the awful thing is that he's become a democrat and operates legally, and his conversion is legitimate. They even say he's become pious. Who wouldn't want to resort to the ax? "I'd rather die in Nicaragua than live here"—that's what Hilde said. She sat for days at her mother's bedside, and when her mother died she simply said, "She's redeemed." Redeemed? I've never had much time for Christianity. Of course, I've been to all their ser-

vices and solemn masses, though I've never seen anything in it all, and I'll go on attending—after all, it's one
of my obligations as a director. But there was one man—
there *is* one man—whom I believe to be sincere and who
struck me as the one Christian among them: my old
friend Heinrich von Kreyl. His faith had credibility, and
now *he* says he's no longer a Christian. Where shall I
find another?

KARL *and* HEINRICH VON KREYL *enter together, Karl carrying
a heavy valise which he puts down beside the piano with some relief.*
KARL VON KREYL: He actually intended to walk into the
Rhine, wearing a lead vest and with lumps of lead in his
pockets. And do you know what stopped him?
HEINRICH VON KREYL, *laughing:* The first thing was the
prospect of a state funeral. Although Karl has promised
to speed me on my way when I'm dying and to have me
buried in the place I come from, by the local priest in the
presence of the local congregation, Chundt and Blaukrämer would have been sure to stage a solemn requiem,
complete with a catafalque, and some people might have
believed I was in it. I wouldn't put it past Blaukrämer to
bury the empty catafalque or have my body exhumed.
And the trouble is that their grief would be genuine. No,
the risk of a state funeral was too great. But the other
thing, the really decisive thing, was this: it struck me that
being alive was better than dying, and that I might rediscover what I'd lost. I thought of casting dice to find
out in which direction I would be going, but there are
six faces on a die, and only four cardinal points on the
compass. So I went up on the roof, and when the wind
dropped I turned the weather vane several times and got
it spinning, in the hope that it would come to rest pointing to the south or the east, but it came to rest pointing
north. So that's where I shall go—to the land of the

heathen. You can have the lead as a present from me—
lead at the beginning, lead at the end. And Karl here
won't play any more symbolic games. And now let me
go before I start crying. You'll be hearing from me: we'll
meet again. *(Embraces them both and leaves the room, only to
return.)* Karl, will you play me a few bars of Beethoven
before I leave? *(Karl sits down at the piano and plays the
beginning of a Beethoven sonata. Heinrich von Kreyl raises his
hand to stop him and picks up the ax from the piano.)* I'd better
take this with me and throw it into the Rhine. *(Exit.)*

KRENGEL: We'll be seeing him again. *(Laughs.)* Imagine
somebody deciding not to commit suicide in order to
avoid a state funeral! That's so like him—I've known him
a long time. *(He is silent for a few moments.)* I'm very sorry
I couldn't persuade Kapspeter to take Katharina on; a
man like him could hardly accept her, with a dossier like
hers. What are you going to do?

KARL VON KREYL: I've got a job. Grobsch has taken me
on as his assistant. I'll also do a bit of work for Wubler.
We'll survive. Katharina's left the Wublers voluntarily.
The Sponge got too nasty.

KRENGEL: So she no longer wants to go away, then?

KARL VON KREYL: No. She says her Cuba is here, and her
Nicaragua—Lore and her family. Also, her doctoral dissertation has been accepted. The Sponge now has an additional image, that of the romantic lover. He quite enjoys
hobbling around on crutches. A real heartbreaker! And
Bingerle's going to be Blaukrämer's undersecretary of
state. It's all taken care of.

KRENGEL: So now he's hobbling through the corridors of
power like a martyr to true love. His crutches are just
what he needed to play the part. He travels to New York,
and he travels to Moscow. He's probably deposited a pile
of Heaven Hint shares in Switzerland for the gentlemen
of the Kremlin. You know, Karl, your father has always

been the living embodiment of the parable of the young man who had many possessions. The only one that applies to a banker is the parable of the talents—five talents plus another five—and I wasn't much good even at that. I'm glad you and Katharina are staying. You'll get along all right with Dimpler. He thinks you're crazy and likes to have you as window dressing in the midst of all the tedium.

KARL VON KREYL: I'm not going to be window dressing or a window dresser any longer. He'll find me tedious too, if I ever get to see him. Blaukrämer and Bingerle will join forces and give Chundt the chop, and then things will get even more tedious. Let them suffocate in their tedium! I'll take care in future not to speak of such a thing as the heart of money, which I wanted to break by playing silly games. Dimpler sees money as something rational and inorganic—and how could money have organs? No, I'll be a dry-as-dust lawyer, the sort that Grobsch needs. And our Nicaragua is Lore and her whole clan, who are constantly in need of an attorney. I hope you're not worrying about your daughter. She won't die there: she'll go on living, all right.

KRENGEL: Will you visit me now and then and play me some music, with Eva and Erika, perhaps? And of course Lore will be welcome too. Will you?

KARL VON KREYL: Yes, I could also do for you what I did for my father. *(Makes to pick up the valise.)* Shall I take the lead away with me?

KRENGEL: No; leave it here. There was a lot of lead at the beginning, at the Johanneshaus, and there should be lead at the end. That's in keeping with my leaden existence.

EUROPEAN CLASSICS

Honoré de Balzac	*The Bureaucrats*
Heinrich Böll	*Absent without Leave*
	And Never Said a Word
	And Where Were You, Adam?
	The Bread of Those Early Years
	End of a Mission
	Irish Journal
	Missing Persons and Other Essays
	A Soldier's Legacy
	The Train Was on Time
	Women in a River Landscape
Madeleine Bourdouxhe	*La Femme de Gilles*
Lydia Chukovskaya	*Sofia Petrovna*
Grazia Deledda	*After the Divorce*
	Elias Portolu
Aleksandr Druzhinin	*Polinka Saks • The Story of Aleksei Dmitrich*
Venedikt Erofeev	*Moscow to the End of the Line*
Konstantin Fedin	*Cities and Years*
Fyodor Vasilievich Gladkov	*Cement*
I. Grekova	*The Ship of Widows*
Marek Hlasko	*The Eighth Day of the Week*
Bohumil Hrabal	*Closely Watched Trains*
Erich Kästner	*Fabian: The Story of a Moralist*
Ignacy Krasicki	*The Adventures of Mr. Nicholas Wisdom*
Miroslav Krleža	*The Return of Philip Latinowicz*
Karin Michaëlis	*The Dangerous Age*
Andrey Platonov	*The Foundation Pit*
Arthur Schnitzler	*The Road to the Open*
Ludvík Vaculík	*The Axe*
Vladimir Voinovich	*The Life & Extraordinary Adventures of Private Ivan Chonkin*
	Pretender to the Throne